Lord of California

a novel

ANDREW VALENCIA

PUBLISHING

New York, NY

Ig Publishing
Box 2547
New York, NY 10163
www.igpub.com

This is a work of fiction. Names, characters, businesses, places, events and
incidents are either the products of the author's imagination or used in a
fictitious manner. Any resemblance to actual persons, living or dead, or
actual events is purely coincidental.

ISBN 978-1-63246-059-2

CONTENTS

I will listen
as though you spoke and told
me all you never knew
of why the earth takes
back all she gives and
even that comes to be enough.

—Philip Levine

There is blood, there, he says
Blood here too, down here, she says
Only blood, the Blood Mother sings

—Juan Felipe Herrera

LORD OF CALIFORNIA

ELLIE

Daddy was a fancy man. He used to come around twice a year to see us kids. Each time he'd walk through the door hauling a stack of presents so high you couldn't see but the point of his head over the gold and silver-wrapped packages. Jessie would work herself into a stink all year waiting for him to show up, and then once he appeared she'd get so excited about the doll or dress he brought her that she'd forget she was ever mad at him to begin with. The last time Daddy came home, Mama whispered to me that a woman ought not to be as forgiving as Jessie, or else she'll be setting herself up to always be wronged. I'd just turned thirteen and the way Mama talked to me had changed. Time before that she'd scolded me for saying I was too big for the doll Daddy had bought me and that I'd never liked playing with dolls to begin with. Should've seen the look on her face then, after she'd shushed me and dragged me squirming into the kitchen. Nowadays most girls get stuck playing with knock-off Barbies from the supermarket, she'd said, and so I should be grateful to have a daddy who could afford to buy me real porcelain beauties from a specialty store on the coast. Six months without seeing him, two months without a word, and that was the lesson she decided to take from the situation. That was Mama. There was always a war waging inside her, with fear on one side of the battlefield, and self-respect on the other.

I say Daddy was fancy on account of no other man I ever knew dressed as well as him or smelled so clean all the time. As seldom as we saw him—as seldom as we had new clothes—we got to notice how different he was from us and Mama and everyone else we knew in the valley. Even though, according to Mama, not all of our neighbors were as well-off as us, or as dignified. Back when we were farming down in Hanford, there was a family that settled one winter on the parcel next to ours, the Mendeses—mother, father, and kids all working together in the orchard alongside their aunts, uncles, and cousins. No hired laborers, no foremen. Me and Jessie used to play sometimes with the Mendes kids, Javier and Ruby, but Mama didn't like us to. She never tried to keep us from seeing them, but we were forbidden from running around the orchards barefoot like they did. Way she put it, any girl who goes barefoot outside is bound to have elephant soles and bunions by the time she's thirty. Try getting your man to rub your feet then, she'd say, even though we'd never seen Daddy do anything of the sort for her. I tried telling her that the Mendeses let Ruby go barefoot whenever she wanted, but that only proved her case as far as she was concerned. With her dark arm hair and graceless paunch, Ruby Mendes was everything Mama feared we'd become if we had to grow up poor. And even after we left the farm and moved on to other things, the memory of that homely, ham-fisted little girl seemed to vindicate for her all the choices she'd made up to the moment Daddy died, as if her prudent thinking was made evident in the softness of our hands and disinclination toward lesbianism.

Little while after Daddy had gone, one of his other wives invited us up to Reedley for the most awkward family reunion imaginable, a chance for the Temple kids to get to know all the half-brothers and half-sisters we'd only just found out about. Without saying a whole lot, Mama ironed our best clothes and piled us into the van for the short trip north to Fresno County. Between Daddy's passing and the discovery of the other wives, these past months had hit Mama hard, launching her into one of her sad stretches so that she kept to the bed most hours of the day while I cooked the meals, managed the foremen, and looked after Jessie and little Gracie. There was no consoling Mama when she got like that. But once the other Mrs. Temple called and the obligation to be civil was on her again, she roused herself out from under the covers and took the reins of the family back up like nothing had ever happened. She was even chatty on the drive up, pointing out certain spots along the roadside and remarking on how much the land had changed since disbandment and the founding of the Republic. I peered out the window and tried to imagine the old interstate highways and national retailers the way she described them, but there was nothing in that boundless dry country to inspire dreams of former glory, nothing to suggest a bond of greatness so strong its likeness could remain visible so long after its breaking. All we saw were a hundred other little farms just like ours, a hundred other families struggling to get by on whatever they could reap from year to year.

Such was the farm where we realized for the first time the full scope of Daddy's legacy—four wives and nine kids, not counting us, all congregated on the gravel yard of a country ranch house, under the shadow of a paper banner with *WELCOME TEMPLES* scrawled across it in craft paint. Katie was a real personable old girl, more lively and energetic than Mama even though she was at least ten years older. She spent the first part of the afternoon tending to the chicken on the charcoal grill and knocking back bottles of homebrewed porter with Dawn, the youngest of Daddy's brides. No sooner had Mama added her macaroni salad to the table than Katie swooped in for a hug. She was full-bodied and strong enough to knock the wind from her system, so it was a relief to see Mama feigning cheer to get through this first encounter. I knew it couldn't have been easy. Even on good days, it was sometimes hard for her to let me and my sisters get close like that.

Hello there, Katie said, squatting down to the same level as Gracie. What's your name?

Gracie grabbed Mama's leg and hid behind the skirt of her sundress.

She's being shy, Mama said.

Katie stood up straight. I understand, honey, she said. And this must be Ellie the genius. Your mom said you were as smart as they come, girl, but I wasn't expecting to find you looking like a magazine fashion model as well.

I was never one to blush, especially at the flattery of strangers, but the idea that Mama was bragging about me to one of Daddy's other wives had me feeling as shy as Gracie all of a sudden. Thank you, Mrs. Temple.

Katie, she said. Aunt Katie, if you want.

Thank you. Katie.

We so appreciate you having us over, Mama said. I know it couldn't have been easy to organize something like this, what with everything that's happened.

It's no trouble, honey, Katie said. Can't tell you how happy I am to have us all together in one place. Almost makes me wish it had happened a lot sooner.

She winked at Mama, who laughed falsely and excused herself to go freshen up.

We ate dinner around a long picnic table, the whole Temple clan packed together yet still separated according to which mother we had come with. The one I felt worst for was Dawn, who had no children of her own and sat drinking beer and nibbling fruit ambrosia at the far corner of the table while the other wives made chitchat about TV series and summer vacation schedules. Claudia, Daddy's wife from Dinuba, sat across from us with her brood of three lanky boys and one slobbering two-year-old girl. Her oldest boy, Anthony, kept giving me the stink eye throughout the entire meal. Finally I dropped my plastic fork and leaned over to him.

You got something you want to say?

Anthony looked up from his plate and glared at me. It was weird seeing Daddy's eyes in someone else's head. You Catholic?

No. Why?

Your mother. Was she married to our father by a priest?

Not that I know of.

That's what I thought. My mother was married to him by a priest in a Catholic church. That means she's his real wife before the eyes of God.

What're you talking about? Daddy wasn't Catholic.

Doesn't matter. He still got married in a church.

I looked to see if Mama had heard us. Fortunately, she was preoccupied watching Anthony's mother fuss over the toddler Karina. I set my chin on her shoulder to catch her attention. Can I go look around, please?

You've barely eaten anything, she said.

Please? I'm tired of sitting still so long.

Well. All right. But don't wander too far.

After putting the full space of the yard between Mama and me, I kicked off my fancy dress flats and let my bare toes luxuriate in the loose soil by the edge of the orchard. Up close as I was, I came to notice that the trees on Katie's property were plums instead of nectarines, and it got me thinking about all the ways Daddy had diversified his investments over the years—different crops for different families, different wives for different children. In my solitude I felt the pang of real sadness come over me for the first time since Mama opened up about his lies. All those months I had held on to the hope that eventually someone, whether Mama or one of the other wives, would explain everything to me in a way that made sense, and then I would finally understand how he could do that to us for so long, and how he could leave us with such a mess on our hands. I'd been waiting for one of them to set me straight, but now I was starting to get it. They could smile and talk over a plate of barbecue, but they were every bit as lost as me.

•

The sun set slow over the valley, with a few dry clouds hanging in the sky, and the day's heat stinging our skins. The mothers herded the little ones into the backyard with the older kids assigned to watch them.

I kept waiting for Mama to send me out to keep an eye on Jessie and Gracie, but instead she had me stay close by as she and the other wives settled onto cushioned chairs and sofas in the living room. Katie's boys, Logan and Will, also stayed behind, as did her daughter Beth, who was only a year ahead of me but already so filled-out that she could've passed for a sixth wife if no one knew better. Anthony had refused to hang around inside with the women, mumbling something on his way out the door about wishing he'd stayed home. I was glad for his absence, frankly. I'd spent enough time looking after Gracie to know when somebody's on the verge of a tantrum, and the way that boy was going, it wouldn't have taken much to set him off.

I suppose it's time we got down to business, Jennifer said. She opened her leather satchel and took out a manila folder stuffed with papers. We only had four channels on the TV at home, but Jennifer reminded me of every lady lawyer on every crime show I'd ever seen.

Hope business wasn't hanging over your head all through dinner, Katie said. I thought it'd be nice to hold off on the serious talk until evening. Sorry if it made you antsy.

Oh no, Jennifer said. I'm fine. It was a lovely meal. I just assumed we were all eager to get the nitty gritty details out of the way. That is why you asked us to bring copies of our parcel allotment forms, right?

I was wondering about that too, Dawn said. Her back grew stiff as all eyes converged on her. I was hoping somebody could explain how all of this works. Elliot and I never discussed the property papers. We'd only had the farm a year or so before he went away and got sick.

All afternoon, none of the other wives had spoken Daddy's name. Now the whole room became charged with a fearful energy, as if Dawn had unknowingly let in some venomous insect that we were all trying to veer away from. She gripped the allotment forms tight between her fingers.

We'll be getting to that in a minute, honey, Katie said. First off, I think we should take a second to clear the air. Get out anything we're holding back that might keep us from reaching an understanding.

I'm not sure what you mean, Jennifer said. We've only just met one another.

True. But I doubt there's a woman alive who could find out her husband was keeping four women behind her back and not come away with some pretty nasty preconceived notions about the other gals.

Again the energy of the room seemed to dip toward nervousness. I could already tell I liked Katie a lot, but she was maybe too direct for the rest of the wives. Mama especially was more likely to let her feelings fester than to open up a wound. I listened close for changes in her breathing, for signs that she was gearing up for another episode.

I'm not saying we need to quit being angry, Katie continued. To the contrary. Far as I'm concerned, that man deserves to have his name cursed for as long as it's remembered, deceased or not. What I'm saying is, we don't have the time or luxury to sit around acting catty and pretending like everyone else involved is a lying slut. That's not going to help us, and it's not going to help our children. Fact is, we've all been hurt by this man. Hurt about as bad as a wife can be by her husband. And the way I see it, we have a choice about how we can face it. We can either go ahead on our own, spend nights crying over our wine bottles, and call each other bitches behind our backs. Or, we can accept that we've all been hurt, that all of our pain is equal, and that together our pain makes us sisters in a way. And then we can move on together. What do you say?

It felt oddly satisfying to hear Katie talk about Daddy like that, if only because no one else had even dared to admit they were upset. I wanted to clap my hands and cry out in agreement, but it was awkward when I was child to the man along with three others in the room. Mama had let me stay because she thought I was grown-up enough to handle their talk, but I didn't know where my place was at when it came to speaking up. Daughter, sister, half-sister, and victim. Each new title seemed to eat away at my freedom to decide for myself. I don't know how the wives and mothers stood it.

I'm sorry, Jennifer said. I know you mean well, and I agree that none of us are at fault. But as for the sisterhood, you'll have to count me and my children out. I agreed to come here today because I thought they had the right to meet their siblings, and I knew eventually we'd have to iron out the details concerning Elliot's estate. But as for working together from now on, I don't see how it could help any of us in the long run. Take away the common thread and we're all very different women with farms in different parts of the state. We can get together now and then for the children's sake, but beyond that I don't see any point in pretending we share anything more than a dead husband and the same last name.

I don't see the point either, Claudia said. She had been sitting as peaceably as a portrait angel up till then. Now she uncrossed her legs and scooted to the edge of the seat cushion, looking out at the other wives until all their attention was hers. The man we called husband committed a terrible sin, she said, and now he's receiving judgment for it in the afterlife. It falls on us to raise our sons and daughters according to how we see fit, and for me that means raising them in a Catholic household. I know the rest of you don't share my beliefs, and that's your right the same as mine. We should hold parties once in a while like we did today, and when the children are older they can decide for themselves if they want to have relationships with their half-brothers and sisters. But five different women, working together, and raising their children in common? Sorry, no. That's Mormon talk.

Even Katie laughed at the joke. I wasn't suggesting we all pile in under one roof like hippies on a commune, she said.

I'm sorry, but what exactly are you suggesting? Mama had jumped into the conversation so suddenly it startled me. I'm afraid I don't understand, she said. Now that Elliot's gone, why wouldn't we just continue managing our farms like we've been doing? Let's be honest. As often as he was away, his death doesn't really change anything.

Exactly, Jennifer said. Not to give Elliot any credit, but he arranged his little operation so that each family would be self-sufficient. Different parcels, different bank accounts, different expenses. The new arrangement pretty much writes itself. What we need to decide is whether there are any assets that can be rightfully claimed among the five of us, and then figure out how we want to divide them.

Quit stalling, Mom, Beth said. She had a strong, carrying voice like her mother's that made me feel even more childish by comparison. Tell them what you told us a month ago. Logan and Will nodded their approval, arms crossed over their flannel shirts like a pair of old-timey bartenders from TV.

You ladies make some good points, Katie said. But what you're taking for granted is that you each have a farm to call home and nothing can change that. And that's where you're wrong. What we really need to decide is whether we can stand the chance of losing everything now that the son of a bitch is gone.

Chance, Mama said. What chance?

I see that look on your face, Sandra. You're scared. You know exactly what it'll mean for your children if you can't find a way to hold on to your land. Problem is, the Republic of California isn't as concerned about your children as you are. Way they see it, farming is the only thing this valley is good for, and they mean to see each parcel turning out as many crops as possible. Now, the Congress up in Sacramento is liberal, but parcel allotment is handled through the state and county ag bureaus. And as far as the State of San Joaquin is concerned, an unmarried woman has no business running a farm on her own. Especially if she has kids.

She's right, Dawn said. Neighbor friend of mine had her husband run out on her last year. When she went to file her taxes, the county cut her land parcel in half, set her back to ten acres. Said twenty was too much for her to handle.

None of the wives spoke for several seconds. I watched their beseeching, desperate eyes move from one face to another in search of answers.

No one can turn a profit on ten acres, Claudia said.

Not if they want to eat, Katie added.

Dear God, no, Mama said. She bent forward so that her hair fell across her shoulders and hid her face from view. I set my hand on the ridge of her spine and stroked it up and down.

It's okay, Mama, I said. We'll figure something out.

She sat up straight and brushed the hair from her eyes, but I could tell from her open mouth and vacant gaze that she was far away from everything that was happening inside the living room. All through my childhood, every time nectarine prices fell or a bad harvest came in, I had to listen to her fretful exclamations about going broke and winding up on the streets. There was nothing in the world she feared more. And now, with this latest piece of news, her nightmare of poverty must have seemed so close to becoming real.

It's the same story all over the valley, Katie said. Men in charge decide how to divvy up the land, and they don't want anybody farming who doesn't match their idea of what's decent. No gays, no illegals, and no unwed mothers. Doesn't matter if we're widows. Way they see it, if we really cared about our kids, we'd remarry in a hurry.

And they call themselves Christians, Claudia said.

Katie looked around the room. How about it, ladies? After all we've been through, you ready to find yourselves another husband in time for tax season?

Not particularly, Jennifer said. But if worst comes to worst, I have a trustworthy foreman I can probably talk into marrying me in name only.

Smart girl, Katie said. That was my idea too before I started reading up on California ag law. Then I stumbled on something so worrisome I had to invite you all up for a barbecue just to sort it out. It might be nothing, but if what I suspect about Elliot is true, we'll be lucky to come out of this with ten acres between the five of us.

Get the fuck on with it, Mama cried. Now all eyes were on her.

You're overheated, Mama, I said. You know how your head aches when you get too hot. Without drawing any more attention to us, I hurried to the kitchen and fixed her a glass of red wine to sip on. When I returned, Dawn was flipping through the stack of papers on her lap.

Take your time, honey, Katie said. It should be a long blue document with a date stamped at the bottom.

Found it, Dawn said. She held the form in front her as if to prove she was being truthful.

That's good, Katie said. Now go ahead and read out the name printed on the first line. Right above your own name.

Dawn turned the document around and squinted at the carbon impression at the bottom. E. F. Rabedeaux, she said. Same as the signature.

Katie touched her face and sighed. That's what I was afraid of, she said.

Who is it? Jennifer asked. Who's E. F. Rabedeaux?

Elias Rabedeaux, Mama said calmly. That was Elliot's real name. He changed it when he moved out from the coast.

For a second there, Claudia and Jennifer both appeared dumbstruck. I tried putting myself in their place. It was one thing to know you'd been lied to when four others had been deceived the same way. It was another to find out you'd been deceived just a little bit more than the others, that Daddy had tipped the scales by adding at least one extra lie to their plates.

Elias Rabedeaux was the name he signed our parcel papers with nearly twenty years ago, Katie said. What about the rest of them? How many names did he have going in all?

Amid the sudden outcries and shuffling of papers, the full picture of Daddy's corruption gradually came into view. Twenty years earlier, Elias Rabedeaux had applied for a land parcel in Fresno County, aiming to grow plums with his young wife Katherine. But by the time he married Sandra and turned his eye to Kings County and nectarines, Elliot Temple was the name he was using on the paperwork. Year by year, county by county, wife by wife, his territory had expanded out across the entire length of the valley. Elias Temple applied to grow grapes in Tulare County with his wife Claudia. Eli Temple preferred almonds, Madera County, and Jennifer. When the time came to bring his new wife Dawn to Merced, E. F. Rabedeaux decided to try his hand at peaches. None of the wives had any idea what the *F* stood for, though I'm sure they could've offered a suggestion.

I know it's hard to accept, Katie said. But it's obvious we weren't the only ones being duped. He wasn't carrying on as a bigamist just for fun. There was a financial motive as well. Not many people know it, but the parcel program only allows each family a certain number of acres in total. In most counties the cap is at sixty, but anything more than thirty is usually pretty hard to come by. And here he was with a hundred acres of land under five different names.

It's a fraud, Beth said. He was defrauding the state. Sort of thing people go to prison for.

That's right, honey, Katie said. At best, we're looking at heavy fines, back taxes, and censure. And that's on top of eviction. Any time someone dies and leaves a bunch of land behind, the government's bound to start poking around. All it'd take is a few phone calls and a state audit for the whole house of cards to come crashing down.

Claudia shuddered briefly and retreated to the kitchen. I thought she might've been done for good until she returned carrying the wine bottle and four long-stemmed glasses. None of the wives bothered with decorum. Us kids waited silently for the slow gulping to cease.

You still haven't answered my question, Mama said. What are you suggesting we do to try and fix this?

We cash out, Katie said. We sell our land back to the state while we still can. Take the money and start over someplace else.

Mama showed a painful smile. Start over, she said. Does anyone here really have the energy to go through that again?

If it's between that and eviction, Dawn said, I think I could manage.

Of course you'd say that. You're what, twenty, twenty-five years old? Everything's still an adventure to you. If farming doesn't work out, you can just go back to working at whatever hole-in-the-wall dive Elliot found you in.

I took the glass of wine from Mama's hand and set it on the table.

She looked at me. Mama, I said. You owe Dawn an apology. Katie's right. There's no use fighting among ourselves.

In the space of a few blinks, Mama's eyes turned glossy. You don't—

Mama. Apologize. Please.

She looked at Dawn with the corners of her mouth turned down. I'm sorry, she said. Please try to understand. That farm's been my home for eighteen years. Good and bad, my whole life's been built around it.

It's all right, Dawn said. I know what it means not to have a home.

Katie stepped up to the coffee table. There was only a little bit of wine left, and she didn't seem to mind drinking straight from the bottle. You asked me what my suggestion is, she said. Still figuring that out myself. But here's what I think. If we were to throw our lots in together, we could apply for cooperative status and get a whole new parcel to start on fresh. We could deal directly with the national ag bureau, bypass the good ol' boys at the local level. And there'd be no limit to how many acres we could buy.

That's because we'd be selling short, Jennifer said. That's how these co-ops operate. The government pays them to sell their produce for less than it's worth.

And we'd be at the mercy of our pickers and packing house boys, Claudia said. They'd all be shareholders under the law.

Watching Katie kill the bottle gave me a giddy little thrill. Ladies, she said. Wives, women, whatever. Listen here. Whether we want to admit it or not, there's a reason the five of us ended up together in this room. You'll know what I mean when I say Elliot was never a heartthrob, even as a younger man. It doesn't make me proud to say, but I was in desperate straits when I met him, and at the time just about any man with a bit of money and an eye to settle down could've won me over the same way he did. He was my golden ticket out of the Kingsburg tavern I was working in at the time. I believed in him, and here's where it got me. Here's where belief landed me in my middle age.

Katie shook the bottle to see that it was empty. Then she walked to the side of the room and stood with her arms crossed over her chest like her sons.

So how's about we try believing in ourselves for a change?

•

It was still light out when the meeting adjourned. Mama took Gracie to wash up and use the restroom before we headed home. She said to give her a while, that she needed to get her head together before she got back behind the wheel. I left Jessie with Beth and headed out under the twilight sky, following an old American irrigation ditch about a quarter mile into the orchard. That time of year, it wasn't much different from our orchard at home—horse-flies clustering around stray dog turds, fermented fruit and pits hardened into a dark macadam. Not the best smelling place for a girl to grow up, but good for losing yourself in a day-dream. I wandered barefoot with my shoes dangling from my fingertips, toes slapping on the hard dry ground.

Suddenly a voice called out to me, Goddamn you're heavy-footed.

I stopped and turned in time to see Anthony slipping out from behind a column of leafy branches, kicking up globs of dirt with his sneakers.

If you were a deer you'd be shot already, he said.

What the hell do you know about hunting?

A lot, he said. I've got a .22 at home. Foreman taught me how to use it.

Good for you and your foreman.

He smiled and circled around me a couple paces. How old are you, anyway?

How old are you?

Sixteen.

Well, I'm thirteen. What of it?

You're pretty scrawny for thirteen. You a hermaphrodite or something?

A what?

A he-she. Born with a dick as well as a pussy.

You're an ass.

Maybe you are and your mom never told you. Maybe that's why she gave you a boy's name.

How do you know what my name is?

My mom. She said one of my new sisters was named after our dad. I figured she must be a real beast.

Elliot can be a girl's name too.

Then how come you never see any girls named it?

I dropped my shoes on the ground and slipped them on. Since third grade I had gone up to my teachers on the first day of every school year and asked them not to call me by the name listed on the roll sheet. Now the most annoying boy in the world had found me out, and I wasn't going to stick around to hear what else he could make of it.

Where are you going?

Home. Mama's waiting for me.

Anthony laughed. Don't go away mad, he said. Who knows when we'll see each other again?

We'll be seeing each other a lot from now on. Unfortunately.

How's that?

Our moms decided on it just now. Daddy was breaking the law with his parcels, so they're selling the farms and buying a new place for us to live on. The whole family. I started walking, but he grabbed me by the arm and pulled me back around. Don't touch me, I said, and yanked my arm away.

What the hell do you mean they're selling the farms?

It's happening. We all agreed. Katie says if we get the papers filed right away, we should have the new place up and running by the time school starts.

He set his hands on his sides and gawked. Son of a bitch, he said. No one asked me how I feel about moving.

Guess you shouldn't have run off, then.

A drop of sweat rolled down Anthony's face. His eyes, Daddy's eyes, appeared suddenly hollow, like egg shells or paper mâché, like one hard blow could cave them in. When he started to move, I feared he could come at me, but instead he turned and took out his anger on the nearest pair of trees. In a rage he tore away handfuls of plums and leaves and snapped the narrow laterals so that they hung fractured with only slivers of bark holding them to the branches. I stood watching his tantrum play out until his fingers were green and dirty and he was all out of steam. And then he was down on his knees with his face in his hands, crying like a baby.

Did that make you feel better?

He didn't answer. I took a few cautious steps forward until I was standing over him. His soft, defeated style of wailing reminded me more of Mama than of Gracie. I tried stroking his back like I did for her, but he pulled away.

Listen, I said. Moving's going to tough on all of us. I'm not wild about changing schools myself. But everything will be okay.

He wiped his nose on his arm. It's not that, he said. I can't help it. I've been going back and forth like this for a while now.

How come?

What do you mean? Anthony looked up at me with his eyebrows wedged in confusion. Our father's dead, he said. And he was a liar and a cheat.

Oh. That.

He stood and shook the sand from his pant legs. Fuck is wrong with you? You're younger than me, and a girl. My kid sister. You're supposed to cry and I'm supposed to say everything will be okay.

I don't know what to tell you.

You know what the saddest part is? When he was alive, he hardly ever gave me the time of day, but now that he's dead it's like I'm the only one who cares. I'm the only one who's broken up about it.

That's not true. You should have been in our house when Katie first got word to us that he was gone. Me, my sisters, and Mama, all crying at the same time. The pickers could hear us way out in the orchard.

I guess I'm just soft, then.

With the dusk light fading to darkness, I nodded toward the house and started walking in that direction. Anthony followed behind me and sped up until we were side by side. It was the first time a boy had ever walked me home at sunset. All sorts of new circuits were firing up for me that summer, and I had to remind myself that he was my brother.

You're not soft, I said. And you're not the only one who's sad about Daddy. It's just hard when you know he was lying to us and our mothers the whole time. Almost like it cancels out every nice thing he ever did.

In the near-dark, Anthony's shuffling footfalls seemed to grow louder. He never did that many nice things for me, he said. And after meeting his other wives, I think I get why.

Why's that?

Think about it. My mom is the only Mexican woman in the bunch. Why would he spend time with us when he had four white families to choose from?

Dawn isn't white. She's part Asian at least.

Okay, fine. But notice he never bothered to get her pregnant.

I don't think Daddy was a racist. He may have been a lot of things, but he wasn't that. Why would he marry your mama if he was?

Anthony snorted up a loogie and hocked it into the brush where it was too dark to see it land. He was after farms, he said. If you want to farm in California, Mexicans are the way to go.

We kept walking at the same pace even as the trail in front of us fell out of clear view. Mama was bound to be mad at me for going off so far without permission. I knew it from the moment I stepped out from Katie's porch. In the summertime, the hour or so before total dark was my favorite time of day. The heat dropped off and all the valley around us sparkled with little red and yellow lights from the neighboring farms. It was the same on Katie's land as on ours. Same rich smell of wood smoke, same warm air on the skin. Having Anthony there got me to wondering about how different life was bound to be on the co-op, and how much harder it would be to find solitude with eleven siblings running around instead of two. Just thinking on it had me feeling claustrophobic, but I decided all the same to give my new family the benefit of the doubt. Katie was right again. Sometimes being a sister is as easy as recognizing that someone else has the same pain as you.

Look, I said. If it makes you feel any better, you should know that Daddy wasn't much for giving me and my sisters the time of day either. In thirteen years, I don't think I ever saw him more than once every six months.

Anthony perked up. So you're saying he didn't single out me and my brothers?

I'm saying if he hated you all for being Mexicans, he hated us just as much for being girls.

Thanks. And I'm sorry for what I said. The Catholic stuff, the he-she stuff, and everything else. It's been a hard couple of months. But it's no excuse for being rude to you.

Thanks. I appreciate that.

Can we start fresh, then? As brother and sister, I mean.

Yeah. We can start fresh.

Good. I'm glad. And you're right. The months ahead are bound to be tough on everybody. How do we even begin? How do we begin to build a home out of so many broken pieces?

I don't know. But we'll try our best.

We came up from behind the house in the pitch black and ascended the steps to the porch. Dawn and Jennifer's cars were gone, but Mama was sitting in a folding chair by the door with Gracie asleep on her lap. She didn't scold me for making her wait, or even cast me an angry look. Instead there was a tired sadness in her eyes that made me feel guiltier than I'd expected to. I put my arm around her shoulder and she wrapped hers around my waist. Anthony tipped his head to us and went inside.

You're not a little girl anymore, Mama said. She sounded dazed and dehydrated.

I haven't been one for a while now.

I know. I'm sorry. It's my fault for being useless so much of the time.

It's all right. It made me strong. I'm just starting to realize that.

Mama smiled and pressed her cheek to my stomach. Across the road and through the trees, bonfire lights flickered dimly from deep inside the orchards. Strange music in the distance, drunken revelry of the day laborers. And nothing for us to do but sit and wait, and hope that somewhere in that darkness was a place we could call our own.

•

We stopped going to church after Daddy died. I don't think Mama ever liked going, but Daddy made a point every time he visited to make sure we were in regular attendance. He said a farmer ought to be involved in a local church, that other farmers would take notice if his family didn't keep the Sabbath. And though he never made it himself to any Sunday service, he had Mama give his best to the pastor, and mention a church in Sausalito he supposedly went to when he was out on the road. Of our neighbors on the surrounding parcels, only the Mendeses were Catholic. The rest included fellow Baptists, Methodists, and Southern Baptists, as well as one old Mennonite couple who'd somehow managed to hold on to their place through drought, disbandment, and the rise of the parcel program. In town you heard rumors of secular families, but out in the country you'd be hard-pressed to find a soul at home on a Sunday morning. Or at least that was the case until God fated Daddy's appendix to burst and freed us from the obligation forever.

I started cooking a big breakfast to cap off the end of the week. It gave Mama the chance to sleep in and made the girls happier than cold cereal. Plus I liked experimenting with different recipes and ideas of my own. Cinnamon pancakes with baked-in nectarine slices proved less tasty than I'd hoped, but bacon waffles were a surprise hit. One Sunday in July a neighbor woman came by with six jars of strawberry preserves from her summer pantry. I remembered her and her husband from church, and even though we were set to move in less than a month, I figured it was smart not to burn too many bridges.

You let your mama know we're praying for her, sweetheart, and hope she feels better real soon. We miss seeing you all at service.

The next Sunday I tried putting her preserves to good use. I'd seen an old movie on TV where a French cook made these thin pancakes with fruit rolled up in the middle, but my own attempts didn't turn out half as fancy. No matter how little batter I used in the pan, they were too thick and heavy to roll up properly. They ended up breaking apart and oozing strawberry like bloody road-kill. And the cakes the French dude made were so light and fluffy he could flip one in midair and catch it on the griddle. Made it look easy too.

They taste good, Jessie said.

I know. Just wish they'd come out looking better.

I took a napkin to Gracie's face so the jam on her cheeks wouldn't dribble onto her clothes. Walking back to the stove, I caught sight of something peculiar through the kitchen window. Jessie, I said. Come here a sec.

What is it?

I lifted her above the sink and pointed out at the driveway. You ever see that car around here before?

No. Who is it?

I don't know. You remember what to do if someone tries to get inside?

Lock the doors, take Gracie to Mama's room, and call the sheriff.

And what else?

She lowered her eyes and thought a moment. Call Tyler or one of the other foremen and tell him to come over quick.

Good girl. Now stay here with Gracie and keep an eye out.

The dusty black Mitsubishi hadn't moved since I started watching it. The glare of the morning sun on the windshield made it impossible to know if there was even someone inside, watching our house, or if some drunkard had mistook our driveway for an empty ditch and left the car there overnight. I stepped out onto the porch with one of Mama's American baseball caps pulled down low over my forehead. Almost immediately the driver's side window slid down and a small hand was waving at me. I pulled the cap off and ran down the steps and across the gravel drive. Dawn got out of the car and laughed as I ran into her arms.

I wasn't sure anybody was at home, she said. Must've spent ten minutes deciding whether or not to knock on the door.

It's so good to see you, I said. And I wasn't being polite. Since Katie's barbecue, I'd been thinking about the other wives and their kids nonstop. It was strange how one massive secret could make you feel closer to near-strangers than to all the friends and neighbors you'd grown up with your whole life.

Good to see you too, Ellie. Is your mama at home? She and I need to talk.

She's still in bed. Have you had breakfast yet?

The way she devoured my pancakes and eggs, I gathered Dawn hadn't eaten a solid meal since leaving Merced. I poured her a second cup of coffee and went back to wiping down the counter. From the last time I saw her, she seemed somehow younger and more tired-looking at once. It took me a while to finally place it—she wasn't wearing makeup.

These strawberries are great, she said. Can't remember the last time I had them.

I folded the towel over the edge of the stove. Round here we call strawberries a lady crop, I said. County won't subsidize em, so they're mostly grown by women in small family gardens.

Dawn shook her head. So many things people used to take for granted are so hard to come by nowadays. When I was a kid we used to have a store in the neighborhood that sold factory-made fruit pies for a dollar apiece. Apple, chocolate, lemon, cherry. I don't remember strawberry, but I wouldn't be surprised.

Wish there was a store round here close by. It's a pain having to go into town every time the milk runs out.

Least you grew up with it. Moving up here for me was like coming to a foreign country. Took years just to get used to the little differences.

You're from L.A. originally?

Near about. We moved around a lot when I was little.

How come?

She shrugged. I was the same age as your sister Gracie. I forget most of it.

Whether she'd heard her name or not, Gracie came pattering into the kitchen like she'd been called. She hugged my leg and buried her face in denim. Shy as she was, it was going to be interesting to see how she adjusted to having so many people around all the time.

You already sold the farm in Merced. That's why you're here, isn't it?

Dawn set her fork down on the plate. I didn't have anything or anyone to hold me to the place, she said. Just a lot of smashed dreams and a foreman I never felt comfortable talking to. So I filed the papers with the county the day after Katie's party. I didn't want to wait.

Mama will understand. At the very least, she'll be glad some of the money's been freed up for the co-op deposit. I gave her a smile as a show of goodwill, but right away it was clear something was off. She pushed her plate away and folded her hands in front of her face. She wasn't crying yet, but the change in her breathing was enough to signal its approach. I touched her arm. It's all right, I said. You can tell me.

She dabbed the skin beneath her eyes with a napkin. There's no money, she said. The deposit on the farm is all gone.

I fixed her a glass of white wine mixed with orange juice and led her from the kitchen into the living room. If Mama got up then she got up, but in the meantime I needed to know what happened so I could figure out how to break it to her and the others. I let Dawn have the good sofa while I sat on the other one with Gracie on my lap, hiding the ripped cushion with my thighs.

I feel so stupid, Dawn said. After the barbecue, I let myself believe that everything was going to turn out fine, that for once I'd have some real stability in my life. I even started thinking up ways to make the co-op nice when we moved in. I wanted to surprise you kids with a swimming pool. Now I can't contribute anything.

It's okay. We'll find a way to make it work. Just tell me what happened.

She picked her glass up off the coffee table and finished the rest of the drink in one go. Your daddy was borrowing against the farm, she said, panting. When I filed the release papers with the county, the balance of the deposit was nothing compared to what he had first put down. I figured there had to be some mistake. But then I checked with the ag office, and they showed me the receipts for all the times he took out loans over the past year. There must've been six or seven of them in total. And they all had his signature.

What was he using the money for?

I don't know. I never knew about our finances. You must think I'm naïve, but understand that your daddy had a way of presenting himself that made me believe we never needed to worry about money. In the year we were married, he traded up cars twice. Anything I wanted, anything he thought I needed, it was mine. Clothes, furniture, appliances, food. Maybe that's where all the money went. Keeping his young wife happy so I wouldn't stray while he was gone.

I took her glass to the kitchen and fixed her another drink. Even with the wall separating us, I could still hear her gasping and sniffling from the other room. I waited a full minute before going back in, and this time I brought the bottle with me.

I want juice too, Gracie whined.

This is grown-up juice. And anyway, you had enough to drink with breakfast. Go find Jessie and ask her to play for a while.

Dawn watched her scamper off toward the back of the house. You're really good with her, she said. And you're a good daughter too.

I know how to look after neglected women, I said. Comes with the territory.

She laughed above the rim of her wine glass before taking another sip. I am sorry for inconveniencing you all like this, she said. I'd planned on showing up at Katie's place, but when I got to Reedley I was too scared and embarrassed to see her. I didn't know where else to go when I remembered you guys lived down by Hanford.

Did you just get in this morning?

Last night. I didn't want to barge in after dark, so I slept in the car.

You didn't have to. It could've been three in the morning and we'd have still let you in.

That's kind of you to say, but you can't speak for your mama. And you can't speak for the others. When they find out I'm broke, they'll vote to cut me out of the co-op plan. Katie might show me some charity, but Jennifer won't stand to see me involved without cash on hand. You remember how she was at the meeting. The rest of us only matter to her as long as we're able to chip in.

Maybe there's another way for you to get the money together. What about all the stuff Daddy bought you? That's got to be worth something.

It was, but I had to sell most of it to pay down the interest on what he borrowed. All that's left is that old car out front and a suitcase full of fancy clothes and makeup.

What about the bank? Didn't he leave anything in the farm account?

A few thousand dollars. Just enough to pay off the foremen. Severance was written into their contracts. Nothing I could do.

I shook my head. Daddy always made sure his foremen were taken care of. Funny that's where he chose to put his loyalty.

Well, of course. They ran the farms in his absence. No way we could compete with that.

I picked up the wine bottle and refilled her glass. It was good that she was feeling resentful. Rather have that than tears. No one's going to squeeze you out if I can help it, I said. You've got as much right to a share as any of them.

I know. But how do I get the others to agree?

You don't need to worry about it right this second. You've been through an ordeal you didn't deserve. Right now you need to rest up and get your strength back. You have another glass of wine and get yourself a hot bath. There's a lock on the bathroom door, so no one'll disturb you. I'll bring your suitcase in from the car so you have something clean to change into. Tonight you'll sleep in my bed and I'll bunk with the girls.

Dawn drew her lips into a straight line and wiped the corners of her eyes. How old are you again, Ellie?

Thirteen. Fourteen in September.

She shook her head. Thirteen. Lord. If I was already as grown-up as you when I was your age, I don't think I would've ended up in this mess. You've got a good head on your shoulders, and don't let anyone tell you different.

I don't intend to.

Dawn took the wine bottle with her into the bathroom. I waited until I could hear the water running in the tub before making my move for the telephone. It was an old landline model with a cordless receiver—the last of the cell phone towers in the valley had shut down around the time I was eight. I took Mama's address book out onto the porch and dialed Katie's number. It rang three times before one of her sons answered.

This is Ellie, Sandra's girl. Is this Logan?

It's Will. How you doing, sis?

Fine. Is your mom at home?

Sure. Just a sec.

I heard Will call for his mother, and then a muffled exchange of words leading up to Katie's voice coming through on the line.

Morning, Ellie. How's it going, babe?

Hi, Katie. Sorry to bother you, but this couldn't wait.

It's no trouble. What happened? Is your mama all right?

She's fine, but Dawn is here trying her damnedest not to break down crying.

I explained everything to her the same way it had been laid out to me, about Daddy and the loans, the squandered deposit, the severance pay, and Dawn's painful trip down the valley. Katie didn't say a word, just listened with her slow breathing rustling in my ear. She even waited a few seconds after I was done talking before jumping in.

That poor girl, she said. I wish she'd come to me with this. Tried my hardest to prove to you all that you could trust me.

She trusts you, I said. She's just afraid of what'll happen when the others find out.

So am I to be honest. Jennifer and Claudia are already on the fence about going in on the co-op. This is only going to discourage them even more.

We might have bigger problems on our hands than what to do about Dawn.

If you know something else, honey, then spill it.

I glanced through the kitchen window and carried the phone down the steps to the drive. Way I see it, if Daddy could take out loans on the Merced farm without Dawn finding out, he could've done the same to all of us. We could be sitting on a pile of debt and not even know it.

Lord, Katie said. That'd put a wrench in everything.

I know it. That's why we've all got to check to see how much of our deposits are left intact. I'll find a way to do it without Mama knowing, you work on Claudia and Jennifer.

You mean to say you haven't told your mama any of this?

No, and I don't plan to until we know for sure what there is to tell. I've already got one worry-sick widow to deal with, I don't need two.

Right. I guess you should do what you think is best.

I will. And you should get on the others right away. Sooner we know how much we have to work with, sooner we can plan our next steps.

The ag bureau opens tomorrow at nine a.m. Should be able to check the balance before noon. I'll make the calls to Jen and Claudia tonight.

Good. And there's something else I'd like you to keep in mind.

What's that, hon?

I was walking down the drive to the Mitsubishi, the sun already stinging my face as early as it was. It was going to be one of those dry, miserable summer days in the valley, with a cloudless blue sky faded partly white, where even the breeze on your skin felt hot. I opened up the backseat and heaved Dawn's suitcase onto the ground. There were so many stones leading up to the house, I knew the pullout handle and wheels wouldn't count for much.

Do you take my word seriously?

Sorry?

I know I'm young. But do you care about what I have to say?

Another long pause on the line. Of course I do, Katie said. As much as I care about what anyone has to say.

All right. Then you should know that, whatever happens, I won't stand by and see Dawn cut out of the deal. You may think it's not my place to decide, but I've been hurt by Daddy as much as any of the women he was married to, and I say Dawn deserves a piece of whatever we manage to get. It's not her fault that Daddy left her without a leg to stand on. Nor is it to our credit if it turns out he left us flush. This co-op idea wasn't supposed to be about money and company shares. It's supposed to be about raising ourselves up alongside the only other people in the world who know where we're coming from. If I've got the wrong idea about that, then I'm not sure I want Mama getting us involved with it. And you know I could probably persuade her either way.

Yeah, honey, she said. I know you could.

All right. Just so we're clear.

We're clear. You look after your mama and Dawn, let me worry about Claudia and Jennifer. I'll be in touch when I have their answers.

Sounds good. Talk to you soon.

Bye, honey.

Goodbye.

I pulled the suitcase up to the porch one step at a time. The house was dead quiet when I came in, which likely meant Jessie and Gracie had been making too much noise right up to the moment they heard me open the door. I left Dawn's luggage outside the bathroom and went to check on Mama. Even with the ceiling fan on at full blast, the air in her bedroom was muggy and stagnant. I was opening the window when Mama poked her head out from under the comforter.

What time is it?

Little after ten, I said. Already hot out.

Did you find something to eat for the girls?

You know I did.

Thank you.

Mama rolled over onto her side. I slipped off my dusty sneakers and climbed into bed next to her.

I love you, Mama, I said, spooning her from the outside.

She took my hand and squeezed it gently. Love you too, kiddo.

Dawn is going to be staying with us for a little while.

Mama lifted her head and turned to face me. What are you talking about?

It'll only be for a few weeks. She can help look after Jessie and Gracie, and when we get ready to move she can follow us to the new place. It won't be any trouble.

But why is she here? I don't understand.

Because sometimes, when you're learning to stand on your own, you trip and fall instead. That's when you need a little help getting back on your feet.

Her crusty and bloodshot eyes stared back at me. She scrunched her face together and massaged her forehead like she had a headache. I don't know what's happening around here anymore, she said. I just don't understand it.

I know, Mama, but please trust me. You'll see. Soon we'll be living at the new place and everything will get a whole lot easier.

Mama rolled back over and nestled her shoulders against my chest. I folded my hands over hers and rested there with the smell of her hair seeping in with each breath. Mama, Jessie, Gracie, Anthony, and now Dawn. We hadn't even moved yet and already the list of people I had to look out for was getting longer by the day. Pretty soon it might encompass the entire Temple clan. All those years being dragged to Sunday service, I'd never felt any kinship with the other Baptists assembled in the pews. It took becoming a heathen for me to find my true congregation.

•

It was two days before Katie got back to me. When I called the county ag office, I managed to disguise my voice enough that they believed I was Mama checking in on the balance of our deposit, which, as it turned out, had remained untouched these past eighteen years. For one reason or another, Daddy had seen fit not to burden us with his debts. That bit of relief came on Monday morning, but it wasn't until Tuesday evening that the rest of the situation was revealed.

I'm sorry for keeping you all on pins and needles down there, Katie said, but it took longer than I expected to get everything sorted out.

But everything is sorted, right?

As well as it can be. The bad news is, it looks like Dawn got singled out for the big screw job. None of the other farms have any record of Elliot borrowing against the deposit. In fact, right up to the day he died, he'd never so much as been late on the rent.

Well, I said. If that's the bad news, then things certainly could've been much worse. What's the good news?

We reached an agreement, Katie said. And as it stands, it looks like we're okay to let Dawn have a stake in the co-op, no down payment required.

That's great. But how much did you have to give up?

Give up?

I figured we'd have to make deals to get Jennifer and Claudia to go along with it.

Right. Actually, it didn't take as much as you might think. Claudia surprised me with how understanding she was of Dawn's plight. Think she felt partly responsible for Elliot's shady dealings since she was married to him at the time. Jennifer was less gracious at first, but I got her to come around.

How'd you manage to accomplish that?

I heard Katie sigh and then laugh through the earpiece. That woman, she said. She tried dodging me at first, acting indecisive so I'd let up on pushing for Dawn to have an equal share. Finally I threatened to come up there and work it all out with her face to face. That's when she let the cat out of the bag.

She's been keeping secrets. I could've guessed as much.

I doubt you'd have guessed right. First off, she's been hiding the true size of the farm in Madera from us this whole time. I always thought it was strange that Elliot never tried to grab more than twenty acres per parcel. Turns out he had her fixed up on a farm sixty acres square.

I backed away from the stove and leaned my hands on the kitchen counter. You've got to be kidding me, I said. He bought up all those extra acres just for her?

A moment's silence on the line. Apparently, Katie said, sixty was what they started with when they got married.

I set the receiver down and took a deep breath. Jessie came running in with pouty lips and crocodile tears in her eyes. One look at my face sent her shuffling back into the living room. She tried to cheat us, I said. At the barbecue. She wanted us to go our separate ways so she could walk off with the biggest piece of the pie.

That's more or less what I accused her of myself.

Tell you right now. If she thinks those sixty acres are going to win her a controlling interest in the co-op, she's got another thing coming.

Hold on now, honey. I don't think we should antagonize her anymore than we have to. She's already backed into a corner.

Bullshit. She thinks she's got leverage over the rest of us, and someone needs to set her straight. She can try to write off her blessings on the grace of God, but it's the grace of Elliot Temple that's left her feeling high and mighty. And that shouldn't count for anything.

We've got our own leverage at play here, Katie said. That's the other thing I wanted to talk to you about.

What? Did Elliot give her ten children instead of the two we know about?

No, but she does have more dependants than we thought. Her parents are still alive. Both of em. They've been living with her on the Madera farm these past several years, and now she's fixing to have them come and stay with us at the new place.

How old are they?

Not sure. In their seventies, I'd imagine.

That's pretty old for this area.

They're not from here originally. Jennifer grew up in Irvine.

Right. Coastal money, higher life expectancy. That makes sense.

Since her parents weren't part of our plan, and they're not even Temples, we agreed they cancel out whatever burden Dawn might pose by not being able to pay in to the deposit. It all evens out in the end.

Don't see how that math works, I said. Dawn's only one person, and she's young and healthy enough to contribute. Can Jennifer say the same about her folks?

I'm not going to ask her that. Besides, it's only two more than we expected. They won't be any trouble.

We can hope. Personally, I've never cared for old timers. They smell bad. And some of them make racist comments.

Katie laughed heartily. God bless you, honey, she said. You're all right.

I know I'm coming across as an icy bitch right now, and I don't like it anymore than you do. But this is what my situation has led me to. You have no idea what it's like to have to take care of everyone, manage the farm, and go through puberty all at once.

No laughter this time. You're right, honey. It's not fair, the lot you've been handed. That's why I'm working so hard to lighten the load.

For all of us.

I backed away from the counter. Through the window I watched Dawn lead the girls around the side of the house and out onto the grass in front of the packing shed. And I appreciate everything you've done, I said. Lord knows if you hadn't taken the trouble to track Elliot down, we'd still be waiting around for him to call.

I know I'll never be a real mama to you, honey, she said. You've already got a mama, and I wouldn't try to step over that line. Same time, if you ever need anything, even if it's just to talk, I'm always here for you.

Thank you, I said. I'll be in touch.

Please do.

Goodbye.

Bye, honey.

I hit the end call button and secured the phone to the wall charger. Invoking my hormones felt like a desperate move—I was already kicking myself for stooping to it. I paced the kitchen floor with my hands on my lower back, trying to ride through the shame and anger like I did with the pain of a sore tooth. A rare summer cloud moved in front of the setting sun, and as I was looking outside I noticed Dawn sitting cross-legged on the grass with Jessie and Gracie playing beside her. I tried slipping my sneakers on without undoing the laces, but I couldn't get one to fit over my heel. So instead I kicked them both behind the trash bin and left the house with my feet unencumbered.

Walking toward her, I could see that Dawn was fiddling with something in her lap. It wasn't until I was standing over her, though, that I saw clearly what it was. She had picked several blooming dandelions from different spots around the lawn, and was in the process of weaving their stems together to make a braided bouquet of sorts. Noticing the shadow that had fallen over her work, she looked up at me and smiled.

Hey, she said. What's up?

I plopped down on the grass and crossed my legs in the same style as hers. Katie called, I said. It all worked out. You'll be coming with us to the new place.

Dawn's face went suddenly blank. For real?

It's true. You're entitled to a stake in the co-op even if you can't pay into the deposit. That's what we all agreed on.

She sprang up onto her knees, spilling the flowers to the ground, and wrapped her arms tight around my back. Thank you, thank you, she whispered, and I could feel her tears trickling down my neck. This never would've happened if you hadn't stood up for me.

You're welcome, I said. There's no way I would've let them cheat you out of your claim.

Dawn slid her hands to my shoulders and pulled her head back. She stared into my eyes. What's wrong? Why are you so angry?

It's nothing, I said. Just some stuff I don't understand.

Tell me. Maybe I can help.

I glanced sideways to check on Jessie and Gracie. They were playing out beyond the edge of the grass, hitting a partially deflated beach ball back and forth off their fingertips. I don't understand why you ever agreed to marry my father, I said. I don't understand why any of you did. I hate him. I hate his memory, his blood inside me. If he had one, I'd hate his soul.

Where's all this coming from?

I told her everything, about Jennifer and the sixty acres, about her richie rich parents from down on the coast. The whole time Dawn kept nodding and listening calmly even as I worked myself into a bigger and bigger stink. By the time I'd told her all there was to tell, I wasn't sure if I was more likely to punch something or break down and sob.

I know you have a lot of hate in your heart right now, she said. You've got as much right to it as anyone ever did. But my hope is that eventually you'll learn to let go of the anger. Nothing good'll come of it. That's what I believe, anyway. All the rage I had inside of me, I've tried to give it up.

How could you? After everything he did?

He's gone now, Ellie. Hating him would only mean giving him more time and energy than he already took from me while he was alive.

You don't still love him, do you?

Dawn laughed and stretched her legs out over the grass. Honestly, Ellie, I'm not sure I ever loved him.

Then why did you marry him?

Lord, she said. I don't know if I should be talking with you about this. You're still young. I wouldn't feel right if I made you cynical about romance all together.

My father had five wives, I said. You think I'm not already soured on Prince Charming?

Fair enough, girl. Fair enough.

Just tell me the truth. Was it like Katie said? Was his money the only draw?

No, Ellie. Money helped, but it wasn't the only thing. If money was all I was after, I could've made it a lot easier as a sex worker.

You mean a whore?

I don't like that word, but yeah. If I'd played it smart, I could've had a lot more fun than I did being married to your dad, and I'd have had control over my own income.

They why didn't you? Be a sex worker, I mean.

Dawn sighed. Like I said, money wasn't the only thing your dad had to offer. Sex worker or not, there was still a chance I'd have wound up raped if I'd kept on living like I was.

My mouth fell open before I knew what it was doing. Couldn't be helped. *Rape* wasn't a word that Mama used herself, and she wouldn't have tolerated hearing it used inside the house. On the TV news, they used *violated* instead. As in, *Unidentified woman found violated and murdered in tavern restroom outside of Clovis.* All over the valley, in the country dives and back roads between towns, there was always some fresh violation going on.

You were homeless, weren't you? Before you met him?

I wandered for a long time, she said. These days lots of people have to wander to find work. The single men have it easier than the women. They can land jobs as pickers or fruit packers on farms like this. But for a young girl without a family, and without any money, there's not much this valley has to offer. Besides the hope of finding a man and settling down.

I know what you mean, I said. Before Mama was married, she wandered for two whole years starting when she was seventeen. She met Elliot at a state-run gas station near Willows. She was hitchhiking south and he was the first person to offer her a ride.

That sounds like him.

She wasn't always homeless, though. My grampa was in the American Army before disbandment. I never got to meet him, but Mama says he was an important officer who was stationed in Alaska and Poland. She used to travel around with him when she was little, before my grandma died. Then they moved back to Chico, and grampa got cancer too. I don't think Mama knew what to do after they were both gone, when she was all alone for the first time.

Being orphaned when you're young is never easy, Dawn said. Now imagine it happening at the same time your country is coming apart, when there are no jobs to speak of and everyone you know is going bankrupt.

I know it was hard, I said. I can see the toll it took on her all these years later. Still, it just seems like a bad reason to marry somebody.

It is. As bad as any. But until you've walked these dusty roads for miles at a time, and fallen asleep clutching the knife in your pocket, there's no way you can know what you'd do if you found yourself in the same spot.

I get it. She did what she had to to survive. But what about after that? She was married to him eighteen years. Eighteen years and all she could think to do was hide away in bed with her sadness. Never once tried to leave him, never told him to stay away. She even stood up for him against us girls, any time we got upset that he was gone. Your daddy has to travel to make money for us, she'd say. Right up until the day she found out about his other wives.

You talk like she had so many other choices, like she's weak for not leaving him a long time ago.

She's my mama, I said. I know she's weak.

I think I surprised her with that. Dawn opened her mouth like she was going to say something, but instead closed it again and looked down at the grass. It's easy for me to forget you're still a child, she said finally. Until you go and say something like that.

It's not childish to call it like I see it. If it's not weakness that's kept her here all this time, then what is it?

Love. Love for her babies. Fear, of what would happen if she had to try to support you all on her own, knowing how she gets when the depression takes over.

Love and fear. Is that all I have to look forward to when I get older?

I wish I could tell you it's easy to pick up and leave when the situation turns ugly. But there's a whole lot of people in this state who'd try to make things difficult for a single mother and her children. You and your sisters might never fully appreciate just how much worse women have it nowadays than in my mother's day, or in my grandmother's, even. We're well into the twenty-first century now, but for the women of San Joaquin it might as well be the 1950s. My mom used to talk about birth control like it was a carton of milk, like when the time came she could walk into any drugstore and get whatever she needed to protect herself. These days you could probably find it on the coast easy enough, but here in the valley you'd be more likely to get arrested than to find a pharmacist who'd be willing to help you out.

In that instant it was too much to feel Dawn's eyes on me, scolding me silently for making judgments about things I could only grasp secondhand. I started thinking about the pills Mama used to take to even out her moods, and how it became harder and harder for her to find them until finally she was forced to do without. And all the while the women at church said it was lack of faith that made her sad all the time. They laid hands on her and prayed that she'd take Jesus into her heart, as if that organ hadn't been hurt enough by the other man in her life.

I'm never getting married or having kids, I said. Not even if I fall in love.

Dawn nodded slowly. That's your right, she said. But folks'll make you pay a price for it all the same. They'll call you a spinster and a dyke.

I don't care. People can say what they want.

They will. And if you're half as strong as you think you are, you'll have to build up a wall against their b.s.

I know. I've already started.

I figured as much. Just be careful. Walls keep out more than just the bad. Day might come when you wish you'd let in more of the good.

We'll see.

That's right we will. In the meantime, don't fault your mama for what she didn't do. She's lost so much already, she doesn't deserve to lose your respect as well. Besides, she might surprise you one of these days.

You mean she might get out of bed for good?

Maybe. And if not, well, there's more than one way to be strong.

She picked the yellow flowers up off the ground and resumed her careful work of weaving the separate, hollow stems into a single dense braid. After sitting quietly for a while, I stretched my body out over the grass and rested my head on Dawn's leg. I listened to her soft humming, to the frenzied slapping of Jessie and Gracie running through the yard in their sandals. We didn't say anything for what felt like a long time, and then I told her I was sorry. It's okay, she said, and nothing more. It made me anxious to leave it like that, with her moving on from the topic and me wondering whether I'd tainted her feelings toward me forever. I was all set to apologize again when she sang out a note of pride and pinned the finished wreath to my hair.

•

After so many weeks of thinking about the new place in the abstract, it felt strange come August when it finally became real. The co-op papers went through at the end of July, and by the start of the new school year we were all set to relocate to a hundred and twenty-acre spread north-east of Orosi—half nectarine orchards, half apricot, with a small pasture at the center for grazing livestock. The tract had been cobbled together from a half dozen smaller parcels whose previous owners had either cashed out or been forced out by the county for failure to make rent. There were quite a few failed farms in that part of the state, such that the minute we arrived we were greeted with envy and suspicion from nearly every neighbor in a twenty-mile radius. Most went out of their way to avoid us. Others erected brand new barbed wire fences along the property lines and posted signs warning SOLICITORS NOT WELCOME, as if we aimed to expand out further like a cancerous growth and swallow up all the land we could get our hands on. Our first and only visitor that summer was an elder from a local LDS congregation. He drove up unannounced in a refurbished Buick, asked to speak to the man of the house, and left in a state of confusion after Katie came out to meet him.

For all the land that was suddenly ours, there was a surprising shortage of living space to go around. Three of the previous owners had lived out of camper trailers or Winnebagos rather than pay the county's price to have a proper house constructed. Another had watched a perfectly good home consumed in a brush fire with no insurance or money on hand to replace it. That left two one-story, US-era ranch houses for five families to fit into. Separated by a hundred yards of upturned and sandy topsoil, the houses were too close for privacy and too far away for convenience. Sun-baked hornets' nests hung plastered under the eaves and behind the rain gutters, and inside the carpets were so matted with dust that in a certain light they appeared to be steaming. After some dispute, it was decided that Claudia's family would come to live with us and Dawn in the bigger, uglier model while Jennifer and Katie would squeeze their broods into the smaller, slightly nicer one. As soon as the funds were available, we'd file the papers to build a third. From the beginning, all of the major decisions were decided by a vote among the five Temple widows. Us older kids could sit in on the debates and chime in if we wanted, but suffrage was granted only to those who had suffered through marriage to Daddy.

One of the tougher decisions that had to be reached early on was what to do about finding schools for the eight of us that still needed educating. Jennifer was adamant about sending Lewis and Jewel to the private K–12 academy in Visalia, and after all the fuss it had taken just to get her this far, the other wives chose not to begrudge her that privilege. My sisters and Anthony's brothers were sent to public elementary schools on opposite sides of the county—our mothers had decided on separating them to avoid drawing extra attention to the co-op, and to spare them the embarrassment of having to explain their half-siblings to the other kids. At fifteen, Will was legally old enough to make up his own mind about school, and in the end he opted to stay on the farm and learn machine repair from his brother. That left me, Beth, and Anthony to attend the local high school, to ride the sweltering yellow bus eighty minutes each way in the early morning and late afternoon. Hardly anyone asked about our shared last name, and when they did we said that we were cousins. As popular as she was from the start, Beth had a way of making people take her at her word, and as for me and Anthony, we didn't talk much.

The high school was situated on a concrete and asphalt slab northwest of Tulare, surrounded on all sides by short, untended grasses that were yellow-brown twelve months out of the year. You could ride the bus for miles in that part of the county and see nothing at all until finally a cluster of green, pagoda-shaped buildings rose up out of the ground and the silver mirage peeled back across the basketball courts. Even though Anthony was two class grades ahead of me, we had the same homeroom every morning and History twice a week after lunch. Beyond that, we each had some version of Math, English, Ag Science, and PE. Some of the classrooms were over twenty years old and still equipped with internet outlets, and gas ranges for science experiments we would never learn. The oldest rooms were sealed-off and used for storage space. Even then, there was no danger of overcrowding. Most of the kids in the area would follow Will's lead the minute they turned fifteen. Our freshman class was already larger than the rest of the student body combined.

Our History course included students from all four grades. Only one semester of History was required to graduate, but some of the older kids retook it two or three times for the easy elective credits. The teacher was seventy-four years old and kept an American flag pinned to the wall above the whiteboard. He'd talk for thirty minutes on the lesson of the day and spend the rest of the time cursing dead Democrats and explaining how the US had perished through sin, decadence, and decay.

As the welfare state grew more unwieldy, he said, traditional values were torn down and replaced by whatever ideas were popular at the moment. Through the atheist media, millions of people were taught to worship the extravagance of the big cities. Pimps and prostitutes were built up as idols. One in three children was murdered in the womb. Men fornicated with their fathers' corpses. That's right. Corpses.

At least once a month we were marched into the cafeteria for special assemblies that were the closest we got to actual health classes. Itinerant speakers—balding, energetic, and middle-aged men—came in to lecture us about the changes that were going in our bodies, about the perils in store for those who didn't abstain, and about a host of other scandalous topics that left us snickering between slideshows of cankerous private parts. In the same cafeteria, three or four times a semester, the school held Friday night dances to give us the opportunity to socialize properly, to give farm boys and farm girls the chance to slow dance to old country songs while chaperones stood guard to uphold the dress code and check our breath for alcohol and weed. These extracurricular events, more than any of our actual classes, affirmed for us the real lesson we were supposed to take away from our time in school—that the true purpose of youth was coupling, that sexuality was only safe within certain parameters, and that severe consequences awaited those who veered too far outside.

I went to one dance, toward the end of my first term, and never went to another one afterward. Anthony borrowed his mother's car and drove us down in the early evening dark with shreds of tattered fog obscuring the road for miles at a time. Though neither of us cared about the dance itself—we were both going stag—we were still dressed to fit in with the rest of the preening and awkward teens, him with a stiffly ironed flannel shirt tucked into the waist of his best jeans, me wearing a skirt for the first time since Katie's barbecue nearly six months earlier. I'd borrowed some of Dawn's eye shadow and a lacy brassiere from Beth. The cups were two sizes too big for me, and after tugging at the straps the whole ride down, I wound up ditching it in the backseat before we went in.

Being the winter dance, and the last big activity before the long break, the cafeteria was decorated to the point of gaudiness, with construction paper Santas dangling on strings alongside gold and silver garlands, and every table and flat surface dusted with a layer of twinkling glitter. Me and Anthony made our rounds separately, saying hi to the various boys and girls from our grades, pretending it was a pleasant surprise to find them there of all places. Eventually, though, we settled into an empty table at the back, watching from a distance as Beth swayed from side to side with her arms around the broad shoulders of her new beau, Eric, a beefy-looking junior who'd driven her to the dance in his own secondhand car.

You let me know when you're ready to go, Anthony said. I can leave any time.

You're not going to ask one of the girls to dance?

Anthony sneered. There's only two girls here who I'm sure know my name, he said, and I'm related to both of em.

You got to try and put yourself out there, I said. If that's what you really want.

Maybe I do, maybe I don't. But what does it matter? Even if I found a girl who liked me, she'd run off scared as soon as she learned about our family. And then the whole school would know. You want that?

No. But how are you going to find someone if you never trust anybody?

Fuck that. Trust is for our mothers. And look what it did for them.

Anthony snatched the plastic cup off the table and drank the rest of his punch in one long chug. Times like this, it was no wonder he still hadn't made any friends at school. But neither had I for that matter. Not really, anyway. There were two boys in my grade who I was on friendly terms with, one in my English class and one in Ag Science. We shared sarcastic comments when the teacher's back was turned, but that was it. Where they went at lunchtime, or what deeper thoughts lay behind their snarky expressions, I had no idea. All I cared from day to day was that they were cool enough not to drag me down, but so goofy that they never stirred up any strange feelings. The more determined I became about my future spinsterhood, the less willing I was to risk spending time alone with boys. And since boys were all the girls in my grade ever talked about, I spent most of my time out of class reading library books and hanging out behind the bleachers with Anthony, around whom I had built a wall of sexlessness appropriate for male relatives.

We haven't really talked about it, I said. But do you think you'll stay in school long enough to graduate?

I don't know, he said. If it wasn't for my mom, I might've dropped out already.

What would you do instead?

Get the hell out of the valley for starters.

All right. Then what?

Not sure. Join the Army, maybe. I already know how to shoot.

I pushed aside the plate of sugar cookies and leaned forward with my arm on the table. You're a smart guy, I said. You'd be wasting your time in the Army.

He glared at me. I suppose your grampa was wasting his time in the service too, he said.

That was different. The California Army's nothing but a bunch of thugs. All they do is camp out along the borders and chase down illegals. You might as well join the skinheads.

It's not all like that, he said. I might get stationed somewhere in Sierra. They have snow up in the mountains. You ever seen snow?

No.

Me neither. But I want to. He reached for one of the cotton balls glued to the paper tablecloth. He pulled some of the fibers loose and tossed them above his head. We watched them float down to the floor and settle between our feet. Real snow's not like that, he said. Real snow melts in your hand if you try to catch it. Our old foreman told me all about it.

The same one who taught you how to shoot?

That's right.

Sounds like a cool dude. What happened to him?

What do you mean?

Why didn't he come over to the new place? Like Jennifer's guy.

Anthony spun the empty cup on the table with his index finger. Even as he was looking at me, he seemed to be staring straight through my eyes and into some far off and mysterious void. He quit before dad died, he said. Moved on to another job up north.

Bummer, I said, and Anthony nodded his agreement. You ever think about staying on at the farm? After you're done with school?

He glared again. You saying I couldn't do any better than this?

You know that's not what I meant. It's just, you've got a big family here now, and we'd miss you if you were gone. I'd miss you. Who am I going to hang out with if not you?

I see, he said, and he flashed me a cocky smile. Over the past few months, he had gotten really good at showing me the amused yet condescending affection of a sister's older brother. Sounds like you're the one who needs to put yourself out there.

Oh, right, I said. That's just what I need. Some pimple-faced dude begging me for handjobs all the time. Thanks but no thanks.

Anthony laughed. I guess that's what I should want to hear from my kid sister, he said. Just maybe not put that way exactly.

Tough shit. You want subtlety, try Jessie or Gracie.

He stood and pulled the wrinkled ends of his shirt out from underneath his waistband. Fuck this, he said. Let's get some Chinese. There's a place on the way home that's open late.

I looked over my shoulder and surveyed the dance floor, but it appeared that Beth and Eric had already left. Okay, I said. You buying?

I waited for one of Anthony's standard foul-mouthed quips, but for once he didn't seem in the mood to play along. He looked down at me with solemn eyes, already holding the car keys. Why not, he said. This might be the closest either one of us ever gets to going out on a date.

We reached the front entrance right as the music was changing from a slow rock ballad to some kind of pop country track that would've been harder to ignore. The school, the music, and the other sounds of the dance all receded behind the taillights as Anthony drove us back into that dark and seemingly limitless countryside that separated our lives' points of interest like the sea separated the ports in this old sailing novel I'd checked out of the library a while back. This time of year, even the orchards were dormant, the leafless trees sticking out from the ground like skeletal hands grasping for the sky. Sometimes it was oppressive, having to pass through so much dead space each day on the way to school, but just then it brought me an odd feeling of relief, sitting quiet in the car with the radio turned off, and only the lights of the dashboard to disturb the comforting darkness.

You still think about Elliot much?

Anthony kept his eyes fixed on the road ahead. I try not to, he said. But it's hard with his wives and kids around me all the time.

Is that why you want to leave the valley so bad?

It's part of it.

I gave him time to say something else, and when he didn't I turned to face the window, to watch the circle of moisture on the glass expand and shrink with each warm breath I took.

•

We arrived home a little after nine and set up shop in the living room with our cartons of sweet and sour chicken and a crime show on TV.

Those days the networks in L.A. were all about cop dramas, mid-budget serials about grizzled country lawmen busting meth cooks and smugglers in shanty towns along the Mexican border. The only one that was any good, that didn't have the same stale formula each time, was called *Peacemaker: San Bernardino County*. It was about a county sheriff in the days following disbandment, when the roads were teeming with the homeless and unemployed and most small towns could only afford to offer the most basic police services. In each episode, the hero sheriff, Dick Moseby, had to reckon with some new tragedy that had befallen the townspeople, usually a kidnapped child or drug deal gone wrong, and hunt down the villains responsible. What set it apart from other shows was that Moseby changed a little bit after each episode, so that if you followed the series close you could see him transform from a clean-cut, by-the-book lawman into a guy struggling to keep his family together without turning into a villain himself. Me and Anthony watched the show regularly, and were afraid it wouldn't get picked up for another season.

You ever go out to eat with dad?

I dropped my plastic fork in the carton and whipped my head around. Hell no, I said. Why? Did he go out to eat with you guys?

Sure. All the time.

You got to be kidding. I don't think I ever saw him in a restaurant in my life.

What did you guys eat, then, when he would visit?

Whatever he told Mama to make special, I said. His homecoming was always a big to do. She must've slaughtered fifty chickens in his honor over the years.

He always wanted Chinese when he was with us. That's how I first got the taste for it.

Maybe he didn't like Mexican food.

My mom never cooked Mexican food.

Then what did she cook?

Same stuff she cooks now. Steaks, burgers, and hotdogs. And

sometimes chili beans without any spice to them.

I meant to find out more about Elliot's tastes, but the show was just starting to get good. Sheriff Moseby had tracked the Mexican drug cartel to an underground bunker in the Mojave Desert, and was faced with the choice of waiting for reinforcements to show or going down to confront the gangsters on his own. There was a tight close-up on his face as he descended the ladder rungs down into the bunker. All the space below was hidden in darkness, and before the commercial break you could really hear his breathing getting louder as each step brought him closer to the danger inside. Then the show cut out and we were back in the real world, fishing pineapple chunks from pools of red sauce as a local car salesman hollered about financing options for the latest Korean sedans on his lot.

When the phone rang, I jumped up and hurried to the kitchen before it could wake up the whole house.

Evening, Ellie, Katie said when I answered. Sorry to disturb you all so late.

It's no trouble, I said. What's up?

I was just wondering if Beth was over there with you guys.

No, it's just us.

Okay. Did she say when she expected to get back?

Sorry. We left before we could talk to her.

That's fine. The dance ends at ten, right?

Yeah, but I think she might have left early. Probably getting a bite to eat with Eric.

Right. That makes sense. I won't wait up for her, then. Thanks, babe.

No problem. Have a good night.

You too.

As I hung up the receiver, I could tell from the sounds of gunplay that something pretty spectacular happening inside the living room. I sprinted to the sofa and plopped down on the cushion next to Anthony, who was bent forward with his eyes on the screen.

What I miss?

He gestured to the TV with his fork. Moseby snuck up on em while they were cleaning out the lab, he said. Now he's pinned down in the corner.

Shit. There's not enough time. They're going to carry it over to next week.

Anthony nodded and stuck his empty carton behind the end table. Sure enough, the *To be continued* caption appeared on screen right as Moseby was laying down his sidearm. After that there was nothing but news on all four channels, so we switched off the set and broke out the card deck. We played gin rummy and blackjack until after midnight, when we both started to doze off. We may not have been cool enough to break curfew, but, damn it, it was Friday night, and we weren't going to bed any earlier than we had to.

Hope you didn't get Beth into trouble with her mom, Anthony said.

I switched off the kitchen light. Oh, that girl, I said. Causing scandals left and right.

Settling down for the night was always tricky. I shared a bedroom with Jessie and Gracie, and unless I wanted to have to coax one or both of them back to sleep, I had to be quiet as possible unrolling my sleeping bag. There was one queen-size mattress for the three of us, and from the start I let the girls have it and settled for sleeping on the floor like a kid in a Japanese cartoon. It was rough at first, learning to sleep with the floor under my back, and in a new house no less. After a while, though, I got used to it. Later that night, in fact, when Dawn came to knock at our door, I was sleeping like a baby.

What's going on?

Dawn held her yellow bathrobe over her shoulders with one hand, staring at me deeply. Katie's here, she said. You better come out to the kitchen.

I staggered down the hallway rubbing the crust from my eyes and found the mothers all seated around the big table where we ate most meals. Mama and Claudia were both wearing their nightgowns, long and shapeless pieces that made them look older than they were. But Katie appeared to be wearing the same clothes from that day. Jennifer had sweatpants on and her hair in a clip, the first time I'd seen her looking so ordinary. It was three in the morning and cold out, and I was afraid to know why they were all awake and in our kitchen. Anthony stood alone in the corner, looking over at me with so much concern in his eyes I barely recognized them as Daddy's.

Sweetheart, Mama said. We need to ask you some questions about Beth.

I sat down and laid my hands flat on the table. Where is she?

Dawn set a cup of coffee down in front of Katie. She still hasn't come home, she said.

Did anybody try calling Eric?

Yeah, Katie said. His parents said he left the dance hours ago. He told them she got a ride with some other people. He wasn't sure who.

Katie took a sip of coffee and kept her face down over the mug. She seemed to be trying very hard to stay calm.

I only saw her for a minute at the dance, I said. I'm not even sure if she was still there when we left.

Did you see any other boys talking to her?

Shush, Claudia, Jennifer said. Beth is a responsible girl. I'm sure she wouldn't do anything to jeopardize her future.

Katie looked up suddenly. I don't care if she comes home pregnant, she said. So long as she comes home safe.

The other mothers traded looks and closed in around Katie to comfort her more closely. All except for Mama, who'd taken hold of my hand and seemed incapable of letting go. I touched her wrist and stroked the short white hairs along her arm. I hadn't told her yet about my plans for spinsterhood, and wasn't sure if they would ease her fears or make her more worried than ever.

We might be fretting over nothing, I said. She probably fell asleep on somebody's couch. Sometimes there are house parties after the dances.

She would've called, Katie said. It's not like her not to.

Claudia glanced around the table with a nervous grimace, and then looked straight at me. You're a good girl, she said. Tell us the truth. Do you know if she's started drinking?

I already told you, Anthony said. Beth's not into that sort of thing.

As far as you know, Jennifer said.

That's right, I said. As far as we know, Beth hasn't done anything wrong.

Jennifer threw out her hands. And yet here we are, she said. Here her mother is worrying herself sick.

You're not listening to me, Katie said. I'm not worried about whether or not she's experimenting with alcohol. She could come through that door right now plastered out of her mind and I wouldn't even chew her out till morning. All I care is that she's safe. That nothing bad's happened to her.

We should call the police, Dawn said. They might know something we don't.

I already tried, Katie said. They haven't had any accidents tonight. If she doesn't turn up by morning, they said to come in and file a report.

Anthony walked to the center of the room and stood crouching over the table. Tell you what we need to do, he said. We need to get out there and search every back road and ditch within forty miles. If there was an accident in the country this time of night, the cops might not even know about it till morning. Beth could be lying hurt somewhere with no one around to help.

Logan and Will are already out looking, Katie said. They been gone nearly an hour.

Anthony shook his head. There's too many places between here and the school, he said. One car ain't enough to cover all of em. Tell you what. You all can stay here and wait for her to show up, but I'm going out and bringing her home myself. Don't try to stop me.

I'm coming too, I said, and pulled my hand free of Mama's grip.

We both started for the door at the same time. Claudia stood up from the table in such a rush that she lost her balance and almost knocked a chair over. Anthony, she said. We've already lost one child tonight. We don't need two more out there to worry about.

I'll go with them, Dawn said. He's right. We need more than just one car looking.

Before any of us could make another move, Katie scooted her own chair out from the table and rose to her feet. Mama and Claudia edged in around her, like they were afraid she might fall. If you find Beth safe, she said, let her know that she can always come home. Tell her I love her, and no matter what the problem is, it's nothing we can't solve as a family.

The roads through the country seemed even darker somehow than when we were coming through the first time. Anthony sat hunched forward with both hands on the wheel, holding steady at forty-five as he scanned the roadsides for any gleam or shimmer from his headlights. I'd offered the front seat to Dawn, but she opted for the back instead. Even after all the time I'd spent taking care of Mama, it felt strange to me that, in a crisis where one young person was missing, it should fall on the other young people in the family to lead the charge.

Whose underwear is this? Dawn asked, holding the lace brassiere up to the rearview.

That's Beth's, I answered. She offered to let me borrow it for the dance. She said it would make me feel grown up and full of confidence.

That was sweet, Dawn said. She folded the brassiere in half and stowed it carefully on the empty seat beside her. Though I could only make out the broad details of her face through the mirror, it was clear that her face didn't have much to show at the moment anyway. That worried me more than the notion that me and Anthony were in charge. Dawn was never without expression. Happy or sad, angry or fearful, she always wore her feelings more vividly than any of the makeup she'd brought with her from Merced. Now she reminded me of one of the homeless veterans camped out behind the ag bureau, staring a hundred yards ahead but seeing only inside herself. I checked the clock on the dashboard.

How're we supposed to know she isn't back at the house already?

Anthony breathed through his nose in a slow, deliberate way. I don't really believe she was in a car accident, he said. I just framed it that way for Katie's sake.

Then what do you think happened to her?

Come on. Girl like that, dressed how she was. One way or another, she got herself into some trouble.

I turned around in the seat to check on Dawn. You might've thought she was sleeping with her eyes open, the way she let her head hang back with her neck bent like a spring. I'd been afraid that Anthony's assessment would shock and upset her, but in a way this was worse. What're we doing out here, then, if she wasn't in an accident?

Anthony took a right at the next intersection, the first turn he'd made since we got on the road. We're looking for signs of suspicious behavior, he said. People driving with their lights off, idling in orchards with their windows fogged up. We'll circle round the area moving inward like a spiral. If we don't find anything, we'll head back to the house and wait for the cops to wake up.

I looked at Anthony for a while with the shadows of the land moving over his face. Without realizing, I let my head sink back against the seat cushion until finally I'd assumed the same dejected posture as Dawn. I don't know whether to be impressed by you or worried, I said. Either way, you've seen too many episodes of *Peacemaker*.

He said nothing. Just kept on driving as the early morning frost settled over the ground.

•

The first light of day was breaking out over the foothills when we arrived back at the farm. Logan's car was parked out front by the bigger house. We could see it as we were heading up the drive, and by the time we got there Anthony was so anxious that he swerved onto the lawn and shut the engine off without bothering to shift into Park. We all piled out and headed for the door. Will came out onto the porch to meet us.

We found her, he said. She's all right. She's got some bruises on her face, but she's more shook up than anything. So when you get inside, try to stay calm and keep your voices down. She's been through a lot.

We followed Will into the kitchen and found Beth sitting at the table with Mama and the other women all crowded around her. I was relieved at first to see her alive and all in one piece, but then she turned her head and I got a full look at the damage. The whole left side of her face was swelled up to the point where she couldn't even open her eye. All the tears she shed from that side seemed to trickle forth from the ends of her eyelashes. The other eye was unharmed, but so red and puffy from crying that it was hard to look at it directly either. I found myself looking at the floor, where I noticed the second skin of grime that had crept up over her ankles and calves all the way to the torn and soiled ruffles of her skirt hem. Katie knelt by her side with a dish cloth and a pot of warm water, readying to scrub the filth from her daughter's scraped and blistered feet. She sniffled loudly and looked up at us where we stood.

She fought back, she said, her voice oddly proud through the convulsive panting. He tried to take advantage of her, and she fought back. My girl. She stood her own and didn't give in.

I wanted to do something. Even now, it's hard to fathom how, as hot-tempered and protective as I was, I could just stand there gawking while a girl barely older than me, who shared my blood no less, was forced to suffer through the pain of something so horrible even her mother could only speak of it in euphemism. I wanted to go up and comfort her any way I could, but as it happened Dawn, of all people, was the first of us to take action. She took small, shuffling steps across the linoleum floor, then bent down over Beth and softly touched the unbruised side of her face. From the state of numbness she was in moments before, she broke out into full unrestrained sorrow, cradling Beth's sore and assaulted body in her arms, crying into the dust-stained fabric of her party dress. I watched her sink down and kneel on the floor beside Katie, take the damp cloth in her hand, and commence to bathing Beth's legs with her own tears falling drop by drop into the water pot. I remember thinking at the time, Is this all we can do when one of our own gets wronged? To weep and wail together, and wash away the stains like the wrong never happened?

I don't know how long it was before Beth had settled down enough to get some rest. After Dawn finished consoling her, we all did what we could in our own way to follow suit. Mama gave up her bed and even tucked her into the covers like she used to do for me and Jessie. We didn't have any aspirin in the house, so Claudia gave her some white wine diluted with water and honey. Jennifer summoned Jewel from the second house and got her to take the little kids over there and fix them breakfast. I admit I was impressed by that. Jewel was snotty even by eleven-year-old standards, and in all these months had never looked at me or Beth or any of her half-sisters with anything but the most hateful and accusing eyes, like every breath we took was spent plotting ways to upstage and outshine her. But now, in this crisis, she did her part for the rest of the family, and didn't even complain. That earned her my respect, for what it was worth. Actually, if there was anyone in the family who disappointed me, it was Anthony, who, faced with the reality that he had been right about Beth, seemed to close in on himself and shrink once more into the corner. That didn't earn him any points in my book. He could sulk and stew and wear that scowl on his face all he wanted, but when all was said and done, he still hadn't done squat to help Beth, or the situation in general.

For the second time that morning, all the Temple women gathered around the kitchen table. This time they were all drinking coffee, or rather, four of them were drinking it while poor Katie held onto her mug with both hands, letting the heat rise up and over her beleaguered face. All her thought and energy seemed to be focused on keeping her wits together, for Beth's sake, or perhaps for the sake of the family at large.

It was Eric who did it to her, she said. All at once the mugs hit the table and the other women looked at her aghast. The little bastard lied to his parents. Or they lied to me on the phone. Either way, he and Beth did leave the dance together. He drove her halfway home and then turned off-road into a peach orchard. He took her way out past the tree line where no one could see them parking. They started to fool around in the backseat, and when he tried to make her go all the way, she told him to stop. That's when things turned ugly.

Sitting next to Mama, I noticed she had covered her mouth with her hand, and hadn't moved it since Katie started talking. All of them, in fact, had locked their bodies into rigid, unnatural postures, and seemed set on staying that way for the time being. Even Dawn had reverted back to her statue-like gaze from the car, hearing every sordid word that was said, but reacting to none of it.

She did exactly as I taught her to do if she ever found herself in that situation. She went for his balls. Gave em a good kick from the sound of it. But then, as she was trying to get the door open to run away, he came up from behind and jumped on her. Hit her so many times she thought she might faint. Then he kicked her out onto the dirt and drove off. Left her to walk home alone in the dark with her face all battered and one eye swollen shut. She said the only reason her brothers found her was because by then there was just enough light that she could make out their car on the road. Before that, she'd ducked out of the way any time someone was coming up behind her on the road. Too scared to take a chance on a passerby.

The whole table was silent for what felt like a long time. When Katie finally took a sip from her mug, the others seemed to regain their awareness of their own bodies and started moving around. Dawn reached for a napkin and dried her eyes. Claudia made the sign of the cross on her chest. That one small gesture appeared to do wonders for relieving her pain, or at least it gave her what she needed to keep the pain inside. She slid her arm over the table and took hold of Katie's hand.

He didn't succeed, though, did he? Her purity is still intact?

Katie didn't look at her. She didn't seem to be looking at anything, as a matter of fact. She's still a virgin, she said. If that's what you mean.

Claudia patted her wrist. Well, she said. We can thank God for that.

Dawn pushed her chair back from the table so fast that one of the legs scraped the floor. She took a few hurried breaths and started walking to the other end of the kitchen. We've got to do something, she said. We've got to call the police.

She was halfway to the phone when Jennifer slipped in front of her and blocked her path. Not so fast, Jennifer said. We have to discuss this. We have to talk about it rationally.

There's nothing to talk about, Dawn said. She looked down at Katie and then at the rest of the mothers. Then at me. My God, she said. This could've happened to any one of the girls. It could've happened to Ellie. We can't just sit here while that little monster is out walking free.

Calm down, Jennifer said. Please. There are things we have to consider before getting the authorities involved in this. First and foremost, we need to think about what's best for the children. All of them. Including Beth. After everything that's already happened, there's no sense in dragging her through another ordeal.

I want justice for her, Katie said. She pushed the coffee mug away and scanned our faces. For a moment, at least, it looked like the indomitable old Katie had returned. She deserves justice for all she's been through, she said. That means seeing the boy punished for what he's done.

Jennifer came and stood by her. There are different kinds of justice, she said. We've got to ask ourselves whether it's fair to the other children to make them all suffer simply to win justice for one of them.

Mama stood up suddenly and started pacing the floor with her wooly house slippers smacking her heels. I don't see what good it does any of them to try and sweep this under the rug, she said. That's no sort of lesson to be teaching them, that they need to hide their heads in the sand anytime someone wrongs them.

From the look on her face, I gathered Jennifer was mighty surprised by Mama's reaction. She wasn't the only one. Most of the time it was easy to regard Mama along the same lines as a potted houseplant, as a delicate thing that you kept in a room and tended to constantly without expecting anything but passive endurance in return. But now here she was laying it on the line for what she really cared about. Dawn's prediction had come true. She'd finally surprised me.

The lesson we need to teach them, Jennifer said, is to weigh the costs and benefits of a decision before rushing ahead with it. You all talk about justice like it's simply a matter of calling up the sheriff's office and watching them drag the boy away in chains. But it's so much more complicated than that. If we press charges, there's going to be a trial and hearings and all the questions that go along with that sort of thing. The lawyers will call Beth to the stand and pick her story apart piece by piece. Long before that, though, they'll try to get at us any way they can. We already know the boy's parents have strong ties in the community. Wasn't that one of the things that impressed you, Katie, when they first started dating?

Our eyes turned back to Katie, whose spirit had once again receded. Eric's father sits on the city council down in Visalia, she said. He runs a trucking company that moves goods and produce between here and the coast.

Jennifer nodded. He's well-off, then, she said. Well-off and well-established. The sort of man who wouldn't stand to see his family's name being tarnished. You think he'll sit by and watch his son get hauled off to juvenile detention?

He can try to fight it all he likes, Katie said. But what does it matter? You saw her face. It's obvious the boy's guilty.

It's Beth's word against his, Jennifer said. That's all a judge and jury are going to care about. And some people might take issue with the fact that she let herself end up in that orchard to begin with. They might wonder what sort of girl sits in a parked car with a boy late at night, and how many boys there were before this one.

Katie opened her mouth very slowly. That's way out of line, she said. She's fourteen. Who would think to shame her like that?

I'm not saying it's right, Jennifer said. I'm just laying out exactly how things will unfold if you call the sheriff. Go ahead. Tell me I'm wrong.

She has a point, Claudia said. You know how people get when there's a scandal in the air. Especially when it involves a young girl.

That's exactly right, Jennifer said. What's more, you all seem to be forgetting that our families have more reasons than most to keep out of the spotlight. We've been fortunate so far, even with the whole community whispering about us behind our backs, but that fortune won't last if something like this comes out. To begin with, the local news stations are going to have a field day. They're going to send reporters and cameramen out here to question all of us and our neighbors. And sooner or later they're going to look into our pasts to try to figure out how five single women ever managed to get a hold of a farm this size. Our worst fears will become realized. They'll find out about Elliot and the other parcels, and then we'll be the ones on trial. That's the nightmare that's in store for us if you go ahead and call the sheriff—our children ostracized and abused, while government auditors come in and strip away everything we have. I'd be curious to hear how you could justify even the possibility of that happening.

I waited for Katie to fire back at her. Or Mama. Or anyone else, really, just so I didn't have to try and stand up to her myself. Jennifer had changed since the summer, or maybe I had. Either way, it wasn't like Katie's party this time around. There was too much cold logic in what she was saying, too many legit reasons to follow the cautious path. For years I had prided myself on being able to hold my own against any adult in the room, but now that no one was treating me like a child, the thrill of being included in the discussion had finally worn off. If anything, I found myself feeling jealous of Jessie and Gracie, safe and happy in the smaller house with all the other little kids. They probably didn't even know that anything was wrong, or at least they had no clue of the compromises the adults were preparing to make on their behalf. I was flirting with the notion of going over and joining them when all of a sudden Dawn let out a long and miserable-sounding groan. She fell into Mama's vacant chair and pressed her palms to her forehead as if to keep her face from hitting the table.

What's the point? What's the fucking point of any of this? She raised her head and looked out at the rest of us with tear-rimmed eyes. This farm was supposed to be a safe place, she said. This was supposed to be a place where no one could hurt us. Not Elliot, not anyone. What's the point of holding on to the farm, this hundred and twenty-acre monstrosity that everyone in town hates us for having, if we can't keep our children safe? What's the point if we can't have justice when one of our own gets treated like a piece of meat? Why even bother?

Heartbreaking as Dawn's questions were, they didn't have any effect on the rest of us beyond making us feel even lower than we already did. Jennifer stood with ice water in her veins, arms folded across her stomach like a peeved schoolteacher waiting for her class to settle down. Mama had taken a seat back at the table, and Anthony might as well have been a piece of decoration on the wall for as much as he contributed. As for me, I could already tell where the debate was headed, such that it seemed cruelly procedural when Jennifer called for a vote to settle the issue. Dawn's arm was the first to shoot into the air, followed a moment later by Mama's. Whatever hesitation she might have had in casting her vote in favor was likely erased by the realization that the nays had already won. Katie's vote was the final one cast, several long seconds after Jennifer and Claudia had raised their hands. Afterward she let both arms fall down at her sides, as despondent in victory as if Beth's assault had been carried out all over again.

I'm going to feel guilty about this for the rest of my life, she said. Even now I don't believe it's the right thing to do. But I'm responsible for more than my own here. I can't ask you to risk the wellbeing of your kids just to do right by one of mine.

Those final words of concession stung worse than anything else that was said that morning. They placed the outcome squarely on the shoulders of those of us who had no say in the matter, declaring once and for all that we were the ones intended to benefit from denying Beth a chance for justice, regardless of how we felt about receiving the favor. The precedent had been set, and all future votes were proactively rendered meaningless. From now on, the women were subservient to the needs of the children, and we in turn were ruled by invisible enemies from outside the borders of the farm. While Mama and the others were slow to get up from the table, I left immediately after the vote was concluded, too overloaded with my own angst to do anything but let it fester on its own.

•

It was early afternoon when again someone knocked at my door. I threw a pillow over my head and shouted to whoever it was to leave me alone and let me sleep. Of course I hadn't really been sleeping, but if Mama got to spend days at a time lying awake under the covers, feeling like shit, then I believed I was entitled to at least half a day of regrouping in the same fashion. The door creaked open and I sensed a pair of feet coming toward me across the thin carpet. I sighed into the sleeping bag and prepared to cuss out Jessie or Gracie for ignoring my demands. But when I threw off the covers, I saw that Anthony was the one standing over me. The look on his face was deceptively vacant. Most people wouldn't have thought twice about it, but I'd spent enough time around him the past few months to know when he had something on his mind.

Christ, man. I could've been nude.

His face didn't change. Come with me, he said. I have something important I need to do, and I can't do it alone.

I'm not getting out of this bag unless you give me a good reason to.

Just come on. Please. I was going to ask Will, but I don't know if I can trust him.

All right, all right. Give me a second.

I pulled my jeans on and followed Anthony to the bedroom he shared with his brothers, Sebastian and Mark. The whole place stank of boy, of dirty socks and B.O., with an undercurrent of spray deodorant that did nothing to mask the other smells. Anthony began fishing through the wadded clothes on the floor at the bottom of his closet. He uncovered a grungy duffle bag and set it down carefully on the edge of the bed. The mysterious silence he was holding to was more off-putting than anything. Before unzipping the bag, he wedged a laundry hamper against the door to obstruct anyone who might try to surprise us.

If you're thinking of showing me your secret porn collection, I said, you picked one hell of a weird time.

He acted like he couldn't hear me. Stay by the door, he said. Keep an ear out and tell me if somebody's coming.

You're going to have to explain what this is or I'm leaving.

Not so loud. Just keep listening to the hallway.

I waited and watched as he opened the duffle. Inside there were other wrinkled clothes, old shirts and cotton shorts worn down to mere rags. Anthony tore several layers off the top of the mound and threw them onto the bed, paying no mind whatsoever to what he was digging through. He forced his whole hand inside and grabbed hold of something at the bottom. After some initial stubbornness, the rifle came loose and slipped out from under the pile of clothes like a newborn calf bursting free from its mother's pelvis. Anthony clasped the wooden underside of the rifle in his other hand and stood with the piece angled diagonally across his chest. Regardless of how he might have pictured himself, he looked less like a soldier or hunter and more like one of the illustrations from his brother's picture book, *Peter and the Wolf*. If I hadn't been so afraid of what he planned to do with the rifle, I almost certainly would've teased him about it.

Listen, I said. You need to take a second to calm down. We've all been through a lot today. But whatever you're thinking about doing, get it out of your head right now.

He took a deep breath and held the rifle closer to his chest. I know what I'm doing, he said. I know what I have to do.

Oh, really? And what do you think that is?

Isn't it obvious? Our families have been insulted. Yours, mine, all of us. Somebody's got to make Eric pay for what he's done, and I'm the one to do it. And I want you to come with me. To keep a lookout.

Lookout. Jesus. You really have been watching too much *Peacemaker*.

Anthony took a step forward and repositioned the rifle with the barrel across his shoulder. I've got it all planned out, he said. We'll wait until dark and then drive up onto his family's property with the head-lights off. Depending on how much tree cover is available, I should be able to sneak up on the house without being spotted. When Eric passes in front of his bedroom window, I'll plug him in the back of the head. By the time his parents discover the body, we'll already be gone.

I pressed my back against the door. The stink of dirty socks and underwear was radiating from the hamper, but it would've taken a lot more than that to get me to move aside. I should've known you'd take this badly, I said. Earlier, when we first got a look at Beth, I admit I was annoyed at you. It annoyed me that everyone else was doing their part to make her feel better and you were just standing off by yourself, not helping. But now I wish you'd go back to sulking in the corner. At least then I didn't have to worry about you doing something crazy.

This is my way of helping Beth, he said. It's for her sake that I'm prepared to shed blood.

No, it's not. You just said it. You want to go off and murder Eric because you believe he insulted the family. You want to shoot him to make yourself feel better.

Anthony scowled at me with anger boiling up from behind his eyes. I'm not a kid anymore, he said. I'm a man. It's my responsibility to protect this household. Somebody has to.

Our mothers just did what no mother should ever have to do, I said. They sold their souls to keep a shit storm from raining down on us. And now here you are, fixing to bring another storm down on top of us.

If you're not going to help me, fine. I'll do it on my own.

No. You won't. You're going to put the rifle away, and you're going to stay clear of Eric and his family.

What're you going to do? Pry this thing out of my hands?

No. I'll do what you're really afraid of. I'll tell your mother about your plans.

Anthony blinked a few times without saying a word. Then he smiled. Go ahead, he said. I don't give a crap if she knows.

Yes, you do. Or you wouldn't have set me to listening for her footsteps in the hall.

The smile vanished as quick as it came. He slid the rifle off his shoulder and held it loose with the barrel dangling an inch off the floor. I trusted you to help me with this, he said. You wouldn't really go and tattle on me like that.

The hell I wouldn't. If you wind up arrested for murder, it won't be long before word gets out about Elliot's parcel fraud. Then where will we be?

I won't get caught. I've got it all planned out.

You don't even know what his family's property is like. They'll nab you for trespassing before you get anywhere near Eric.

He clenched his teeth and swung the rifle onto the bed. God damn it, he cried. Why are you being like this? Why are you being such a little bitch?

As he turned his face to the wall, I seized my chance and pounced on the rifle before he could get his hands on it again. I pulled back the lock to inspect the chamber. It wasn't even loaded. Anthony paced the room with his hands balled into tight little fists. Every so often he paused to punch the air and let out a high-pitched groan. For as much as he was worried about me making noise, he didn't seem too concerned about someone overhearing his hissy fit.

You don't understand, he said. None of you understand a damn thing about what I'm going through. I can't just stand by feeling helpless while that asshole gets away scot free. A man protects his own. I wouldn't respect myself if I didn't.

You need to quit worrying so much about how you feel about it, I said. You weren't the one he tried to rape. You didn't get beat up, and you didn't have to walk home alone in the dark. If all you can think about at a time like this is how you're going to prove yourself a man, then you've got the same head sickness as Eric as far as I'm concerned.

Anthony slammed his fist into the wall. From the way he winced afterward, it looked like it hurt him a lot more than it did the wall. All right, he said. What, then? What do I do to make this right? And don't say let it go. I've had enough of that shit from our mothers.

No one expects you to let it go, I said. If you really want to help, you can do what you should have done from the start. You can put the rifle away and come with me to Katie's place. You can help to make Beth feel better. That's what she really needs right now.

He stood with his hands in his pockets, looking down at his sock-feet. I wouldn't be any good over there, he said. I wouldn't even know what to say to her.

You were ready to kill for her sake, I said. But you can't even stand to face her. Is that what being a man means to you?

Even with Anthony acting quiet and moody, I felt a whole lot better about the situation once the rifle was back inside the duffle bag, hidden away in the closet. Anthony put his shoes on and followed me across the yard to the smaller house. There were dark clouds across the sky and in front of the sun, but still he kept his head down and eyes turned away from me as we walked. We approached the house from the front. Jennifer's parents, Grandma Alice and Grampa Reid, were seated in canvas camping chairs positioned side by side on the porch. Before we could even begin to mount the steps, Beth came outside carrying a plate of saltine crackers and two plastic cups of wine. The bruises on her face now showed the same deep red color as the drink. She had on a pair of gray sweatpants and one of her mother's button-up shirts, but her hair was still done up the way it had been at the dance. She glanced at us briefly, then set the refreshments on the folding table and squatted on the boards beside the old couple.

There's lemonade in the kitchen if you guys want, she said. Mom likes to keep some on hand even on cool days.

No, thanks, I said. We're not thirsty. We came to see how you were doing.

She turned the bruised side of her face to us and shrugged. You're looking at it, she said.

I sat down across from her with my back against the porch railing. Anthony remained standing, leaning on the painted support column at the top of the steps, his head angled so he could only see us through the corner of his eye, if he saw us at all. Jennifer's parents or not, we didn't have to worry about saying the wrong thing in front of Grandma Alice and Grampa Reid. Alice hadn't spoken a word since her laryngectomy years before, and Reid's mind was so drifty most days he could barely remember who we were. Alice reached a veiny hand out and raised the cup of wine to her lips. Her husband smacked a saltine into mush between his gums, crumbs cascading onto his face and clothes. Beth took the napkin off his lap and wiped his chin for him.

You shouldn't have to look after them today, I said. You need to rest.

I've rested enough. She folded the napkin over and laid it across Grampa Reid's thin leg. Besides, Jennifer pays me good money to take care of her folks on the weekends. She has ever since we moved in.

Can't she get Lewis or Jewel to do it?

Beth laughed. Lewis is too busy spanking his monkey to be of help to anyone, she said. As for Jewel, she'd be happy sticking her grandparents in the ground a few years early just so another bedroom would open up. I guess Jennifer cares enough about her mom and dad not to place their wellbeing in her own kids' hands. Anyway, she pays well, and I don't mind it.

I pulled the brassiere out of my back pocket. It unraveled instantly and hung limp and wrinkled from my fingers. I wanted to make sure I got this back to you, I said. The cups didn't fit right, so I didn't end up wearing it in the end, but I wanted to say thanks all the same. It was a nice thing for you to do.

She took the brassiere and folded it into her shirt pocket. Sorry it didn't work out, she said. Sometimes it's nice to feel sexy just for the hell of it.

Anthony cleared his throat in a way that made me wonder if I'd made a mistake bringing him along. Here it was supposed to be his chance to make her feel better and all he could do was stand around looking sour like always.

We wanted you to know that we're both sorry for what happened, I said. We wanted to say that if you ever want to talk, we're both right across the way. Right, Anthony?

He pivoted on his heel and made eye contact with Beth for the first time since we arrived. For sure, he said. You need help with anything, let us know.

That's right, I said. In fact, Anthony, why don't you ask your mom if she can start lending you the car during the day? That way you can drive us to school and we won't have to bother with the bus anymore.

Anthony nodded. Yeah. I'll try asking her.

That's sweet of you to offer, Beth said. But I'm not going to need a ride to school from now on.

I turned my head and gaped at her. Why not?

I turn fifteen in a couple of months. Mama says they won't kick up a fuss if I leave early.

She's making you drop out?

No. This is my own choice. I may not get the chance to see Eric behind bars, but I sure as hell don't have to see him again either. Or any of them for that matter.

I watched her dry her eyes on the sleeve of Katie's shirt. She shuddered from touching the bruised half of her face, and afterward she let the tears on that side fall where they may.

Seems like a shame to leave school on his account, I said. What're you going to do, then, if you're done taking classes?

I don't know, she said. But I'll tell you one thing. Soon as I'm old enough, I'm leaving the valley for good. I'm sick of it.

Where would you go?

Somewhere on the coast. A real city.

Think you'd do well over there, Anthony said. He stepped away from the support column and took a seat under the window sill next to Beth. I wasn't sure if he was doing much to help her feel better, but from out of nowhere his own attitude had suddenly perked up. I hear there are towns on the coast where they still have internet, he said. Everybody's connected to everybody.

That's what they say, Beth said.

Not to mention the food. Every kind of restaurant you can imagine. Chinese, Japanese, Indian. After disbandment, all the good cooks in the valley packed up and headed for the ocean.

Beth looked out across the field with a far and dreamy look in her one good eye. With the wind picking up, the rows of topsoil had suddenly come alive, shifting and falling in place like lines of sand on a rattling tray. I'd just like to live in a place where there's something going on, she said. Last year for my birthday, mom drove us up to Fresno to see a movie at the only theater left in the county. It'd been a long time since we were up that way, and when we got there the theater was all stripped down and boarded up. Big *For Sale* signs hanging in the windows.

Mama took us to see a movie down in Bakersfield once, I said. The faces on the screen were so huge Jessie thought they were going to gobble her up. Started crying so hard we had to leave after ten minutes.

It costs money to live in a city, though, Anthony said. A lot more than it does to live here. You'd have to find a good-paying job to make it.

I'll find a way, Beth said. Anything's better than sticking around here waiting to grow old.

I've been wondering, I said. When Elliot was alive, did he ever let you guys come with him to the coast?

Not me, Beth said.

Same, Anthony added. He always said the coast was no place for farm people.

There was a bitterness in Anthony's voice that I worried would swing his mood back around the other way. Still, it was something like a relief to know that Daddy hadn't excluded me and my sisters in particular, that he'd kept all his families equally confined to our humble lives down on the parcels.

I used to dream that someday he'd drive up to the house and take us away to live with him in a big city, I said. But now that I'm older, I'm not sure I'd be comfortable living in an area like that. They say people on the coast look down on folks from the valley. You might end up feeling lonely and out of place all the time.

Beth clenched her jaw and continued to stare out across the land. No one would need to know where I really come from, I said. I'd tell em I grew up someplace else.

Where?

Depends. If I lived in San Francisco, I'd say I was born in L.A. And if I was in L.A., I'd say San Francisco.

You'd be okay doing that? Lying all the time?

Everyone lies about something, she said. We're lying right now about our father and where the money for the co-op came from. Our father lied to us and our mothers every day of our lives. Eric lied when he said he cared about me. What's the point of being honest when the dishonest people always get what they want?

God's the point, Anthony said. He judges everyone in the end.

I don't believe in God anymore, she said. God is just another old man who's never been there for us.

I watched Anthony's eyes widen and his face go blank. For all he knew, this was the closest he'd ever been to an outspoken non-believer. I know what you're talking about, I said. But I don't agree about the lying. At the end of the day, I've got to believe there's a way to stay honest even without some big man with a beard watching over us.

Good luck with that, Beth said. In the meantime, you'll have one less Temple to run into at school, cause I'm done with it. I'll stick around doing chores for mom and Jennifer until I've saved up enough money, then I'm gone.

You should try talking to Dawn about this, I said. She's got a lot of experience living on her own. Might have some good advice for you.

She's an angel, she said. Spent all morning looking after me. Tired herself out so bad mom finally made her go lie down in the bedroom.

You should talk to her before you decide to leave. What she has to say might be worth thinking about first.

See, that's your whole problem right there, Anthony said. You keep looking to yourselves and your mothers and each other for answers. But God's the only one who has any answers to give. Two thousand years before any of us were born, He laid out the correct path for us to follow. He's with us now even if you don't accept it.

Right, Beth said. Then I guess He was with me in the orchard last night too. He was right there watching while Eric beat on me.

Anthony scowled. It's not His responsibility to explain why bad things happen, he said. The burden's on us to keep faith in His word.

His word, I said. You mean like, *Vengeance is mine, saith the Lord*?

A shamed look I'd never seen on him before came over Anthony's face. He hid his mouth behind his knees and hugged his legs to his chest. I thought he might've been praying at first, but his eyes were open and he wasn't making a sound. With him crawling back into his shell, I hoped Beth would feel like talking some more, maybe opening up about what Eric's betrayal really meant to her. But instead she went back to cleaning up after Grampa Reid, who had red wine dribbling from the corners of his mouth, making a mess of his shirt front. The wind continued to pick up, sending a current through the leaves and teasing the parched earth with the promise of rain. And still more clouds came rolling in from the west, though, like most things, they never stuck around the valley longer than they had to.

•

All told, it was a bad winter to try and get a farm up and running. The temperature dipped into the low twenties at night, and every morning the frost settled on the grass in crisp white blades. Neighbors who specialized in citrus watched helplessly as their winter crops came in hard and flavorless and gray. Most of the orange growers in Orosi had cashed out by the end of January, and with their departure the pickers at the state camp packed up and headed south for the season, leaving no one to prepare the land for spring. So many of our own laborers pulled out that we had to start paying their deposits back out of the household account. The big breakfasts I liked to cook on Sundays disappeared, replaced by morning after morning of farina and other packaged cereals that could be purchased in bulk at the local grocery. When Gracie outgrew her winter jacket, I took Mama's sewing machine down from the closet shelf and altered Jessie's to fit her. In turn, I gave Jessie my own heavy jacket and made do myself with one of Mama's old coats. Without telling anyone, Dawn sold the rest of the clothes and makeup Daddy had bought her to a second-hand store in Tulare. We tried to refuse her money, saying she should've kept the clothes to have something nice to wear. She replied that, come summer, it didn't matter if she had to run around in her chonies, so long as we were able to get by till then.

The first apricot was at least four months out, but still the trees needed watering and tending to make it through the winter. Jennifer's foreman, Dale, really proved his worth in those uncertain days. Even with the state labor camp deserted, he used his connections to round up a team of hired hands to work off-the-books pruning and irrigating straight through to the first blossoming. Taciturn men with prison records and no proof of citizenship, they nonetheless knew how to keep an orchard in good health, and to keep out of sight if the county inspector came snooping round. Not everyone was thrilled to have them on hand, though. After what had happened to Beth, Mama said that none of us girls were allowed to play outside when the workers were in the orchard. We tolerated her command, as we'd tolerated her fear of the Mendes children, and spent our afternoons inside watching TV or doing homework.

Money and labor problems aside, I looked forward all day to coming home again. Even after pulling straight A's in the first semester, school began to lose the value it once held for me. The frost had taken its toll on so many families in the area that come January fewer than half the upperclassmen returned from break. Most of the Math and English faculty were let go and the juniors were lumped together with the freshman and sophomore classes. I'd hardly seen Beth at school before she dropped out, but now I could feel her absence everywhere on campus. Each room I entered made me pause to wonder if she'd taken a class in there before. I spent my breaks and free periods hiding in the library and behind the cafeteria, avoiding anywhere my peers congregated in groups of two or more. Any time I thought I saw Eric coming toward me in the corridors, I turned and hurried off in the opposite direction or ducked inside the girls' bathroom. I could never be sure if it was really him, but I wasn't about to take the chance. Not surprisingly, I started to gain a reputation as a weirdo. With a small student body pulled from a handful of small farming towns, it didn't take much to get labeled as one. Kids went out of their way to avoid sitting next to me in class, and on the bus ride home other girls burst into muffled laughter as I stomped through the aisle to the open seat at the far back. Once I overheard a pair of sophomore boys whispering a few seats ahead of me. One of them turned and looked back at me real fast. That's the one I was telling you about, he said, and his friend glanced over his shoulder and laughed in my general direction.

I might've been spared these afternoon bus trips if Anthony hadn't decided right out of the blue to go out for the wrestling team. After having her ear whined off all December long, Claudia finally decided that she couldn't afford to lend the car to Anthony during the day—not if she was going to keep up her routine of giving confession at the local church three times a week. Fortunately for him, Dawn overheard their bickering and offered to let him borrow the Mitsubishi on weekdays. For a brief moment, I thought my days on the big yellow limousine were at an end, but then he went and decided he'd rather spend his afternoons getting manhandled by a bunch of sweaty dudes in leotards. There weren't enough schools nearby for them to wrestle competitively, but the team still met for practice in the gym Monday through Thursday. Anthony would get home around seven and collapse in a chair at the dinner table. He'd spend another half-hour hunched over the plate of food his mother saved for him, too exhausted to do more than eat a few bites and wash them down with a gallon of ice water. I never came out and asked him why he bothered with it, but I never stopped being curious either. The longer I knew my brother, the more it seemed that his passions always led him to pursuits that excluded the company of women and incorporated violence in some crucial way. I couldn't help but feel uneasy about the way he chose to spend his time. Still, if wrestling kept his mind off the rifle in his closet, that was good enough for me.

I found him on the bleachers one afternoon during free period. His practice didn't start for another ninety minutes, but he was already dressed in the red spandex and black socks of his team, in the same uniform he wore around the house, against his mother's wishes, whenever he was too lazy to change before heading home. He appeared to be killing time watching a freshman PE class run laps around the track, though he might've been spacing out instead. I tend to believe the latter, seeing as how he didn't seem to notice me approaching until I was already sitting down next to him.

Aren't you cold in that getup?

He shrugged his bare shoulders and rubbed his hands together. Cold's bracing, he said. Makes you stronger.

I guess. Feels like I hardly see you around anymore.

I've been busy.

Busy wrestling?

Busy getting into shape. I got to toughen up.

So you're still planning on joining the Army?

Soon as I'm old enough. Or as soon as I can pass for old enough. Whichever comes first.

Right. Well, let me know when you decide to sign up. Cause I'm dropping out of school the very next day.

Anthony finally looked at me directly. As dark as he was, his cheeks still showed red in the cold. Is that your way of trying to guilt me into sticking around?

No, I said. I just don't want to go through this alone. You're my only friend here.

That's no reason to drop out, he said. You're brainy. You could do a lot with a diploma.

Like what? College?

Yeah. You might get a scholarship someplace good.

I shook my head and drove my fists deeper into my coat pockets. College is for rich kids in other states, I said. Round here they're bull-dozing colleges to free up space for more farmland.

So move to another state, he said. What's wrong with you? The valley's no place for somebody with your smarts.

I've got Mama and my sisters to worry about. I can't just up and leave them.

That's a shitty excuse. I think you're just afraid of trying to make it on the coast.

Maybe I am. So what? Elliot came from the coast, and look at what a monster he turned out to be. Antony looked around the empty bleach-ers, as if to make sure no one was listening in. All this time we'd kept to an unspoken agreement never to talk about Daddy at school, and my sudden breach of the pact was clearly making him nervous. But he was worrying for nothing. The only students within a hundred yards of us were too busy sweating and panting on the freezing cold track to give a crap about anything we had to say. I know I sound like an obsessive, I said. But I'm trying. I'm trying every day to get him out of my head.

I didn't know he was still in there. Thought you got him out a long time ago.

I quit mourning real fast, but that was because I was so angry and hurt by what he did.

Anthony stretched his arms out over his head. He didn't have much yet in the way of biceps, but his chest looked fuller and less boyish than it did before he started training. You wouldn't feel hurt if you didn't still care about him, he said. It's the way we were created. Everyone wants to be loved by their fathers and by God. Can't fight the human condition.

I can harden my heart, I said. Same as how you're working to make your body tougher.

Yeah, I guess you could.

I've already made progress. When we first met, I could hardly stand to look at you, because you have his eyes. Now they don't bother me a bit.

His arms fell down at his sides. He looked at me and seemed on the verge of laughing, though his lips never cracked a full smile. I really do, don't I? Have his eyes?

Of course you do. Why would you think otherwise?

Dad never said they looked the same, and mom's color blind so she can't tell. I always thought we had the same eyes ever since I was little, but no one ever came out and said it, so I wasn't sure if I was right. I used to look at myself in the mirror and try to remember what he looked like. That was when I was eight or nine. Six months felt like forever then.

They always felt long. His away stretches.

That's why even now I don't mind the winter, or the hottest days of summer. Because he used to come home in January and July. We always had new clothes, toys, and Chinese food around those times.

As I listened, I tried not to show how this new bit of information made me feel. I must not have been doing a very good job, cause right away he shot me a concerned look. January and July, I said. Funny. We usually saw him around March and September. Right as the cold was dying off, and right as the heat was fading.

I never thought about that, he said. Guess he must've had a whole schedule mapped out for when he would visit each family.

It's time to be honest with ourselves, I said. His being on the road all the time was never about making money or improving our lives. He just had a lot of families and farms to manage, and needed to ration the time he spent with us.

Anthony put his heels up on the bench and stared down at the soggied laces of his wrestling sneakers. He didn't say anything for a while, and neither did I, and in our silence the steady thumping of feet on the track seemed amplified to an absurd degree. I thought you weren't angry at him anymore, he said finally. What happened to getting him out of your head?

I don't feel anything about it either way, I lied. I'm just stating a fact.

Yeah, well, let's see how you feel come March. This'll be your first spring without anything to look forward to.

I'll be fine. He gave terrible presents anyway.

Anthony smiled and nodded his head, and just like that I had confirmation that Daddy had been as thoughtless with his other kids' gifts as he'd been with ours. The more stuff I found in common between me and my siblings, the sadder I felt for us all. What Anthony was going through was enough to break your heart all on its own. He really seemed to believe that, somewhere up there, God was looking down and taking stock of everything he did. And even if he believed, as Claudia did, that our father had been damned to the flames of hell, I'm sure there was a part of him that believed Daddy was somehow able to sit in judgment of him as well.

When the PE class had finished, Anthony bolted upright and commenced to sprinting around the track in full gear as a warm-up for his practice. I stayed and watched him as long as I could, until the clouds broke open and a cold rain began to fall. He was still running when I left.

•

As expected, March came and went without any of the fanfare of previous years, without any of the cooking, cleaning, and anticipation that Daddy's arrival had provoked in our old way of life. I warned Jessie and

Gracie not to let their disappointment show, lest they make Mama and the other mothers feel bad. Forget about how things used to be, I told them. We've got new things to worry about now. Which was true. The worst frost on record had left Tulare County bleak and neglected. The last of our neighbors finally cashed out, and we found ourselves with unoccupied parcels bordering three of the four sides of our property. We joked that, if we wanted to, we could buy up more and more land until our cooperative had consumed the entire county. Then we could rename the towns and landmarks any way we liked. Temple City. Mount Dawn. The Gracie River. We joked about it, but there was no money for land, or even to begin construction on the third house like we planned. Until the summer harvest came in, money would continue to go out, and the vastest empire we could hope for was a full dinner table.

Day by day the weather turned hotter, and slowly the state laborers returned to the area. Dale cut the scabs down to a skeleton crew and prepared for the blossom season and the constant irrigation and pesticide spraying that would accompany it. All across the valley things were starting to pick up even as rumors began to fly from the mouths of farmer and worker alike, whispers of trouble on the coast and big changes in Sacramento. Anyone with any connection at all to the ag bureau suddenly became an expert on California farming politics. They all claimed that something big was coming down the pipeline in Congress, though not a one of them was clear on the details. The TV news, meanwhile, started carrying reports of strange insects from Asia contaminating local orchards, forcing already struggling parcelites to quarantine and destroy hundreds of acres of trees before the first nectarine could begin to swell. Other stations pointed to low levels at the national aquifers and prophesized a summer of water rationing and withered fruit left to rot on branches. The county slashed prices on parcels for the first time in over a decade, and still the neighboring plots remained unoccupied.

Not even my classmates were oblivious to the fear in the air. To the contrary, we all seemed to internalize our parents' worries, filling the corridors at school with a morose and nervous atmosphere that made our already stressful days positively nerve-wracking. Most of us found ways to cope with the added anxiety. Others reached their breaking points and never looked back. It seemed like every other day a fight broke out on the quad during lunchtime. The siren would go off and the attendants would usher the whole student body into the classrooms for lockdown. One time we heard police cars coming up the road and by the next day eleven members of the freshman class had been expelled. Another time, on the morning of the national standards test, one of the boys in my exam room started trembling all through his body ten minutes into the first math section. The girl sitting next to him told him to quit it, at which point the boy stood and threw his chair against the wall so hard it left a ten-inch crack in the dry erase board. The proctor ordered us outside, and while we waited for the attendants to contain the boy's outburst, the sky itself burst open and commenced to pummeling the campus with hail pellets the size of cherry stones. They fell off and on for over an hour, after which the sun came out and the temperature rose to the mid-seventies.

I started playing hooky sometime after Easter vacation. It wasn't like how it was with the other kids who ditched, who took their cars out for lunch or free period and never came back for the rest of the day. On mornings when I didn't feel like putting on a show of being alive, I slept late and asked Anthony to pick up my homework. Mama trusted me to do what I needed to do, and anyway, she was the last person to judge someone else for staying in bed all day. I always knew there was a chance I'd start experiencing sad stretches of my own. Fortunately, they didn't come anywhere close to Mama's. Most hooky days, in fact, I was up and around before noon, and after lunch I'd head out to the field office to check with Dale on how the spraying and pruning were going. Crazy weather aside, the blossoms were coming in on time, full and fragrant. It was that time of year when the whole valley was in pastels, with mile after mile of trees sporting tiny pink, white, and yellow buds like colored popcorn exploding off the branches. The bees emerged from their winter dormancy and hay fever spread like the plague. That was also the only time of year we saw anything like tourists in the valley, weekend visitors driving in from the coast to gawk at all the pretty flowers, tipping dollar bills to the laborers in exchange for access to the orchards. They wore enormous cameras on straps around their necks and spent hours out there alternating between different sizes of lens. One spring Ruby Mendes and me stumbled upon a pregnant lady standing half-naked between two rows of blooming nectarine trees. She kept one hand over her breasts and held her giant belly with the other as her husband took photos of her from every conceivable angle. Eventually they noticed us spying on them. The lady pulled up her dress and staggered through the soft earth in her flip-flops. The man told us to thank our parents for him, handed us each a stick of gum, and followed his wife to the car.

A few Sundays after Easter, I was sitting on the porch of the bigger house with Dawn and Anthony, sucking on one of the small popsicles we made in the ice cube tray with juice and toothpicks. Anthony had given up sugar for Lent, but even now he didn't seem to have much of a sweet tooth. He sat Indian-style on the boards, whittling a square of wood with his pocketknife, while Dawn used a kitchen knife to slice lemon rings into a pitcher of sun tea. Jessie and Gracie were playing with Mark and Karina on the grass. After months of initial shyness, they were finally starting to come around to their other siblings.

It's a beautiful day, Dawn said. We should see if Beth would like to come over. The sunshine would do her good.

I sucked the last drops of juice from the ice and tossed the leftovers behind the hedge. Ever since the night of the dance, Dawn had remained deeply committed and attentive to Beth. The only reason she thought to make tea, in fact, was probably because she knew Beth liked it.

You know she's talking about running off to live on the coast.

Dawn nodded. We've talked about it a lot recently.

And? What did you tell her?

Dawn set the knife down and rubbed the smell of citrus over her hands. I told her how hard it can be for a young woman on her own. I shared some of my experiences from the years before I met your dad.

That's good. Hopefully you got her to change her mind.

I wouldn't know. That was never my intention.

Surprised to hear you say that. You were the one who told me how dangerous it is out there. She could get really hurt, or worse.

Dawn sealed the plastic lid onto the pitcher. She carried it to the corner of the porch where the tea could soak up the sunlight the whole day through. Any danger out there can just as easily reach her here, she said. That should be obvious at this point.

I know. I just thought you might want to warn her about what she's getting herself into. Seeing as how at the time it was worth marrying Elliot to get yourself out of it.

I never said it was worth it. At any rate, though, it's her life to live the way she wants. After all she's been through, it's not going to do any good to try and keep her caged up here.

She should give her life to God, Anthony said. He shook his head and scraped a particularly long wood shaving from the edge of the block. God's the only one who can take her pain away. He's healed women who have been through a lot worse than her.

How would you know? I asked.

Don't worry about it. I know what I'm talking about. Read the Bible.

I tried reading the Bible once, Dawn said. Gave up after Lot's wife got turned to salt.

All of a sudden there was dust flying up from the driveway and a low rumble that grew louder the longer I listened. I stood and peered out through the gaps in the tree line. Something shiny caught my eye with the gleam of the sun. There's a car coming, I said. Nice one from the look of it.

Turned out *nice* was an understatement. I'd never seen a car as new and fancy as the one that came up the drive just then and parked beside the house. It was a European import, all sleek and automatic, with hardly a speck of dust anywhere above the tire treads. The engine was still clicking when the driver's side door swung open and a pair of clean leather shoes stepped out onto the gravel. A tall young man in a suit and dark sunglasses paced around the yard for a stretch, looking the houses up and down and staring far off into the orchard with a hand shielding his already shaded eyes. I don't think he could've failed to notice that we were there, but he was sure taking his time getting around to acknowledging us.

Hello there, I said, waving to him from behind the porch railing. If you're looking to take some photos of the blossoms, you're welcome to do so.

The stranger turned his head ever so slightly and cracked a smile. I'm not here on vacation, he said. I'm here on business. I'd like to sit down and have a talk with your mothers.

Me and Anthony glanced at each other for a second and then looked back at the stranger. I tried to remember what the inspectors at the ag bureau looked like, and considered how likely or unlikely it was that one of them would be driving around in a German sports car.

Anthony shot to his feet still holding the pocketknife and block of wood. What sort of business do you have with them?

That'll be made clear in due time, the man said. For now, you had best get your people together in one place. Because what I have to say concerns all the Temples.

Such vague menace resulted in a fairly accurate test of how quickly we could get everyone together for an emergency meeting. While Mama and Claudia prepared the little ones for another babysitting session with Jewel, I got on the phone and alerted Katie to what was happening. Whoever this guy was, I stressed, he seemed intimately aware of who we were and what our living arrangement was like. Within ten minutes, all of adults and older children were assembled around our kitchen table, remaining tensely silent as Mama served coffee to our well-dressed visitor.

I don't believe you've given us your name, Katie said. Seems like that'd be a good place to start.

The young man stirred heaping portions of sugar and cream into his coffee. Without his sunglasses on, he looked no older than Logan, and even had his hair combed in the same slicked-back style. My official title is as a contractor, he said. That should suffice for now. At the moment, I'd prefer to focus on who I represent and what they have to offer.

So you have come to make us an offer, Jennifer said. I figured as much.

An offer on what? Claudia asked. What do we have that's even worth buying?

Your property, for one, the contractor said. The Russert Growers Company out of Watsonville has enabled me to speak and act on their behalf. They're prepared to make a very generous offer to you for the farm as-is. That means everything—the land, trees, buildings, and all the equipment and machinery therein. They'd like the place to be ready to hand off before the start of harvesting, and they're willing to compensate you appropriately for a speedy transition.

He folded his arms over his chest and leaned back in his seat. While the rest of the family, including me, stared at him with looks of confusion or fear plastered over our faces, Beth smiled and let out a single condescending laugh.

Mister, she said, I don't know how long you've been working or where you got your information from, but this is San Joaquin. We're on parcel land. That means we can't sell the farm to anybody, except back to the government. Anything else is against the law.

The contractor smiled and raised an index finger in front of his face. Actually, he said, this property is registered as a cooperative. And according to the policies set forth by the national agriculture bureau, any piece of land registered as a cooperative may be transferred from its current occupants to any individual or organization willing to buy them out under the terms of the original agreement. That means the Russert Growers Company is perfectly within its legal rights to assume tenantship of the farm provided that they compensate you for the full amount of your deposit. Now, seeing as how you all have put a lot of work into these orchards over the past several months, the company has authorized me to offer you compensation over and above your initial investment. One and a half times, in fact. For a fifty percent return on what you paid in. No one else is going to give you that kind of deal, I assure you.

I can't see what a big company from the coast would want with our place, Anthony said. Or how they even found out about us.

I alerted them to your situation myself, the contractor said. As to their reasons for making an offer, I believe they see this place as a means of getting in on the ground floor here in the Central Valley. You see, folks, whether you want to accept it or not, the parcel system is a thing of the past, a relic of a more desperate time. Perhaps it was useful in the early days of the Republic, but since then it's become an inefficient boondoggle that keeps the land from being developed to its fullest potential. Our nation has grown up, and agriculture must grow with it. A handful of corporations could do more with this valley than all the tenant farmers and state laborers in the country put together. That's the way the wind is blowing now, and anyone with any sense at all should cash out while they still can.

Even if what you're telling us is true, Mama said, I don't see why we should be in any hurry to sell. Those trees out there didn't bloom by themselves. We deserve to see through our first harvest. Or else all the time and money we've put in will be for nothing.

The contractor smiled, showing a mouth full of perfectly straight teeth unlike anything you ever saw east of the Pacheco Pass. Mark my words, he said. The government is starting to catch on to the untapped potential here in San Joaquin. When the laws change and privatization takes effect, you might end up having to pay a whole lot more than a deposit to hold on to a piece of property this size.

That may be so, Katie said. If and when that day comes, we'll deal with it the best we can. In the meantime, you thank the Russert Growers Company for taking the trouble to approach us, but I'm afraid the answer is no. This farm means more to us than a return on an investment. We're building a home here on this land, for ourselves and for our children. And we don't intend to give it up after less than a year.

I thought you might respond like that, the contractor said. In which case, I'm sorry to say, you've forced me to play my trump card. You understand, it's just business.

I'd finally had it. Even before he started talking, this cocky interloper had irked me something bad, and now that he was being openly threatening, it was too much for me to hold my tongue any longer. You're dancing around something, I said. Go ahead and tell us whatever it is you think you know. We don't deserve to be strung along.

Fair enough, he said, and laid his knuckles down on the tabletop. You purchased the rights to this farm with money attained through fraud and deceit. When he was alive, Elliot Temple was married to five women at the same time. He used each of his wives to apply for a different parcel in a different county, in direct violation of the limits established by the bureau of agriculture. After his death, you used the deposits from his parcels to set up a cooperative farm in your own names. Ergo, this entire enterprise is founded on ill-gotten money. Which, as it happens, is the sort of offense the authorities would be very interested in hearing about.

When he'd finished speaking, I closed my eyes and let out a slow stream of breath. Everyone else at the table appeared similarly stunned, with the possible exception of Dawn, who sat with her head down and a hand over her eyes, feeling whatever reaction is possible when you're proven right about your own vulnerability. And she was right, after all. Without even stepping off the property, the danger had found us once again. Even after all the precautions we'd taken, even after our betrayal of Beth, the life we'd worked to build up for ourselves all these months was on the verge of coming undone. I wanted to run outside screaming and tear every last blossom off every last tree in the orchard. They were as much to blame as any of us—the bright and pretty things in this world always invite disaster.

Claudia held her hands out imploringly. We have two houses full of children on this land, she said. How could you live with yourself if you cast them out of their homes?

The contractor titled his head to the side, looking around at us with an annoyed intensity in his eyes. He pushed his chair out from the table. I can see you need some time to process this, he said. That's why I'm going to give you a week to think it through. I'll be back next Sunday at the same time. For your children's sake, I hope you come to your senses between now and then. Here. Let me give you my business card.

He pulled a stack of cards from his coat pocket and divided it into two even halves like a magician preparing a trick. Go ahead and pass them out, he said. I've got plenty.

The two halves went around opposite sides of the table before converging on Anthony at the end. Each person who took a card paused for a moment before passing off the rest of the stack. They were cream-colored and tastefully understated, with the lettering sunk-in so it felt like the words were trying to evade your touch.

Elliot Temple, Jr.
Independent Contractor

I let the card fall and settle face-down against the table. I felt Mama touch my arm in a way that was somehow different from her usual expressions of anxiety. It took me a while to realize that she, in her own imperfect way, was trying to comfort me this time.

In case there's any more confusion, my newest brother said, let me make myself clear. Don't ever try to assume the limits of what I'm capable of. You'll be unpleasantly surprised.

ELLIOT

I was eighteen years old the summer my father took me on the road with him to the San Joaquin Valley. Dad was in the fruit business and spent most of his time traveling around between the Bay Area and Yosemite. Before that trip I had never been east of the Diablo range in my life, nor had I spent more than a few hours alone with Dad at one time. The car radio died out halfway over the Pacheco Pass, and after driving through miles and miles of pure nothing from Los Banos to Fresno, we suddenly came upon a pastoral landscape where trees outnumbered men by a wide margin. You live all your life on the coast and you forget there are places so different just over the mountains, places without any of the things you've come to expect from a civilized community. No traffic, no sea walls, no gated housing tracts. Nothing but trees and grass and live-stock, and tiny, old-fashioned houses with entire families of people with unwashed hair congregating on their porches like Okies from a social studies textbook. I had plenty of time to take it all in on the drive down; Dad was never one to converse behind the wheel, and after four years without seeing him, my own awkwardness kept me similarly silent right up to the moment we crossed the town line into Porterville. I don't know if it was awkwardness, boredom, or a need to make myself heard, but I turned to him then and said with the eagerness of a younger boy, "The land's so beautiful. It must be nice living here."

Without taking his eyes off the road, Dad gave a slight nod and hummed softly through his nose. I studied his face closely. He was a big man, tall and broad through the shoulders, with a beard of graying whiskers and a mostly bald head that rose to a point at the peak of his crown. Owing to his size, he was capable of imbuing his smallest gestures with the weight of hidden significance, and from the time I was little I was always prepared to try to interpret what he really meant by them, even if there was nothing there to be found.

He said, "The valley's lush, no doubt, but if you had to live here a month you'd wind up suicidal."

I turned away and leaned my shoulder on the window. "The families who live here must have found something to like about it."

"That's different. They're country people. Simple folk. It doesn't take much to keep them happy."

"You've spent so much time out here. You don't consider yourself a country person?"

"I'm an entrepreneur. An educated man. We come from a long line of educated people. Your great-grandfather was a University of California regent."

We drove in silence for another several minutes before reaching the hotel. Pulling into the parking lot, the Ramcharger wasn't the only antique to be found, though it was certainly the best maintained. I didn't know much about Dad except that he insisted on maintaining a certain image and lifestyle; classic cars, custom suits, prime cuts of meat slathered in French sauces. Everywhere he went, he made inquiries into the best places to eat and sleep, and after nearly twenty years on the road, his knowledge of room and dining accommodations was enough to rival that of any agent or travel website in the Republic. For our trip to the valley, he had booked us a room at the Caravan Hotel, a comparatively high-end establishment that catered to out-of-town visitors and others who shared Dad's means and tastes but happened to find themselves stuck momentarily in that otherwise desolate part of the state. On the way inside, he caught his reflection in the window and stopped to adjust his tie. He said, "You and I are going to celebrate tonight, Junior. It's not every day a son of mine graduates high school."

His words struck me as funny at the time, on a couple different levels. I was, as far as I knew, the only son he had, and he hadn't even bothered to attend my graduation. He just showed up out of the blue one day a couple weeks after the ceremony and said he wanted to take me on a trip to see the rest of the country. "It's your choice," Mom told me before we left, "but don't come crying to me if he lets you down." A part of me, the spiteful part, hoped I would have the time of my life with Dad just to prove her wrong. But the reasonable part knew I shouldn't get my hopes up; I'd been disappointed too many times before.

After checking in at the front desk, I thought we were going to go to the room, but instead Dad paid the valet to take our bags up so we could have a pre-dinner drink in the hotel restaurant. A heavyset girl with brown hair and orange highlights greeted us at the door with a stack of menus in her arms. Her name was Kylee, or at least that's what it said on the nametag hanging crookedly over her protruding and lopsided breast. She saw us coming and immediately stepped forward to touch Dad's shoulder and smile up close in his face.

"Been a long time, Elliot," she said in an upspoken, questioning sort of way. "We never see you around anymore."

"Good to see you, Kylee," Dad said. "Sorry it's been so long. I just got into town today after a long stay up north."

"No worries. I figured you were keeping busy."

"You know it. Say, we don't have a reservation, but any chance you could get us a table? We've been on the road all day."

"Sure thing. I'll seat you in my station over by the bar. It'll be quieter there."

"Thanks. You're a peach."

Kylee led us to the back of the restaurant and past a varnish-stained mahogany bar without a single patron or employee on either side. For as much as Dad made it seem like a testament to his charm that we managed to get a table, there was hardly another soul in the place. Dad took off his jacket and draped it over the back of his chair. With no one else around for reference, I couldn't tell if I was underdressed or not.

"Can I get you boys started with something to drink?" Kylee asked.

Dad looked at me from across the table and replied, "Kylee, this is my son, Elliot Jr. Today's his twenty-first birthday."

Kylee's face beamed with false surprise. "Well, happy birthday!"

"The thing is, I was all set to buy him his first drink tonight, but then the big dummy went and left his ID at his mother's house."

"Ah, what a shame."

"Shame is right. We drove all this way before he realized what he did."

Now she put her hand on the crease of my arm and addressed me directly. "You know what I do? I keep my apartment key inside my wallet. That way I make sure I have my money and cards with me whenever I leave home."

Dad pointed his finger at me. "You hear that? The lady's got good advice."

"You're lucky you have him here to vouch for you. Next time you might not be so lucky."

Dad said, "I hope it's no trouble. Any other day and I wouldn't have even asked."

Kylee winked. "It's fine, boys. I've got ya covered." She took out a pen and flipped her tablet open to the top page. "What can I get you?"

"Junior?"

To say I was unsure what to order was putting it mildly. I'd never ordered a drink in a restaurant before, nor tasted alcohol beyond a few stale beers at a house party. I remembered having brunch one time with Mom and her ordering a Bloody Mary, so I decided to go with that. "I'll have a Bloody Mary."

Kylee started to write down the order, but Dad raised his hand to stop her. "Bring him a Stoli on the rocks," he said. "I'll have a double bourbon. Neat."

As Kylee disappeared behind the bar, Dad leaned across the table and looked at me sternly. He said, "You want fruit, order the fruit salad. Don't embarrass yourself and me by asking for a liquor smoothie."

"Sorry. I didn't know."

"Learning to drink responsibly is an important skill to acquire. Your mother's father used to have a full Martini set that he'd bring out on summer evenings or whenever he was entertaining. That was back when British gin was easy to get a hold of. Vermouth as well."

"Must have been nice." I took a sip of water and looked down at the pristine white tablecloth. Half a day on the road with Dad and I was learning more about the older generation than about him. "How old were you when you decided to marry Mom?"

Dad waved his hand in front of his face dismissively. "Who can remember? My mid-twenties, sometime around there. I had already been out of college several years."

"Mom says you graduated from the Cal State system."

"Fullerton," he said. "International Business program. With a minor in Chinese."

"Get out. You speak Chinese?"

"Everyone was studying Chinese in those days. It was practically a prerequisite for any halfway decent MBA program."

Another revelation. "You went to business school?"

"Almost. I had just started my applications when things began to get difficult. Disbandment was still a few years away, but the economy was already in the toilet. Couldn't afford to take on any more debt."

"So you took the job at the assessor's office instead."

Dad stared at me with his shoulders suddenly raised. We had been making steady progress up to that point, and I worried I had driven him back behind the walls of his garrison. "Your mother talks a lot about me, apparently."

I unfolded my napkin and laid it out smooth across my lap. "I don't know. Not really. Sometimes I want to know about you and she's the only one around to ask."

"That doesn't mean it's her place to provide you with answers."

"I know. I'm sorry."

"Right. Well. I'm here now. What do you want to know?"

"Well. *Were* you working for the assessor's office when you met her?"

"Yes, as a matter of fact, I was. Up in San Joaquin County. Local government was one of the few stable lines of work in those days. I did have some private sector jobs before that, though. But they were all dead-end, entry-level positions with a hundred people above me. So I quit them, and never looked back. Even then, with the entire country falling apart, I was determined to make my own way in the world."

Kylee returned with our drinks. She set each glass down carefully with a paper napkin between it and the tablecloth. "This first round is on the house. Happy birthday." I watched Dad raise his glass and sip the lukewarm bourbon. He didn't react to the taste beyond a few gentle smacks of his lips. His eyes weren't even on me, and yet I felt compelled to compose myself in the same way, as though I had been drinking hard alcohol every day of my life for years. There was a lime wedge on the rim of the glass, but, remembering Dad's stern warning about mixing liquor and fruit, I ignored it and took my first drink of vodka with only ice to dull the edge. Somehow I managed to fight through the burn and swallow the entire mouthful without gagging. By the time Dad looked at me again, I had already wiped my tears off on the napkin.

He said, "While we're on the subject of life decisions, I would hope you'd let me in on what you plan to do with yourself now that you've finished high school."

It was the last thing I wanted to do, but I took another drink to buy some time. As the vodka settled inside my otherwise empty stomach, a radiating numbness spread out from my chest and down through my fingers and toes. "I haven't really decided what to do next. Most of my classmates are going away to college, but I don't know if it's right for me."

"You didn't apply anywhere?"

"Stanford. To get Mom off my back."

Dad nodded slowly. "She's proud of her alma matter. She should be."

"She suggested I take the summer to work on my applications and reapply in the fall."

"Right. But what do you really want to do?"

Instead of drinking this time, I raised my glass and held it off to the side with the ice rattling against the edges. I was already learning that drinking came with a performative aspect that could ease the tension in the room as effectively as the drink itself. At that age, thinking about the future not only strained my nerves, it distorted my whole sense of being, as if the very idea of some older, more perfect future-self negated the realness of whoever I was at the present. What I could never admit to Dad, or to any of the adults who took it upon themselves to judge the scope of my ambitions, was the same secret that made my heart race and chest tighten any time I thought about it for too long; namely, that I could not and could never conceive of myself as a grown adult, that I had no more desire to establish a career than to spend another four years inside a classroom, and that no matter how old I got or how healthy I remained, I saw no reason to expect I would ever live beyond my youth. That certainty of my own evanescence informed every other area of my life, such that I could never take questions like "What do you want to do with yourself" even remotely seriously. I was a transient in this world, in my own body, and as such there was no point in trying to plan for a future I knew would never come. All I could hope for was to arrive at a better understanding of the world, and of the limitless mysteries it contained.

I said, "I want to find God. I want to hear Him call my name."

Dad took another drink. He looked at me without speaking. He drank again. "Have you fallen in with the end-of-days crowd since we last saw each other?"

"No. Nothing like that."

"Hippies?"

"No, never."

"So where's this coming from?"

"I can't articulate it properly. Or at least I can only describe it as an absence. I never had any real idea of God growing up. Mom's never been religious, and hardly anyone I knew in school ever prayed or went to church. You'd think it wouldn't bother me, since I don't even know what I'm missing. But it does. Always has. It always feels like there's an emptiness inside of me. I don't know any other way to explain it."

I watched Dad as closely as I ever had, looking and hoping for some small expression or gesture that I could latch onto and interpret. But he remained stone-faced right up to the end, right up until the moment he reached for his glass and, realizing there was nothing in it, started looking around for Kylee so he could order another round. He said, "Emptiness. You feel an emptiness inside." He shook his head and slid the glass to the side of the tablecloth. "I suppose you think it's my fault."

I closed my eyes and held out my hands. "Dad, I never—"

"Empty. My own son tells me he feels empty. That's a fine how do you do. I gave you everything. Even after the divorce, I continued to send your mother child support every month."

"I know, I wasn't—"

"You should try growing up around here. See how empty you feel then. Most of these kids never get beyond the ninth grade. Our waitress was living in a state camp before she started working here. She had two miscarriages in a single year. You want to ask how empty she feels?"

"Dad. Please. I didn't mean it like that. I appreciate everything you've done for me."

"No, you feel empty. In spite of all the advantages you've been given." Dad looked over his shoulder and, finding the bar still abandoned, sunk forward in his chair with his arms crossed over the table. He grumbled something I couldn't hear and didn't particularly want to. "You probably think I abandoned you. As if it was easy for me, putting up with your mother and all her abuse. And trying to start a business at the same time. Oh, yeah. It was real easy."

"I'm sorry. I didn't mean it like that. I was talking about how I feel about God, not you."

"That's no excuse for going around saying you're empty. You have more to be thankful for than most. You have a good father and a mother. That should be enough. Love us and show some gratitude."

"I know. I will. I'm sorry."

"I try to do something nice, share a drink with my son to celebrate his achievements, and this is what I get in return."

"I'm sorry. I'm sorry. I'm sorry."

I could have gone on apologizing a while longer if Kylee hadn't decided to check on us.

"How we doing? You ready to take a look at some food menus?"

Dad pointed to his glass and then at mine. "Sure, and let's do this again. Less ice for him this time."

She grabbed our glasses off the table and left us in the same strained atmosphere she had found us in. It was all I could do to look at him directly, to feel the judgment in those eyes that were the bluest I had ever known. Other eighteen-year-old boys might have stood up and walked away, but I wasn't driven to indignation as easily as them. There was still something I wanted from him. After all those years without him, I still wanted my father's approval, and longed to know him as a part of myself, as any namesake would. To get there, I would endure his bitterness as best I could. I saw judgment in his eyes, but also a chance for enlightenment.

· ·

For a man who worked at a glass desk in a glass office in a mostly glass building, Mr. Russert wasn't as transparent as I would have preferred. Not that he needed to be given all the attention he had garnered since his startup in Watsonville, aptly dubbed the Russert Growers Company, grew into a successful business seemingly overnight. The character of agriculture on the coast was different from that of other places in the Republic. Rather than relying on a nomadic underclass of poor whites and Latinos to do their picking, coastal growers brought in foreign laborers from Indonesia and the Philippines, spry little men with their own languages who worked on guest visas for ten months at a time, flying home once a year to check in on their families and reapply. With no parcel program in place, the arable land of every county eventually came to be split among the same half-dozen or so large ag companies. Mr. Russert owned one of the newest and most controversial operations in the country; before I met him, he had made waves in Santa Cruz for buying up twenty thousand acres in just over two years. Now he was beginning to expand into other territories. On the morning of our first meeting, I found him sitting alone in his scantly furnished glass sanctuary, clad in a simple ash-colored shirt with no tie and the sleeves rolled up to his elbows. My initial impression of him offered nothing substantial by which to gauge his attitude, but I remained optimistic that he would confirm my earlier suspicion; that, in his role as upstart newcomer, he would be more willing to accept the kinds of propositions his competitors might deem too risky, and therefore unsound.

He looked me once over and said, "All right. Now that you've got my attention, maybe you could go ahead and tell me who you are."

"My name is Elliot Temple, and I've just come from the State of San Joaquin. That's all I'll say for now. You understand I have to be careful about compromising myself."

Russert shot me a confused look that lasted until the moment he adjusted the almost invisible frames of his eyeglasses. "Where did you graduate?"

"I don't have a degree."

"Interesting."

"I entered the job market early. The classroom environment was too stifling for me."

"Interesting."

I recognized the look he was giving me then. It was one I received often, living in the Bay Area, whenever it became known that I was somehow traversing this globe without the benefit of a BA. Often incredulous, occasionally envious, but always baffled that a species such as me was not yet extinct in this part of the nation.

He said, "Well, Temple. What can I do for you?"

"As I explained over the phone, I've recently come into a situation where I would be able to facilitate the sale of a large tract of quality farmland. In an area of the country where no private enterprise has flourished since before disbandment. And I believe I could negotiate a very reasonable price for you. Much less than you would normally pay for a hundred and twenty acres."

"In San Joaquin?"

"Yes. Don't ask me which county, though."

Russert reached across the desk to a glass decanter full of water and raw asparagus. The asparagus stalks were bound together in the style of a Roman fasces and caused a gurgling sound as he poured. He sipped from his glass and slid the other one over to me.

He said, "Mr. Temple, either you're trying to cheat me, or you've been cheated yourself. I'll be polite and give you the benefit of the doubt. The simple fact is that no one could buy a farm in San Joaquin for all the money in the world. The government's got that whole valley nationalized as part of the parcel program. Country bumpkins packing peaches in rented sheds. That's what the land is earmarked for."

"This isn't a parcel. It's a cooperative, the biggest of its kind. The government makes a special exception for co-ops. They can transfer the lease to anyone, including a private company like yours. All you have to do is buy them out."

"Sure. But I wouldn't really own the land, would I? I'd be at the mercy of the Ag Bureau. I'd still have to pay rent every month, and sell my produce for a fraction of what it's worth."

"In the beginning, perhaps, but then things are more than likely to work out in your favor. You know as well as I do that once the Vandeman Act passes Congress and the parcel program is phased out, all that land in the valley is going to be worth ten times what it is now. I'm giving you the opportunity to step into a new world and plant your flag before anyone else. And I hope I was right in assuming you're an ambitious man, the kind of man who wouldn't back down from the chance to build an empire up from the ground."

Russert laughed. "A hundred and twenty acres is hardly an empire. With all the mountains between here and the valley, it's more like a far-flung outpost. Probably more trouble to maintain than it would be worth."

"As a businessman, Mr. Russert, I can understand why you would try to play hard to get, but I wish you would draw the line at being disingenuous. You can't sit here and pretend your pushing into Gilroy and Hollister isn't part of some grand forward-thinking strategy. I don't need to convince you of what an opportunity this is; you've already realized it yourself. The grower who succeeds in spreading eastward down the middle of this country will have all the blessings of heaven and earth at his disposal. You'll have your army of Asians, the most fertile land on the planet, and equidistant access to the markets of San Francisco and L.A. From there, nothing will be out of your reach. You could probably become president of the Republic if you wanted."

"Flattery and daydreams are two things I simply don't have time for."

"It's not flattery to suggest that a powerful man could become more powerful. Nor is it daydreaming to imagine that same man using his power to gain even more."

Russert turned and brushed his hand over the computer hibernating in a built-in compartment at the center of the desk. Immediately the machine bloomed for him, unfolding silently and contorting itself until the keys were right within reach. He moved his fingers over the screen. Then, as abruptly as he had turned to the device, he shut it away again. The rain, which had been trickling lightly when I first arrived, finally started to pick up, slamming the windows with intermittent gusts of wind rising up from the sea wall thirty miles to the west.

He said, "The state of agriculture in this country. It's like something out of the Dark Ages. I truly believe that a hundred years from now people will look back at this point in our history and wonder how we ever allowed so much valuable land to go underutilized for so long. All that wasted potential. Future generations will mock us for it, and rightly so. Like the Chinese with their Great Leap Forward."

"The valley is a backward place in an otherwise forward-thinking country. That's what my father believed."

He said, "There's one part of this I can't put my finger on. You. What's your stake here? You say you're in a position to help me buy this place cheap, but clearly you're not the one with your name on the lease. Which means you're going through all this trouble for a measly ten percent on the deal."

"I was thinking more like forty percent."

"Forty? Jesus. That's a hell of a finder's fee."

"True, but that's between me and the other party. I wouldn't ask you to front my commission in addition to what you'd already be paying."

"Well. Isn't that gracious of you?" He stood and turned to the wall and looked out at the rain splattering on the outside glass. Seizing the moment, I removed the flask from my pocket and mixed a shot of vodka in with my asparagus water. It had been a few hours since my last drink and I needed to keep my head together. Russert said, "Tell you how I see it. Seems to me like you're nothing but a middleman in all this. What's to stop me from going behind your back and dealing with the tenants directly? A co-op that size couldn't be too hard to find, especially now that I know your name. And whoever the other party is, I can't imagine they're very eager to carve forty percent off the top just to pay your end. So I bet I could negotiate a better deal without your help. What do you think of that?"

I smiled and swirled the asparagus water in my glass. "I think that, without me, there's no way they would ever agree to sell, to you or anyone else. That's the advantage I'm pressing here, Mr. Russert. They won't sell if they don't have to, but I have it in my power to persuade them."

"That sounds pretty sketchy."

"You need not concern yourself with the details. Let's just say my father didn't leave me much, but he left me what I need to get my start as an entrepreneur. You see, I'm after more than just a finder's fee, Mr. Russert. This deal is going to be the catalyst that sets the rest of my future in motion."

"You want to make a career for yourself in agriculture?"

"I want to make money. How I do it at this point is incidental."

"That doesn't sound like a very meaningful way to live."

"I searched for meaning a long time and didn't like what I found. Now I'm focused solely on the living part. Leave the meaning to the ministers."

Russert's eyeglasses slid almost imperceptibly down the ridge of his nose. I would have been surprised to learn that he was a godly man, as opposed to a sometime convert like Dad, or some brand of agnostic like so many in his field claimed to be. He said, "I can't get a clear read on you, Mr. Temple. Can't tell if you're the real deal or some joker off the street."

"In this instance, all I'm asking for is the right to approach the sellers on your behalf. You'll lose nothing if the deal falls through. And if I succeed, which I will, you'll have a leg up on everyone else trying to move in on the valley."

"You're welcome to go and talk with these people, and if you can work your magic on them like you say, I'll consider making an offer. But they'd have to agree to a full transfer of tenancy rights. Land, house, and all. I don't have time to mess with squatters."

"Don't worry. You won't even know they were ever there." I emptied my glass and stood to leave. As I was refastening the middle button on my suit jacket, I looked up suddenly and raised my finger to hold his attention. "One more thing."

He sighed and reached again for the decanter. "Go on then."

I smiled. "Do you know a good place around here to print up some business cards?"

· ·

We were halfway through our second round when Kylee brought our starters out from the kitchen. I was so hungry and tipsy that each bite of carrot soup seemed to replenish something essential in me, without which I didn't know how I was going to survive the rest of the evening. Dad didn't speak for a while after the food arrived. He kept his fork suspended over his plate, delivering clumps of romaine and blue cheese dressing to his mouth with mechanical stiffness. With every sip of vodka that entered my system, I grew angrier and more aggrieved by his stubborn silence. I wanted to lash out at him, to seize him from across the table and demand that he say something, but then the weight of my guilt rolled back onto my shoulders, reminding me that he was paying for my food and drinks tonight, just as he had paid to support me through all the years I was in school. And so I made myself drunker waiting for him to talk, taking hurried swigs from my glass every time the ice had melted enough to offset the burn.

He finally wiped his lips on the napkin and said, "There are only two ways to make a living from God, you know. Being a minister and being a fraud. And maybe selling Bibles."

I smiled. "What about poets?"

Even before Dad glared at me, I knew the joke had been a mistake. He set his knife and fork down and pushed the plate away. He said, "I'm talking about making a living, which is something you should be thinking about from here on out. If you won't go to college, then you'll have to figure out a way to earn your keep from day to day. Unless you plan on living off your mother indefinitely, stringing her along with promises of getting into Stanford one day."

"I'm not a leech. I wouldn't do that to her."

"And what about me?"

"What about you?"

"Maybe that's why you agreed to drive down here with me. Because you thought you could coax me into supporting you until you get on your feet. As if ten years of monthly checks weren't enough."

"I followed you down here because I hadn't seen you since I was fourteen. If I had said no, who knows when we would have seen each other again?"

Dad shook his head and took another drink of whiskey. He was already acting surly, and I couldn't be sure if he had even heard me. "There are times I worry your generation will forsake the rest of us the moment we stop being useful to you. Like those native tribes in the Arctic, where the young people set their elders adrift on the ice so they don't have to worry about being burdened by them."

"I don't know where you get these ideas about me. You're my father. I wouldn't think you'd set your father adrift for convenience's sake."

"Your grandfather died of a heart attack not long after disbandment."

I blinked several times in rapid succession. I never knew about my grandfather or how he died; Mom had never met the man, and Dad hadn't mentioned him until now. That someone so close to me in blood and influence should remain such a mystery seemed wrong somehow, not because I felt incomplete without the knowledge, but because no one had ever thought to satisfy that curiosity they should have assumed I was bound to feel.

But all I said was, "That's sad. Did he lose his business in the crash?"

"He wasn't an entrepreneur. He was a school teacher in Stockton. Eighth grade science. Never had any real ambition."

Kylee's return offered a momentary reprieve from the gloomy streak we suddenly found ourselves on. For dinner we were presented with cuts of pink and charred tri-tip served on heavy cast iron platters with grilled asparagus, potatoes, and mushrooms. Dad waited for her to freshen our drinks before cutting into his meat. I tried forcing some of the starchy potatoes down my throat, but since the soup my stomach had turned around on itself, shedding hunger in favor of mild nausea and disgust.

I said, "It must have been rough, living through disbandment.

When I was younger, some of my friends' parents used to talk about what it was like back then. Sounded like everybody lost something that was dear to them."

Dad nodded as he finished chewing through a bite of steak. "It was the crash that really made things difficult. Your mother and I were living near Carmel at the time and overnight the whole area was overrun with economic refugees from other parts of the state. Davis, Riverside, Fresno. People came from everywhere and flooded the coast looking for work. Used to be that inland folks would say we were crazy living so close to the water. Conventional wisdom said that, when the next big earthquake hit, the entire coast would break away and fall into the sea. Hicks around here, they laughed at us before, but the second things started to fall apart, they came running to beg at our door."

"You've got to admit, though, there is some cause for concern. We might never fall into the ocean, but if the sea walls ever broke, we'd be under water regardless."

"They'd never let San Francisco stay sunk. They'd cut down all the redwoods and raise the city up on a pier first."

"I suppose that would keep the inland people out."

With more than a half a pint of whiskey in him now, Dad started to get sloppy in a way I had never seen from him before. Up to that point he had been so stiff and composed; it was strange to see him roll his eyes back while he was thinking, or run his tongue over his mustache to mop up the stray liquor and grease. He said, "Don't misunderstand me. It was hard times waiting on the economy to recover, but disbandment was still the best thing that ever happened to California. We have our own independent country now. We have the sixth largest economy in the world, and we get to keep all the profits for ourselves. Not like how it was under the US."

I hadn't expected to wind up talking politics with Dad, to say nothing of hearing him express views that were the polar opposite of everything I had been raised to believe. Mom was a staunch Unionist who had marched against disbandment in the streets of Palo Alto and even voted against the California Constitution as a matter of principle. Growing up, ours was one of only a few houses in the development that still celebrated the fourth of July every year by filling the summertime air with the savoriness of barbecued hotdogs and the sulphurous stench of Chinese fireworks. I tried to imagine the circumstances by which they would have moved past their differences, but I couldn't picture either of them being that tolerant and accommodating. Dad must have changed his views since the divorce, or kept his real opinions to himself the entire time they were married.

I said, "We were a whole lot richer before disbandment, though. Or at least America was. I don't know. Maybe it's just nostalgia, but I've always wondered what it would have been like to live back then. To have a whole huge country to see and explore."

Dad pointed at me with his fork. "It was already rotten long before disbandment. That's what happens with great nations, they rot away from the inside. But ask any botanist or farmer and he'll tell you the same thing, that rotting flesh can be used as fertilizer to help new life get its start. Sometime after the fall of Rome, you can bet there were boys like you, longing for the dream of an empire that had collapsed before they were born. At the same time, though, men of talent and ambition looked around and saw that there was fresh opportunity all around them. They worked hard and became medieval lords while the nostalgic ones sat around waiting to be turned into serfs. You think about that."

I thought about it. I thought about what he had said and wondered how much of it was from the heart and how much was the product of the whiskey and his own grandiose self-image. "In school they taught us that the centuries after the fall of Rome were a bad time for everyone. Isn't that why they call them the Dark Ages?"

Dad sneered and wiped his damp mustache on the back of his hand. He said, "That's a myth, a revisionist smear campaign launched by later historians with radical agendas. No one who was alive at the time would have called the medieval period an age of darkness. It's true, the hardships of life were greater in those days, but then so were the pleasures."

I watched Dad's eyes flicker in the diminishing evening light. Outside the big bay windows at the back of the room, the sun had gone down enough that the oppressive heat and brightness of the valley were reduced to far more tolerable levels. And yet Dad seemed more tired and disoriented than he had all day. Even as he carried on with issues of political and historical importance, there was an almost perverse intensity to the way he was behaving, and suddenly I was grateful for the vodka, and for the sleepy-sick feeling it had brought over me.

"Men had real honor in the medieval period. And women knew what it meant to be real women. Each king and each lord ruled like the pure manifestation of God on Earth. That's why, pound for pound, medieval lords were the greatest rulers in history. They didn't just rule well, they ruled totally. Think about it. I mean really think about it. Each lord had total dominion over his land, but his land was nothing without the people who cared for it. He had to rule over his serfs, his servants, his squires, and his knights, as well as his daughters, his sons, the rest of his family, and his wife. Can you even imagine it? There's no way to skate by in that situation. You're either a leader, with talent and responsibility, or you're nothing. Now think about all the sad bastards today who can't even manage to take care of themselves. And then try to tell me the medieval period was a dark time to be alive."

I looked down at my plate and said, "They still had more things to worry about back then. Like bubonic plague. The Black Death."

"Of course you'd bring that up. You're a negative person, you always have been. That's your mother's side coming out in you, depressives and pessimists all through their bloodlines." Dad raised his glass and drained the last ounce of bourbon and swirling grease from the bottom. His food was getting cold as he continued to eulogize. "You know what really happened during the Black Death? The lords and noblemen, basically everyone who was educated and worth a damn, they all fled to their estates in the country, while the peasants in the cities and the hicks in the fields stayed behind and perished. I know what you're thinking. Oh, what a tragedy, oh, what a shame, half the world gone in the blink of an eye. But do you know what happened after things returned to normal, when suddenly the world was only half as crowded as it used to be? The Renaissance happened. The Age of Discovery happened. Suddenly the exceptional men were able to raise themselves up without a whole host of human parasites weighing them down. And now here we sit, in a fine restaurant with steak and whiskey in front of us, indebted to a deadly pathogen from seven hundred years in the past."

Dad exhaled slowly and ran a napkin over his glossy, sweat-covered forehead. I couldn't believe what I was hearing. As a kid, I had known him to say some pretty harsh things about the unemployed, but he never carried it to such an extreme until now. I kept waiting for him to burst out laughing, or to notice the stunned look on my face and admit that he had been exaggerating. When no admission came, I cleared my throat and tried to find my own words.

I said, "If I understand you correctly, you're saying that a huge catastrophe like a plague, or the disbandment of an entire country, is actually beneficial because it weeds out the undesirable parts of the population and leaves behind the strong and innovative people. But that can't really be what you're saying."

Dad huffed irritably like a much older man. The meal before him had barely been touched, but still he folded his napkin over and tossed it onto the plate. He stuck his finger in my face and said, "You weren't there. You don't know what it was like then."

"Right. I wonder how many fathers have said that to their sons throughout history."

"Keep talking, smartass. You only reveal your own ignorance. You've been spoiled by the Republic, the same as the rest of your generation. But you'd sing a different tune if you saw what San Francisco was like in the old days, if you could smell the hot stink of open sewer rising up from the gutters of China Town and Hyde Street. All you've ever known are clean streets and productive people, computer programmers sipping espressos in wicker chairs on Market Street. But what would you do if suddenly there was a bum on every corner? How would you react if you couldn't walk home from school without being mobbed by panhandlers, without smelling the piss and diarrhea on their clothes and the stench of their blackened feet? That's what the city was before disbandment. Bums, addicts, hippies, whores. They practically ran the place before the government changed and the police drove them out. The productive members of society, the business class, they're the ones who saved the city—and the entire country, too, for that matter—when the US fell apart. You look at the rest of the former American states and see how they're doing now. The Plains are in chaos. The South has a GDP lower than Uganda. You believe it was lack of faith that brought them to it? I don't think so. If you can't see the connection between the success of ambitious men and the success of the whole, then you're blind, pure and simple. Or perhaps you think we should have done the Christian thing and built the bums an ark."

"Do you even believe in God, Dad? I'd really like to know."

"Of course I do. In my own way." He licked the corners of his mustache and seemed to zone out for a couple seconds. From across the room, I saw Kylee pass through the main dining room and into the kitchen without so much as glancing in our direction. "I believe He's necessary as a source of hope in most people's lives. I know I wouldn't want to live in a socialist country where people look to the government for answers instead."

"I've never heard you talk about Him. Before the divorce, or after, I don't remember you saying one word about God or religion."

"Rest assured, I have my own ideas about a higher power. It hasn't always been a smooth relationship between us, though. When I was a younger man, I faced some difficult times that led me to seek the truth in His word. The Old Testament, especially, provided me with a great deal of clarity about what it means to be a man and to live in this world. But it seemed like every time I came close to getting serious about my faith, He'd send a message that would make me question the whole thing."

"I don't know what that means, send a message."

"Well, for example, when I was twenty-six, maybe a little older, a friend of mine talked me into accompanying him to a late night service at a megachurch up near Folsom. Everyone was worried about the state of the world then, and new congregations were springing up all across California. We get into the church, which is packed corner to corner with something like two thousand people, and the minister gets up and starts sermonizing all about redemption and salvation and so forth. But what really struck me was that he wasn't the typical kind of minister you would expect to find in that part of the country. He was well-dressed and well-spoken, and he seemed to have had something like a real education, not like some of these hick preachers who have only read the Bible and elementary school readers in the entire course of their lives. And the stuff he talked about, I swear, it sent a chill down my spine. Here was a minister I had never seen before, and it was like he was preaching directly to me. He didn't just talk about spiritual matters, but about wealth and property as well. He went on for I don't know how long about how God rewards the faithful with money and success in this life, not just paradise in the other. That was the whole theme of his sermon, more or less, and I got to say it really hit a nerve with me then. There I was, a young man trying to make a name for himself, and it was like the minister knew in advance that I was coming and designed the sermon for me in particular. I tell you, it was an earth-shaking experience for me, to say the least. I didn't think I'd ever be the same again. In fact, halfway through the service, I turned to my friend and said, from this day on, I'm turning my life around. I even had tears in my eyes if you could believe it."

"Okay. So what happened?"

I heard an abrasive tone in my voice that Dad must have picked up on as well. He had been in a much better mood since he started reminiscing about the sermon, but now he narrowed his eyes and adopted the same accusatory grimace as before.

He said, "I was feeling lighter than air when I came out of the church into the parking lot. I felt so good, in fact, I wasn't paying attention to what was in front of me. There was a flat piece of wood, like a broken two-by-four, just lying on the ground in the middle of the lot. It had a long nail sticking out the end of it, and of all the people who were coming outside at that moment, I was the one who just happened to step on it." Dad reached for his glass again, forgetting that it was empty. He stared longingly into the cold cylinder, then slammed it down hard on the table. "The nail went all the way through my foot and I collapsed on the ground from the shock of the pain. My friend helped me up and drove me to the hospital, but first I just sat there on the asphalt with the nail sticking out the top of my shoe, sensing that this too was a message intended specifically for me. I looked up at the night sky and said, 'Really? This is what I get? This is all the love you have to show me after I decided to give my life to you?' My friend tried to get me to go with him to church again after that, but I'd been put off by the whole experience. I know they say God works in mysterious ways, but there's a fine line between mystery and callousness."

My mouth opened slowly as I tried to comprehend the logic of Dad's testimonial. "If you really believe God was out to get you that night, why do you still believe in him? Why bother?"

Dad shrugged. "He's our Father in heaven. He deserves our respect."

At last Kylee emerged from the kitchen and came over to see how we were doing. Without a word, Dad and I both held out our glasses to signal for another round.

• •

I booked a room for six nights at the Blossom Road Motel in Tulare. I told the manager I would make it day-to-day if I wound up needing to stay any longer. After the eighth night, he leaned his pockmarked and sallow face over the counter and asked if I wanted him to look into more permanent arrangements in the area. I told him, "Don't bother. I'm only staying around here as long as I have to. So this will do just fine." Which isn't to say the Blossom Road was equal in comfort and amenities to the Caravan or other establishments of that sort. Not even close, really. (The US-era linens were so yellow-brown with wear that a coffee stain would barely stand out against the bed sheets, and the shower, so called, was something better suited for hosing down pigs at a livestock auction than for cleaning a human body.) Still, I wanted to keep a low profile this time through. Klyee could always be trusted to keep her mouth shut when it mattered, and to come straight away when I called. She didn't take our professional relationship for granted; there was history there, and besides, any night she was with me she could count on making far more than she ever would from tips alone. She had grown fatter and more morose over the years, but I still paid her a decent rate every time. In general, women could be got and gotten rid of fairly cheaply in the valley, but one you could trust was an investment worth holding on to.

She turned to me once with the morning light streaming through the curtains and said, "How many more nights you gonna want me for? I need to let the shift manager know when I'm coming back to work." She lay on her side with the blanket stuffed between her thighs, her skin bright and doughy from the heat of the room. She had a large tattoo stretched across the back of her shoulder. Supposedly it meant "hope" in Chinese, but considering the sort of life she led, she would have been better off with any random character copied from a takeout menu.

I said, "My guy's going to be here soon with the information I've been waiting for. You should leave before he gets here. I'll call later in the week if I'm still around."

"You gonna be all right on drinks till then?"

"I don't know. How many jars do we have left?"

She rolled onto her opposite side and peered over the side of the bed, at the small washtub loaded with chilled Mason jars and clouded ice cubes from the machine next door. Trails of sweat trickled down the back of her neck. She raised her head and said, "Three and a half. Maybe three an a quarter."

"What day is today?"

"It's Tuesday."

"Plan on coming back Friday. Same number of jars as last time. I'll call if there's a change of plans. In the meantime, pass me the one that's already open."

Ice water ran off the sides of the jar and dribbled onto the sheets and blanket. As clear as the liquor was, I could see tiny particles of dirt and vegetation floating on the surface as I raised the jar to my lips. "Christ that's harsh," I said, then took another long drink and screwed the lid back on. The potato vodka these farm boys brewed was practically lighter fluid, and still I was going through a jar of the stuff a day. After a bad night I would wake up with spasms in my liver seeing all sorts of colorless fireworks exploding across the fluid of my eyes.

"I didn't say get dressed."

Kylee held her wrinkled blouse by the sleeve with half of it still balled up on the floor. "What about breakfast?"

"You can eat afterwards. I'm not finished yet."

"But I'm hungry. My stomach hurts."

"Here. Drink some of this."

"I don't like the taste."

"No one does. That's not why we drink it."

She sucked a few drops of vodka through her pierced lips and gagged almost instantly.

"That's a girl. Now one more for the road."

She dug her knees into the mattress and rested her huge stomach on one of the pillows. When we were done she cleaned herself with a bath towel and reassembled her work outfit from the disheveled pieces strewn across the floor. She looked like a refugee, a victim of a far and unfeeling war.

"You still owe me for two nights. I'd rather get it now if it's all the same."

"How much does that come to?"

"Two nights. Same rate as always."

"Right. And is that more or less than what my old man used to pay?"

She stopped buttoning her blouse and looked back over her shoulder at me. "You always ask about that."

"Yeah. Because you never want to tell me."

"Yeah. So stop asking."

"What if I were to pay extra? Would you let me in on the secret then?"

"I would not."

"How come?"

"Because. That'd be the last money I'd ever see from you."

I smiled. "That's why you're one of the smart ones."

One of the smart ones. That was the truth. Not that it ever did her much good, poor fat creature. I paid her the going rate plus cab fare back to Porterville. With any luck she'd be able to placate her pimp and still have money left over to bribe the manager for the shifts she missed. Then again, she was smart, not lucky.

After she left I showered and changed into a clean pair of underwear. I had planned on finishing getting dressed, but first I sat down on the bed and had a few more drinks from the vodka jar. I don't know when I nodded off, or how long I slept, but when I opened my eyes again Ramirez was standing over me with an amused look on his face.

He said, "Sorry to disturb you. The door was unlocked, so I let myself in."

I moved the blanket off my chest and looked around the room until my head stopped spinning. I said, "I was expecting you earlier this morning. What happened?"

Ramirez took off his Stetson hat and sat down in the easy chair in the corner of the room. Besides my father, he was the best dressed man I had ever seen in these parts, though he kept to a Southwestern style that Dad would have found unacceptably gauche: corduroy jackets, Stetson hats and boots, sterling silver bolo ties. He crossed one leg over the other and rested a manila folder on the side of his calf.

He said, "Something told me you wouldn't be ready for me until later in the day."

I took the vodka jar off the nightstand and choked down a heavy swig. It was almost room temperature by then, and practically cauterized my throat on the way down. "I've been ready the past two days. I'm not shacking up in this place for my health."

"I can see that."

"Cut the crap. Just tell me what you found."

He turned over the top page of the folder and leafed through the loose pages inside. "There are five women all together. Claudia, Dawn, Jennifer, Katherine, and Sandra. They have twelve children between them, ages two to nineteen. Jennifer's parents live with her and Katherine's family in the second house, although I use the term 'live' very loosely in their case. Beyond that, they have the usual crew of foremen and hired laborers, most of whom have only just arrived for the start of the season."

"Twelve children. Jesus."

"That's right. And they're all your father's as far as I can tell."

"As far as you can tell? What does that mean?"

"Well, I couldn't exactly get a hold of any DNA samples, of course, but the birth records all match up with the dates on the marriage certificates you gave me. So it's a pretty good guess they're kin to you."

"You've been through the county records?"

"You asked for thorough, and so thorough is what I gave. County, state, and federal records all the way back through the American era. I even managed to dig up Sandra's father's old military records. Fascinating stuff."

"Great. But aside from the scrapbook material, what else did you find out?"

"You want a particular answer, you're going to have to be more specific."

"What do I need to look out for? And more importantly, who?"

Ramirez took a water glass off the end table and spat a stream of runny brown saliva into it. Until that moment I hadn't noticed the wad of dip packed into the lower recesses of his gums.

I said, "Seriously? You're going to make me stare at your disgusting tobacco juice for the rest of this conversation?"

He smiled and nodded his head gently. "I could smell the stink of sex in here from the parking lot. So let's not quibble over who's making who endure what."

"Just tell me if there's anyone I should keep a lookout for. Any boyfriends or close relations. Anyone who could pose a problem."

"Jennifer has a foreman who came with her from their previous parcel. Seems to be some loyalty there, though she's still got him living in shared quarters at the state labor camp."

"I'm not worried about a foreman. I'm talking about people who can't be bought off. There must be someone you're overlooking."

As quick as it came, his smile disappeared. Apparently I had offended his pride by questioning his vaunted thoroughness. He said, "Well, Mr. Temple, keep in mind, I was only able to observe the goings-on of the farm for a limited time. But from what I can gather, you don't have anything to worry about when it comes to unexpected wildcards. These wives of your father, or should I say widows, are about as solitary as any subjects I've ever investigated. They receive next to no visitors, they have no relatives for you to worry about, and the children don't even seem to have any close friends in the community. All told, you're looking at a flock of sitting ducks ready for an ambush."

"Five women without a single person looking out for them. How is that possible?"

Ramirez rolled the base of his spit cup back and forth over his kneecap. As with the dip, I think he knew it irked me to hear my carefully laid plans described as an "ambush," but he kept doing it for the same reason middle school boys will keep teasing a classmate long after it's ceased to be funny. Behind all his affected manners and speech, there was a child's heart longing for the chance to mess with somebody, to kick dirt onto their polished shoes, if only to prove they never deserved to be taken seriously. He said, "It would seem your father had a taste for vulnerable young women with no real support system to speak of. It makes sense, really. Without anyone else to look out for their interests, these women were at his mercy to provide for them. That would have made them far more pliant in the long run."

"It just seems too good to be true. You'd think at least one of them would have a brother or uncle around to complicate things for me."

"Again, you need to consider the possibility that their rootlessness was one of the qualities that drew Elliot Sr. to them in the first place. You look through these background profiles and a distinct pattern emerges. Tragedy followed by poverty followed by isolation. One of these girls was hookin' it before your father came along. Another was a borderline junkie. Another was on SSRIs for chronic depression. Of course none of this is terribly uncommon with that generation, the ones who came of age around the time of disbandment. But it is significant that your father, a man who, by your own accounts, was something of an elitist in his own right, should decide to marry these women who he all but took in off the street."

"My father was a perverse man. That should have been evident from the start. Six wives, thirteen kids, God knows how many others he strung along who we don't even know about. Anyway, I'm done trying to make sense of why he did the things he did. There's only one thing keeping me in this dusty shithole of a state, and it's tied up in that co-op where I can't get my hands on it."

"I'm guessing you plan on going ahead with the shakedown, then."

"Of course. Why wouldn't I? If what you're saying is correct, then all I have to worry about are five lonely widows and their brats."

"That's so. Although I can't help but feel you may be underestimating what they're capable of, especially if you put them in a position where they don't have any other options."

"They're middle-aged mothers from the valley. Pushovers. They probably don't even keep guns on the property."

"My research suggests they don't. Or at least there aren't any fire-arms licensed under their names in the national registry."

"See? They wouldn't know how to run me off even if they wanted to. Plus, you just said they're more pliant than most."

Ramirez uncrossed his legs and rested his spit cup on the arm-rest. His free hand started fiddling with one of his shirt buttons, pinch-ing it between his nails and drawing it forward as far as the thread would allow. It occurred to me that none of these idle gestures of his ever seemed to stem from nerves or restlessness; it was as if he were in complete control of himself, and yet resolved by choice to expend his energy on actions that served no purpose other than to give his hands something to do.

He said, "When I was working for the government, I learned from doing criminal profiles that you always have to ask yourself the questions that will force you to defy the expectations of who and what you're dealing with. In the case of these five women, I asked myself what it is that they value more than anything else, and the answer jumped out at me almost instantly. Security. Safety. Stability in their lives. They were so desperate for it that they married a man they had known for only a short time, and that was before they were mothers. Now, with two houses full of children to look out for, they might take even more drastic steps to ensure their family remains unmolested. Something you should keep in mind before you go and threaten them with anything."

I smiled and stole another harsh swig from the Mason jar. "Don't tell me you're intimidated by a handful of country widows. Mister big, tough federal investigator."

"A handful of mother hens can peck a fox into submission. Evolution can't help but give the female of the species the tools she needs to keep her babies safe. Call it instinct, call it irrationality, or whatever, but at the end of the day, those with something to live for tend to outlast those with nothing to lose."

"Right. And I suppose that's me in this scenario. The man with nothing to lose."

He looked around at the general squalor of the room, another seemingly idle gesture delivered with clear and deliberate intent. "That depends on how you define the word 'nothing.' For me personally, I have a hard time believing that a man who's shirtless and drunk before noon on a weekday is hiding some inner light behind a bushel. That's just me, though."

Ramirez stood and put his hat back on. I was so angry I could barely stand to look at him, but I wasn't about to let him go away thinking he had left me feeling humbled. I reached into the nightstand drawer and took out a white envelope with several hundred-dollar bills sealed inside.

I said, "Leave the folder on the chair and get the hell out of here. Your money's all there just like we agreed. But don't expect to hear from me again."

He stuffed the envelope in his jacket pocket and sauntered casually to the door. He said, "Don't worry. Illegal or not, your plans are safe with me. That's the deal I strike every time I take on a new case, and I don't mean to go against it now just because you turned out to be an asshole. Just remember what I warned you about. One stitch now could save you a whole lot of them later down the road."

Unwashed and grody as I was, I still managed to get to my feet before he could leave. "You fucked up today, my friend. I've got plans for that money, and someday I'm going to be a very important man in this country. You'll wish then that you had been civil to me, instead of trying to tear me down any way you could. Because I can tolerate a lot of things, but I won't tolerate being belittled by someone who doesn't know the first thing about me. I got enough of that when Elliot was alive."

Ramirez shook his head. After all the snark and stubbornness that had tainted his work these past weeks, it seemed strange to find him suddenly divested of any concern for the situation at hand, standing with his hat brim low over his forehead, already off-duty in his heart and mind. "I worry about you, Mr. Temple. I really do. You're an odd duck with big ideas, dangerous methods, and poor impulse control.

You might end up running the Republic someday or lying dead in a gutter, but not likely anywhere else in between."

I slammed the door behind him. I did so in the spur of the moment, just as he was passing the threshold, and afterwards I felt petty and childish for letting him drive me to such a pointless final gesture. It was the sort of thing I imagined he would have done in the same position, and it left a bitter taste in my mouth for the rest of the afternoon. With enough vodka, of course, almost any shame could be forgotten. But even as I began to make myself very drunk, the thought that he was somehow still in my head, driving me to drink from afar, made the whole thing as joyless as any other chore.

• •

After our plates were cleared away, Dad ordered a glass of brandy to cap off the evening. He told me to order another round myself, but advised that I should "stay with the one that brought me," which I took as an indirect way of reminding me that, regardless of the fact that I had matched him glass for glass over the entire course of the meal, he was still more experienced in these matters than I was, and always would be. He produced a cigar from out of nowhere and lit up right there at the table. Either smoking laws were very lax in San Joaquin, or Dad felt confident that no one in that place, customer or staff, would dare ask him to put it out.

He said, "So. Here we are. A couple of men out on the town. How do you like that?"

I took a drink of water from the overflowing glass in front of me. Every bit of ice had melted since we first sat down and started ordering booze. Seemed like hours had passed in the interim, although in reality it was still barely nightfall. "Can I ask you a question, Dad? And have you answer me seriously?"

Dad blew smoke in my face. I fought the urge to cough. He said, "I don't know about you, but I've been serious this whole time. Go ahead."

I started to speak almost immediately, but my tongue felt strangely heavy and I couldn't get my thoughts arranged in any coherent order. I took another gulp of water and ran my damp hands over my face. "Why does it have to be like this? Why? You show up out of the blue and ask me to take this trip with you. So why do you feel the need to ride me like this all night? Why can't you treat me like a father ought to treat his son?"

The deep red embers pulsated dimly at the end of his cigar. He said, "I could ask you the same thing."

"That doesn't make sense. Ask me the same thing?"

"You know what I mean. You sit here with my food and drink inside you, and you have the gall to ask me why I don't treat you better. But when have you ever treated me like a son ought to treat his father? That's what I'd like to know."

"Jesus Christ, Dad. What did I do? What did I ever do that was so terrible?"

"Don't act like you don't remember. Spitting in my face. After all the effort I put in."

"I never spit in your face, Dad. I don't even know what you're saying anymore."

"Right. It must be some other son I'm thinking of, then. Some other son who takes the present his father gets him for his birthday and throws it away like it's nothing but garbage."

"What present? What birthday?"

Dad lowered his head and hacked violently into his fist. Afterwards he stared at me with eyes full of vindictive rage, as if I had been the one gagging him instead of the cigar smoke. "You really don't remember. The bicycle meant so little to you."

"Bicycle?"

"Yes, goddamn it, a bicycle! A brand new fire engine red bicycle that any eight-year-old boy in the country would have been proud to call his own. Any boy except you, of course. Oh, you pretended to be interested in it. You even took it around the block and made a big show of how much you liked it. But the next time I came into town, it was gone. You had traded it to a Mexican boy down the street. Swapped it like it was a rusty old dime-store piece of crap, instead of an expensive import that took a lot of research and legwork to find. I tell you, I've been betrayed many times in the past, and it stung like hell when it happened, but I never felt as double-crossed as I did the day I came home from the road and found that bicycle gone. It was like even then, at age eight, you were trying to say that you didn't care for me or what I had to offer. It was like you were already laughing at me and you could barely tie your shoelaces."

Dad sloped down low over the table. He had started to chew compulsively on the end of the cigar, staining his teeth with its earthy brown juice. I began to worry that I was in just as bad a shape as him, and that the second wind I was feeling was nothing more than the vodka's way of covering its tracks for the damage it had already done.

I said, "I'm sorry, Dad. I don't remember any of that. Why did I give my present away?"

"I've been wondering the same thing for ten years. It was a beautiful bicycle. It was worth so much more than the monster you replaced it with."

"Did you say monster?"

Without any warning, Dad slammed his fist against the table so hard that our drink glasses rattled. The nearest other diners were all the way on the other side of the room, and still they looked over at us with nervous alarm. Dad took a breath and said, "A fucking iguana. That's what you accepted in exchange for your birthday present. A dirty, disgusting lizard with jagged claws and lumps on its neck like something out of a medical journal. You used to keep him in a glass box with a heat lamp and feed him old cabbage so the whole house stank of rot. Damn thing would pull food into its mouth on the tip of its tongue like a frog. I watched it being fed one time, just once, and nearly threw up from the sight of it. But to you the little bastard was worth more than my gift ever was. It was a good trade in your eyes. That's how little value you placed in what I did for you. That's how little you thought of me."

I sat there stunned, staring into my father's otherworldly eyes and feeling the bitterness that permeated every aspect of his being. An iguana. I had owned a pet iguana as a child. Of course I remembered it all so vividly now, the proud, menacing curve of the creature's back, its slow crawl across the kitchen floor to the sunny spot under the windowsill. But I hadn't thought about it for years until Dad brought it up. I couldn't even remember the name I had given it. Still, it was more than I remembered about the bike. I could have sworn Mom had bought the iguana for me, even though affection for any type of animal, especially reptiles, was completely out of character for her. But no. I had made a deal for the iguana, and in doing so had wounded Dad enough to make him resent me secretly for nearly a decade. What could I even say to make it up to him? The whole episode was a blank for me, a piece of original sin of which I never realized I was guilty. I didn't remember trading the bicycle to a Mexican boy when I was eight. I didn't even remember the Mexican boy.

"Dad. I'm sorry I upset you. I'm sorry I didn't appreciate the bike. I know raising a child is never easy. But come on. I was eight years old. You can't seriously hold it against me. It was just me being a dumb kid. Nothing more."

I really should have known better than to try being sincere with him, at least when it came to something like this. It would have been better if I had lied and said I wanted to hurt him, if I had confirmed his suspicion that the eight-year-old me had been full of contempt, that I had been angry at him for some reason or another, that the lizard was my own cheap way of getting back at him, and then apologized and promised never to hurt him again. He could understand pettiness, and he could understand revenge, and maybe he could have forgiven both. But he would never accept that such a slight against him, even one committed by a grade-schooler, could have been perpetrated thoughtlessly, without intent. It would have meant going against his whole perception of the world and his place in it. If on some cloudy day he had suddenly found himself caught in a downpour, it would have been more comforting to believe the skies held some secret grudge against him than to accept that they were totally indifferent.

He shook his head and said, "Spite. That's what this is. You were a spiteful child then, and now you've grown up to be a spiteful young man. The sort of pathetic person who blames his father for the hair in his soup." He took his sweaty palm off the tablecloth and held it in front of his face. The tips of his thumb and index finger were so close they were almost touching. "I came this close to poisoning your damn lizard. Would have been so easy, too. Just a couple squirts of pesticide in the cabbage and I'd have been rid of that nauseating thing once and for all. Your mother was all that stopped me. Said she'd lock me out of the house if I tried it."

I looked at him for a long second and smiled. I said, "It's funny. Even now, after everything you've said, it still doesn't change the way I feel. I mean, I can think all sorts of nasty things about you, even more so now that we've had this time together, but the core feelings stay the same. I love you, Dad. I always have."

He stared at me for so long after that that a trickle of brown drool began to seep through his lips and soak into his beard. He put the cigar out in his water glass and wiped his face with a napkin. I didn't see him cry that night, nor did he ever give me the impression that he was on the verge of breaking down. But just seeing him flummoxed as he was, taken aback by his spiteful son's words of love, was enough to give me chills. There were some things that seemed too unnatural for me to comprehend at that age; God never dies, the sun doesn't set in the east, and Dad doesn't get choked up. That's the way of sheltered adolescence. All great truths go together, or they were never really true to begin with.

Dad said, "It's been a long time. Since you said you loved me. I can't even remember the last time, in fact."

"When I was eleven, and you took me to see the Russian circus in San Jose. I said it a couple times in the car on the way there. But you didn't like it, so I stopped."

"How do you know I didn't like it?"

"You told me it was peculiar for a son to tell his father he loved him."

"Did I?"

"Those were your exact words."

"Well." Dad brushed his hand through the air like he was shooing away a fly. "As you said, raising a child is never easy. It was my job to make sure you turned out strong enough to make it in a difficult world. I had to be careful not to let you turn soft on me."

"You talk like you raised me up single-handed. But I haven't seen you in person in over four years. I don't see how you can reconcile that with what you're saying."

I expected him to shoot me a nasty glare, but he didn't even look up from the table. He said, "I had to make a living. It wasn't like your mother was going to be able to support a decent lifestyle for you on her own, what with her lack of work experience, and a degree in the humanities. Or perhaps you would have preferred growing up in an East Bay shithole and going to school with a bunch of Nigerian refugees."

"It's not like you couldn't have found a job that kept you closer to home. How was I supposed to feel with you away on business all the time?"

"Grateful. That's how you were supposed to feel. What? You think you're the only son who ever had to make do while his father was out earning money? If you were a Chinese boy, you'd barely see your father's face until you were all grown up. And you'd be proud that he had a job that kept him busy with so many responsibilities."

"I'm not a Chinese boy"

"Evidently. Evidently."

"Please. Let's not get started on another mean streak. I just told you that, despite everything you've said to me so far on this trip, I still love you. I thought maybe you could take the time to say you love me as well."

"Yes. I suppose I could." He took a slow sip of brandy, and afterwards he sat idly swirling the liquor around in his glass like one of the noble lords he admired so much from history. "It's difficult for me to express myself like that. With words. To go around saying how I feel like a woman or a hippie. I've always been more comfortable with actions and gestures, with doing things to show people that I care. That's why I place so much importance on gifts, I think. Because making an effort to do something is the best way I know to let those feelings out."

"I can understand that, Dad. And to be honest, I had kind of hoped this trip would be a way for you to do just that."

"Well. The trip's not over yet. Let's get the check and see what we can do about it."

"You're saying you want to buy me another gift?"

"In a sense, yes. But first tell me something. Are you still a virgin?"

The question was so unexpected I nearly sprayed vodka out my mouth and across the tablecloth. I said, "I don't see what that has to do with anything."

Dad shook his head and smiled enigmatically. "I can tell from your reaction that you are. That's all right. The boys who lose it in high school always peak too early. But now that you're going to be making your way in the world, you'll need to know how to lay your claim when the time comes. I can help you with that. Take the mystery and suspense out of it for you."

"I'm not sure I like where this is going."

He laughed. "Don't be scared. That's the woman's job."

Kylee came and placed our bill between us in a black leather tablet. She smiled with her hands behind her back. "How we doin', guys? Everything all right?"

Dad pulled out his entire bankroll and dealt a few large bills onto the open tablet. He said, "Tell me, Kylee. Any chance those friends of ours are working tonight? At the usual place?"

Kylee glanced from side to side and then down at the roll of money in Dad's hand. "That depends. You got any particular friends in mind?"

"Possibly. What about our acquaintance with the long brown hair? I have a hunch she and my son might really hit it off."

Kylee turned her head and looked at me in a way that I knew was insinuating something. She said, "It's short notice, but I think she might be available later this evening."

Dad dropped several more bills onto the tablet. "We're about thirty minutes away now. See that she's ready and waiting when we arrive."

Kylee took the cash and hurried off to use the phone on the other side of the bar. I watched her as she placed the call, noticing the perfunctory way she carried out the task at hand, no differently than if she were taking down dinner reservations or putting in a produce order. Meanwhile, Dad raised his glass to me and nodded. He said, "Drink up. At your age, liquor can only help you get your money's worth."

• •

We took the main road out of Porterville and followed it I don't know how far into the country before turning onto another road that was completely removed from any reliable source of light. Dad switched on the high beams and switched them off just as quickly. He was sober enough to know not to draw attention to us, but drunk enough to slip up now and then if he didn't keep his attention fixed on what he was doing. And so we drove on in silence much as we had for the better part of the day, him focusing on the road ahead, me half-sick and terrified of where the road might be leading us.

By the time we started heading up a long, unpaved driveway, I realized that I had no memory of actually getting up and following Dad out of the restaurant and into the Charger. The sudden frailty of my mind struck me as both scary and funny, though I lost all sense of humor about everything the moment we reached the end of the driveway and parked in front of a well-lit house with pink curtains in the windows. There were nicer vehicles than ours surrounding the house, as well as shabbier ones, but they all had the same rim of dirt around the tires from making the drive here on the dusty valley roads. After jamming the parking break into place, Dad pulled a flask from his jacket pocket and took a drink, his fifth or sixth in total for the evening.

He wiped his mouth and said, "When we get in there, don't make eye contact with the other men unless they make it first. But treat every woman in the place like she's an old girlfriend from a long time ago. I've already got a date lined up for you, so you don't have to worry about fending off any sales pitches, but as a rule you should act the gentleman to all of them, even the ones who are too worn-out or ugly to earn their keep. You listening to me?"

I nodded gently and continued to stare out the window at the house. It was an old place, pre-Republic, with three stories stacked on top of one another in order of decreasing size like layers on a wedding cake. The pink curtains and bright yellow exterior only added to the impression I had that the whole house was one big frosted confection designed to be gobbled up by greedy children like the witch's cottage in the fairy tale. I listened for screams, for the cat-like moaning of whores, but heard only the faint sounds of an erhu turning out pre-recorded Chinese melodies in a slow and longing style.

Dad said, "Don't tell me you're getting cold feet."

I looked down at the floor mat, but my feet were too drunk to tell if they were hot or cold. "I said I wanted to find God. I don't think this is the place to do it."

Dad gestured outside with his flask still in hand. "God's in there as much as any place."

"How do you figure?"

"He made our flesh weaker than the flesh of a woman. So He's always with us when our flesh leads us to temptation."

"My flesh didn't lead me here. You did."

"That's right. Because I don't want you to get to be in your twenties and be so in awe of what women have between their legs that you become the slave of the first one to let you have it. I'd rather you sinned once tonight and got it out of the way than stay pure and become a lifelong neurotic." He raised the flask to his lips, drank deeply, and coughed so hard that a fine mist of whiskey coated the inside of the windshield. Between the heat of the day and the constant drinking of the evening, his beard had come to resemble something wild and sickly; a gutter animal, rank and matted from exposure. "Though I suppose it's your decision in the end. No sense losing your cherry if you're not man enough to handle it yet. Say the word and we'll drive back into town. I'm sure there's somewhere around here we can get you a hot fudge sundae, if that's less frightening for you."

"No. I'll go inside."

"You sure?"

"Yeah. I just decided. I'll do it."

Dad reached over and patted my knee proudly. He said, "That a boy. You'll see. People make a big deal about it, but there's nothing more natural for a man to do. We were built for it, same as them."

I got out of the Charger and staggered up the peastone walkway with Dad several steps behind me. When I got to the front porch, I waited for him to catch up so that he could knock or ring or recite whatever password would establish him as a member of the club. But then the door opened and a middle-aged Asian woman appeared behind the screen to greet us. She was squat and buxom and wearing a plain black dress that reached past her ankles, but with a makeup job that offset the funereal look of her clothes with muted pastels and eyebrows penciled into Egyptian arches. She seemed to look straight past me, smiling at my father with every tooth showing as her manicured hand pushed the screen door open.

She said, "Welcome back, Mr. Temple. We were pleased to hear you would be joining us. The girls get lonesome when you're away so long."

"I'll bet they do." Dad smiled and winked in her direction. All of a sudden he struck a strange and deceptively casual pose, standing straight with his thumbs hooked through his belt loops, rocking back and forth on the heels of his shoes. He looked like the salesman instead of the customer. "Tonight I'm here to help my son mount his first jenny.

Our mutual friend led me to believe everything would be ready when we arrived."

"And so it is. Livia is waiting in the parlor as we speak."

"Good. Junior and I'll be at the bar. Give us a couple minutes and then send her in."

We stepped through the doorway and into a talcum-scented room with crepe paper lamp shades throwing colored shadows onto the walls. None of the ceiling lights were on, and so the whole interior of the house seemed caught in a state of perpetual twilight that would have been disorienting even if I was sober. Dad stepped in front of me and led us to a bar that consisted of two varnished folding tables fitted together at a ninety degree angle. He must have forgotten his advice about staying with the one that brought me, because he ordered us each of shot of whiskey. A fat Latino nodded and grabbed an unlabelled bottle off one of the shelves nailed into the papered drywall. Dad and I touched our glasses together and tossed the whiskey down our throats. It was the second type of liquor I had ever had, and all it did was make me shudder.

Dad said, "I remember my first time in a place like this."

But he didn't go on. He just stood leaning on the bar, looking out at the rest of the room. While a few of the girls were occupying the laps of other customers, most were spread out over several ancient, floral-print sofas positioned at different points along the perimeter of the room. They sat with their bare feet on the cushions or tucked into their skirts. Some were topless and others covered, but they all seemed to share their madam's affinity for gaudy eye shadow, as though they were franchise workers obliged to wear the same matching uniform. I shook my head and looked at Dad.

I said, "Some of these girls don't look a day over fifteen."

"They're young, but they know what they're doing. Or else they wouldn't let them stay."

"Doesn't seem right. As young as they are."

"It's a different culture here in the valley. Kids start screwing as soon as they sprout their first fuzz."

Before I could begin to wrap my head around the sexual disparities between San Joaquin and the coast, the old madam returned, accompanied by a heavyset young girl with curls of brown hair running down her naked shoulders and back. She was pudgy in the face and a bit snaggletoothed, but pretty enough all the same. For as much as she stared straight at me, I could hardly bring myself to look her in the eye.

The madam addressed me directly for the first time. She said, "This is Livia, Mr. Temple. Livia, may I introduce Mr. Elliot Temple, Jr. Mr. Temple is just in from the coast. I thought perhaps you could entertain him for a while."

The child-whore smiled and said, "I'm sure I could find something to do with him."

Dad laughed in a boisterous, over-the-top sort of way; honestly, I'm surprised he didn't go so far as to actually slap his knee, he was so caught up in the performance of being jolly. After a childhood in which I could scarcely remember him hugging me, he now came up behind me, gripped my shoulder, and whispered, "Go get her, buddy." Livia roped her arm around mine and began leading me upstairs.

The more I replay the events of that night in my head, the more improbable it seems that I could black out some small moments and be able to recall others with such clarity and detail. The hike up the stairs, for example, as well as the first stages of my eventual undressing, was wiped completely from memory by the time I awoke in the morning. The next thing I remember after leaving the parlor was sitting on the side of a queen bed in my underwear watching Livia roll her stockings down her legs two inches at a time. Her legs were fine in the conventional sense, but all I could think of were pale sausages being torn raw from their translucent casings. Perhaps I wasn't really drunk enough to black out. Perhaps it's possible that, in wanting so desperately to forget my first foray into adult sensuality, my brain had tried suppressing everything that happened to me that night, but, finding itself unable to erase the most important and formative events, it settled for omitting the transitional periods, the in-between moments that connected one trauma to another.

Livia stroked my thigh and asked if this was my first time. Already embarrassed, I closed my eyes and shook my head before she had even finished asking the question.

"Who told you? Dad, Kylee, or one of the others?"

"No one told me anything, baby. I was just curious."

"Right. Is that how you got into this line of work? Out of curiosity?" I looked at her again and saw that her smile had vanished. With as much sexual experience as she must have had, it was easy to forget that she was at least a couple years younger than me, that in all likelihood she was just barely old enough to enroll in high school. "Sorry. I didn't mean to be rude. Or if I did, I'm apologizing for it now."

She laughed abruptly, resuming her hand's playful busywork around my swimsuit area. "No worries, baby. You're funny. I like that in a man."

She stood and walked to the old fashioned vanity table and retrieved a condom from the bottommost drawer. From behind, her nudity was frank and unpretentious; thighs and ass and furrowed labia all united in one seamless, all-encompassing erogenous zone. I tried to put myself in the mood to do what was expected of me. It wasn't a physical problem; I had been hard since before she took off her skirt. The difficulty was in shrugging off the feeling of general misery that had been plaguing me since before we arrived, in persuading my mind to enjoy the pleasures of the body when all I could think of was Dad waiting downstairs, drunk and boastful, believing he had succeeded in making his son a man. Livia sat back down on the edge of the bed. She scooted closer and touched my arm tenderly.

"What is it, baby? What's the matter?"

I wiped the tears from my eyes with both hands, but more came pouring out to take their place. I said, "I'm fine. Look away. Just give me a minute."

"It's all right to be nervous. Everyone is at first."

I was practically hyperventilating at that point. I gritted my teeth and dug my fingernails into the mattress. "Could we just sit here? Please? Could we just sit here until the time's up?"

Livia wrapped a strand of hair around her finger and drew the curls out as straight as possible. She glanced nervously at the different walls, as if the place were equipped with hidden peepholes like something out of a campy movie from the last century. She said, "Your dad's already paid up, baby. If I don't deliver and word gets out, the boss'll paint my ass black and blue without a second thought."

"The lady from downstairs?"

"She just keeps an eye on things. The boss is a big guy with a bad temper. I can't risk him finding out we didn't fuck."

My breathing had returned to normal, but still I couldn't stop myself from crying. She leaned into me and pressed her naked breast against my back. I said, "I don't know… I don't know what's wrong with me," and right away she started to hum soothingly while running her soft fingertips down my spine. This wretched young girl, inelegant child of the whorehouse, had become my caretaker in a moment of pain and humiliation. I had gone searching for God, and instead I had found a caricature straight out of pulp erotica, the oppressed and motherly nymphet who could satisfy any number of secret fetishes from the most perverted end of the spectrum. She waited until I had finished bawling before reaching into my boxers and slipping the condom over me.

"That's it, baby. You just lie back and let me do all the work. You know any girl here would count herself lucky to have a go with you. So smart, so sensitive, so strong. A real gentleman. Not like most of the riff-raff we get in here."

I closed my eyes again and felt her wet lips form a suction-tight seal over my neck. I was going to die young, of that I was certain, and in the end all I would ever know about sex would be derived from secondhand gossip and a few minutes of sweaty straddling with an obese harlot. So be it, I decided. It was easier to endure with my eyes closed, resting flat on my back, imagining that the weight I felt pressing down on me was really the supernatural presence I had been seeking all along.

• •

I gave the widows my demands and returned to the Blossom Road to await their response. One week may have been an overly generous amount of time to let them mull it over, especially with Russert waiting to hear from me, but I suspected it might end up working to my advantage; the longer they had to think about it, the more time they had to sweat. The threat of losing everything (farm, money, and all) would be too much for most people to handle, and with five scared women facing down the threat of ruin, I figured it wouldn't be long before internal divisions began to undercut the united front they had presented me with when I spoke to them. As it happened, only two days passed before one of them came to see me in secret. She appeared outside my door in the late afternoon, a gangly roughneck accompanying her for protection.

I cleared some empty jars off the easy chair and said, "Please have a seat. Hopefully we can get this thing squared away before it gets any more awkward for all of us. The moment I saw you, I had you pegged as a refined and savvy lady. I hope I'm right."

Jennifer lowered herself onto the very front of the seat cushion and crossed one leg over the other. Her bodyguard looked all around the room for another chair that didn't exist, then leaned his back against the wall with his narrow thighs abutting the air conditioner. Jennifer said, "All I'm interested in is seeing this mess resolved in the quickest way possible. That, and ensuring that my children aren't cheated out of what's rightfully theirs."

"I understand completely. Before we begin, though, perhaps your associate wouldn't mind waiting outside. We're getting into some very delicate information here, after all."

"You don't have to worry about Dale. He's been my foreman since your father first brought me to the valley years ago. I trust him as much as I trust anyone."

"Fair enough. Would either of you care for a drink? I'm afraid all I have is local homebrew, but maybe I can place an order with the front desk."

Jennifer said, "Thank you, no. I'm fine."

Dale stepped forward and studied the empty jars with his hands in the pockets of his jeans. He said, "I wouldn't mind a little pick-me-up now that you mention it. From the look of 'em, I'd say you got these offa those Sarafian boys up near Minkler. Am I right?"

"I wouldn't know. An associate of mine picked them up while passing through the area. But you're welcome to have some, Dale, as an associate of a wife of my father."

Dale nodded amicably and passed me one of the half-empty jars from the nightstand. I twisted the lid off and passed it back to him for the first lukewarm pull. We carried on like that for a little while, passing the jar back and forth like regular old hillbillies, until finally Jennifer got us back to the business at hand.

She said, "First of all, I want to say that I appreciate where you're coming from, and why you felt compelled to take such extreme measures to get what you're entitled to. There are times when taking the moderate, tactful route only invites others to take advantage of you. I realize that now from bitter experience."

I nodded and set the jar back down on the nightstand. "You can imagine my surprise the day I discovered everything my father had ever earned was tied up in these five small farms in the valley, each one with a different Mrs. Temple at the helm. Now try to imagine what I felt, besides surprise, when I learned the five of you had invested his entire estate in some half-cocked cooperative venture."

"That was Katie's plan. The rest of us were just saps who let ourselves get talked into going along. And I was the biggest sap of all. For bankrolling the largest portion of the co-op, and coming away with a share no bigger than anyone else's."

"That hardly seems fair."

Jennifer crossed her arms over her chest. She was wearing both concealer and eye shadow, but still she looked tired and dispirited. She said, "I have never been compensated appropriately for what I've put into that farm. And I don't believe I ever will be. Meanwhile, a slut who carried your father's name for all of five minutes gets to live off the fat of the land without paying a single dime. All because your father left her with nothing while we were running a three-year surplus in Madera. That's the philosophy of the co-op in a nutshell. From each according to her abilities, to each according to her sob story."

"Interesting. And yet I suppose you must have approved of what Katie and the others had planned. At least in the beginning."

"Believe me, young man. You have no idea how intimidating it can be to face down four women at the same time when all of your futures are on the line. Men think they invented hostility the day Cain murdered his brother, but you can be certain the world today would be an even bleaker and more dangerous place if Eve had given birth to daughters."

"I believe you. That is, I respect you and take you at your word, as a good stepson ought to, I suppose. As I said, I knew you were a class above the rest of them the moment we first met. I don't even have to ask if you're well-educated."

"Before disbandment, everyone in my family was well-educated. At one time we had three generations of USC alumni alive at once: my father, my grandfather, and me."

"That's wonderful. My own mother was a Stanford undergrad in the pre-Republic days."

She gave me a very small, practiced smile. "I have great respect for that particular school. Though growing up we never thought much of the Bay Area in our house."

I smiled. "You sure I can't offer you something to drink?"

"No, thank you. I'd rather return to the issue of the farm."

I sat down on the edge of the bed so she wouldn't have to keep looking up at me. I said, "It's no issue as far as I'm concerned. I want you and the rest of them to sign a contract turning over everything to the Russert Growers Company. If I place a call to Mr. Russert this afternoon, he should be able to have something written up and faxed to me within the next few days so that, come Sunday, I'll have it ready for you sign when I head back out there. But Russert will only go through the trouble of making a contract if I can assure him that a deal has been reached, and I won't tell him that unless I'm sure myself that all five of you will agree to sign. If that's something you can arrange for me, all five signatures on a piece of paper, then I believe you might deserve something over and above what the others would receive. Something commensurate with your contributions to the farm. How does that sound?"

Jennifer traded glances with Dale. Even with a few shots of homebrew in him, there was a shrewd and stoic quality to the old farmhand. Jennifer said, "It sounds to me like you don't really think I'm entitled to a larger share based on what I've already put into the place. You're only open to the idea because I'm in a position to give you something more, to serve as your spy within the farm, so to speak. I'm not sure how I feel about that, to be quite honest."

"I'm glad you said something. Now let me make myself perfectly clear: I'm not going to offer you a larger share simply because you've earned it. I'm blackmailing you here. It's not a fair system. It's out of respect for you and my father that I agreed to see you today, and I'm making you this special offer because you're in a position to help me get the contract signed in the least messy way possible. That's my only reason. And if you deliver on what I'm asking for, you'll get the special treatment you want. It's an indelicate way of doing business, I know, but considering the constraints and risks I'm dealing with, it's all I can do to help us both. If I'm right about you, and the kind of woman you are, then I believe you'll understand."

Without a word, Jennifer rose and walked the dozen or so steps from the chair to the bathroom, Dale following behind her instinctively, without needing to be called, like any good lapdog. I took another swig of homebrew waiting for them to finish their private deliberations. By the time they came out again, I was feeling alert and lucid enough to tackle any roadblock or counteroffer they tried to throw at me.

I said, "Perhaps now we can continue. Or do you need more time with the toilet?"

Jennifer reclaimed her position on the edge of the chair cushion. She said, "I'm not a greedy woman, Mr. Temple. I don't believe in the supremacy of the almighty dollar. It's one of the lifelong burdens of coming from Orange County, people developing these assumptions about you based on where you were raised."

I nodded sympathetically and even showed her a slight frown; to secure a mole inside the co-op, I would have gladly gone along with her act for as long as necessary, coaxing her bloated ego, letting her think she was honoring the valley itself by deigning it with her presence. But I had read the background profiles Ramirez put together. I knew that, despite her upbringing, she was no Southern California elite, and hadn't been for some time. Her parents had been practically insolvent when Dad met her, one of the many families caught off-guard when Wall Street disintegrated and the American treasury dissolved. For so many years he must have held his tongue while she condescended to him, even as he was helping to rebuild her shattered world in the form of a sixty-acre spread with a legion of pickers and foreman for her to look down on. And now here she was, condescending to me even as she pleaded for a larger share of the wealth. I took it all in stride, speaking softly and acting the gentleman, just as Dad had taught me to do when facing an avaricious whore.

I said, "You won't find any negative assumptions here with me. Not after all the hardships you've had to endure since father's death."

She closed her eyes and appeared to hold back a sudden outpouring of grief. Ever the committed actress, the old bitch. She said, "Because I'm not greedy, I won't try to take advantage of the situation by asking for more than I deserve. Even after all the hard work I've put in these past months, I'm willing to walk away with a stake in the property no better or worse than what I had before. Except it has to reflect my initial investment, which of course was never equal to those of the other women. From day one, they were trying to extort something extra out of me, and they finally succeeded when I agreed to pay the slut's share of the deposit. Two fifths of that cooperative belong to me by right, Mr.

Temple, and that's what I'm asking in exchange for helping to secure a peaceful transition. Two-fifths of the total offer, promised to me in writing as part of the contract you want signed. That's my condition. Take it or leave it."

I let her sweat, watching her eyes closely as the resolute expression she was going for began to waiver in the face of my stonewalling silence. As I left her dangling well past the appropriate amount of time needed to consider her proposal, I noticed Dale also started to appear nervous, fidgeting with his hands like he didn't know what to do with them except leave them stuffed inside his pockets. It was like watching a two-headed beast out of mythology.

Finally I said, "It would seem you're asking for more than just that, really. You're also asking us to exclude Dawn from the offer altogether. That extra share has to come from somewhere, after all, and I imagine you wouldn't be heartbroken seeing her left out."

She contorted her face into a look of such pure disgust that I half-expected her to spit on the floor at the mere mention of Dawn's name. "She's an opportunist of the worst kind, a parasite that latches onto a healthy organism and stays until it dies off. First she latched onto your father, and we both know how that ended, and now she's dug her hooks so far into that farm there's no other way I can think of to get her out. She's even started referring to other women's children as her own. 'Our children.' That's what she said. That's when I knew I had to find a way to get rid of her. Then you showed up, and everything became clear to me for the first time in months. Suddenly I understood exactly how to get me and my kids away from that place, and that demented bitch away from us. So, no, to answer your question, I wouldn't care one way or another what happens to her after all this is done."

"I can respect that. Of course, what I can respect and what's in my best interest are two very different things. I'm wondering how you're going to convince the other wives to forsake her. How will you get them to sign the contract if she's left out?"

"Don't worry about the others. Being forced to live next to them all this time, I've learned what I need to know to get them on my side. Sandra and Claudia are ruled by fear, and Katie's been looking for a way out ever since her daughter got into trouble with a boy from school. They're all desperate to make you go away, and to do so they'd be willing to believe anything I tell them. Even if they do read the contract before signing it, and supposing they notice the biggest share's going to me, all I'd have to do is promise to give Dawn half of it once the deal goes through. And then disappear once the money is in my hands."

I laughed and reached under a pillow for another jar. I said, "You make it sound so easy. I'm starting to wonder if I even need someone on the inside."

She shot me a conceded smile. "Don't kid yourself. The only way this plan of yours can go smoothly is if someone helps it along. It's not just the other women you have to worry about. They have lots of children, and some of your brothers and sisters are downright savage."

My own smile disappeared. I poured a huge dose of vodka down my throat and wiped the spill-off onto the back of my hand. I said, "With all due respect, please don't call them my brothers and sisters. Having the same father doesn't make us family. It doesn't make us anything as far as I'm concerned. As far as I'm concerned, I'm an only child. Always have been, and always will be."

Jennifer looked at me. She nodded slowly and said, "If that's how you feel about it."

"Yes. That's how I feel. Thank you." I stood up from the bed and walked to the closet, to the half-emptied suitcase in which my personal effects were stowed. I uncovered the phone, still in its original packaging, and brought it over for her to examine. "That's a satellite phone from Korea. Brand new. Bought it from a retailer in San Mateo on the drive down. I have one too. Once you're certain that the others will sign the contract, shoot me a text message saying so. Then I'll contact Mr. Russert and have him fax over the forms. If I don't hear from you before Friday, don't bother looking for me come Sunday. By then I'll have already notified the Ag Bureau in Tulare about the fraud you've got going on over in Orosi. Three days. That's how long you've got. That's my condition, you can take it or leave it the same as I can for yours."

She looked at Dale, and together they shared a moment of wordless consideration. I was worried they would return once more to the bathroom, but instead Jennifer rose from the chair and reached out to shake my hand.

She said, "You take after him. I don't know if you know that, but I thought you should."

I didn't appreciate her saying so, and was positive that deep down it wasn't true. But still I thanked her, shook her hand, and saw both of them to the door.

• •

Losing my virginity wasn't what I expected. It wasn't anything like what the guys at school made it out to be. I felt nauseous the entire time it was going on, in part because of all I'd had to drink, but also because Livia's thighs kept squeezing my balls as she ground her pelvis into me. When it was over I felt greasy from my navel down to my hips. I think she applied some form of artificial lubricant when I wasn't looking. Probably did the same with all her clients. Now she wrapped herself in a sheer lace robe and began brushing her hair at the vanity.

She said, "Thank you for the nice time, baby. Hope to see you again real soon."

Her polite nudging didn't fool me; the service had been rendered, and now she was kicking me out the door. I found my underwear at the foot of the bed. I stood to hitch them up, but my head started spinning and I fell back on the mattress. In places the sheets were transparent from sweat and other fluids. I turned to the vanity mirror and got my first good look at Livia. Uncomfortable as the sex had been, it elicited a remarkable change in that I was able to see her for more than a second without succumbing to shyness. Now that I had had her, there was nothing about her that inspired any trepidation in me, at least until her eyes appeared clearly in the mirror and I found myself leaning in for a closer look. She noticed and stopped brushing.

"Something wrong, baby?"

"Turn around."

"You feeling all right?"

"Turn around. Look at me."

She set the brush down and did as she was told. I touched her cheek and brought my face within a few short inches of hers; I didn't want to frighten her, but I couldn't help myself. Her eyes were the deepest shade of blue I had ever seen, and I would have recognized them anywhere.

"Where do you come from?"

She pulled away gently. "I don't know what you mean."

"Where were you born? Who are your parents? Tell me. Please."

"Time's almost up, baby. You should get dressed."

My pants were lying on the floor with one leg folded in half like something an amputee would wear. I scooped them up, took out my wallet, and removed all the money I had. I said, "This is almost a hundred dollars Californian. And it's all yours if you just answer me truthfully. That's all I ask."

Livia looked at the money. She was afraid, and her fear was obvious, but still, the look of desperation with which she eyed the money was so much more natural than the faces she made while faking orgasm. What did a hundred dollars mean in her world? What would she normally have to do to earn that kind of tip? She glanced up at me and said, "Your father's waiting for you. He'll start to wonder what's up if you don't head down soon."

"Two minutes. That's all I'm asking for. Then I'll get dressed and leave. And you'll be a hundred dollars richer."

Livia hesitated, but then snatched the money out of my hand. She folded the bills into a small, tight roll and held the roll to her chest with both hands like a woodland animal trying to guard its foraged nourishment. "Okay. What do you want to know?"

I sat back down on the edge of the bed. In my head I worked

backward through the chain of evidence needed to confirm what I already suspected. "How old are you? Really."

She looked down at her bare feet and looked up again. "Fourteen."

"Where were you born?"

"Here."

"In this house?"

"No. I mean here as in the valley."

"In a place like this?"

"More or less."

"So your mother was a whore as well?"

Her eyes flashed briefly with a spark of outrage. She lowered her head and clutched the money more closely to her body. She said, "Mama used to work in a party house up near Parlier. We moved down here when I was little."

"Where is she now?"

"I don't know."

"What do you mean you don't know?"

"She ran off a couple years ago. Didn't say where to. She was in pretty bad shape. Lots of drinking, and meth. Think she knew it was only a matter of time before the boss kicked her out."

I closed my eyes. It was too appalling to be true. Fat and brainless, second-generation whore daughter of a wayward addict. By all rights, the government should have had them both sterilized.

"Who was your father? That's my last question. Answer it and I'll leave. But be honest."

"I've been honest so far."

"Then tell me. Who was he?"

"I don't know that either."

"Your mother never told you."

"I don't think she knew herself."

"How could she not know?"

"It's easy to lose track. Week in, week out, men come from all over the country."

"From the coast?"

"Of course. They're the biggest spenders."

"Right. That makes sense." A speck of doubt glittered in the back of my mind. Of all the hundreds and maybe thousands of men her mother had been with, the odds of my suspicion bring true were about as good as my chances of winning the national lottery, or Livia's chances of finding a man to take her away from all this. It comforted me greatly, the improbability of it all. But then I looked into her eyes again and saw the truth plain as day, the similarities that stood in mocking contrast to all the rules of logic and likelihood. Dad was wrong. Instead of finding a peaceful, loving God in that place, I was staring straight into the eyes of the girl whose very existence seemed to confirm that no such peace would ever be available to me again. I steadied my breathing and said, "Thank you for your time, Livia. After I leave, you won't see me again. So good luck with all of this. I hope it turns out as well as it possibly can."

She watched me get dressed, still holding on to the money like someone was going to try to steal it away from her. She said, "You can't just leave me wondering like this. Why do you want to know about me? What's it to you?"

I was already fumbling with getting my shirt buttoned, and having her ask such questions, when all I wanted was to never hear her voice again, got me aggravated to the point of maliciousness. If such words existed, and if I could have found them, I would have spoken the incantation to wipe her forever from my memory, as well as from the living world itself. I said, "That's not how it works. We had an agreement. You got your money. If you wanted more, you should have negotiated better when you had the chance."

I blacked out briefly on the staircase, and when I came to I was in the middle of the front parlor with Dad standing between me and the door, a drunken smile stretched across his face. He seized me by the shoulders and shook me, looking around at the other patrons who weren't paying the slightest attention to the scene we were making. I couldn't look into his eyes, but I'm sure they were full of pride. He said, "There's the man. How do you feel?"

My heart was beating like I had just gone up fifty staircases instead of coming down one. I said, "Good. I feel good."

"Told you there wasn't anything to it. Most natural thing in the world."

"I think I'd like to leave now."

"In a little while. I ran into some associates from Bakersfield over at the bar. Come have a drink and give us some details."

"I can't take any more drinking tonight."

"It won't kill you. Besides, you never forget your first drink after your first time."

"I said I'd like to leave!"

Dad let go of my shoulders and backed away slowly. I think I startled the whole room with my outburst. The girls on the sofas were all looking around idly, as if they had never seen the wallpaper before, while the men at the bar, Dad's so-called associates, were watching us with their eyebrows raised in cautious bemusement. Dad shook his head.

He said, "All right, fine. Let's go."

I was two steps ahead of him all the way to the door; four steps by the time we reached the Charger. Dad hoisted himself into the cabin and set us cruising back down the driveway. Neither of us bothered with a seatbelt. Glancing through the side mirror at the lighted windows of the whorehouse, the full delayed reaction of everything I had just discovered, the truths and lies and nightmarish implications, came and settled over me like the early symptoms of some debilitating nervous condition. Once as a child I had sprained my ankle playing soccer and felt no pain until hours later when I crawled into bed. That's what it was like. My face and arms went numb, my throat contracted, electric needles danced across my kidneys and spine. I wasn't even sure if I was still drunk. And still the thing that scared me most was the fact that Dad hadn't said a word since we left the establishment.

I could see him on the edge of my periphery, darkness shrouded in darkness, enormous arms gripping the steering wheel, eyes unwavering even as his heart was pumping more whiskey than blood. The farther we drove along that deserted stretch of valley road, the more aware I became of the immense and terrible presence of his body, and of all the terrible acts it was capable of perpetrating, directly and indirectly.

I said, "Dad. It's been a long day. You mind if I grab a quick nap till we get to the hotel?"

He looked away from the road. I was too out of it to realize what an ominous sign that was, or to perceive the narrow tightrope I was walking. "As a matter of fact, I do mind. You don't go to sleep when someone else is driving. It's bad manners."

"Sorry. I didn't think of that."

"Speaking of bad manners, you never thanked me for introducing you to Livia. Seems like the sort of thing you should make a point to do, to show your appreciation. You should do it now, in fact. Right now."

I could feel the tension building the longer Dad waited for me to thank him. It was easy to lie. I was just beginning to realize that. But this time I chose against self-preservation. I said, "Introducing us. So that's how you see it."

Dad started to swerve into the opposing lane. He jerked the wheel abruptly to get us back between the lines. "I'm going to give you the benefit of the doubt and trust you're too drunk to know what you're saying. But whether tonight or tomorrow, come hell or high water, you are going to thank me for all I've done for you tonight. That's not an option."

"Have fun waiting for it, then."

"I'm not joking around. You keep running your mouth and I'll run us off the road."

"Go ahead and do it. See if I care." I stared out the window and waited for the road to disappear out from under us. Of course he would never really do anything so dramatic. Not if it meant putting his own well-being at risk. One day in his company and I already felt like I understood what was going on in his head, even if what lay in his heart remained a fearful mystery to me. I said, "Just tell me one thing. Why her? Of all the girls you could have picked out, why that one?"

I waited for an answer as the Charger continued to barrel ahead through the omnipresent darkness. At long last he said, "I wanted you to enjoy yourself. She's a tight piece of ass with plenty of meat on her. I figured she'd be able to show you a good time. If not, you should've said something while we were there, instead of making a scene."

I sat up in the seat. "How do you know? That she's a tight piece of ass?"

"How do you think?"

"Pull over."

"Christ, you're uptight. What, you think you're the first boy ever became milk brothers with his old man?"

"Pull over."

"If you didn't have fun with the girl, then it's your fault, not mine. It's about time you grow up and stop blaming everyone else for your own problems."

"Pull over! Now!"

Dad took his foot off the gas and eased us over to a strip of ground that sloped down drastically as soon as the asphalt ended. The Charger settled to a stop at an extreme slant, and when I opened the door it was like falling straight down into the upturned soil that bordered whatever kinds of trees were assembled like legionaries in front of me. My feet sank into the earth, and I only managed a few steps before curling over. It was so dark I couldn't see the vomit splattering even as my head hung just a few paltry feet off the ground. A cigar flared in the corner of eye. I looked up to see Dad standing on top of me, puffing away in the darkness.

He said, "I told you to drink responsibly. Maybe next time you'll listen."

I don't remember how I managed to make it to town. I had no money, no directions, and the supermarket parking lot where I awoke was six miles to the north on the edge of a small farming town whose name I only learned because I had to (Western Union and Mom both came through for me in a pinch, though the latter had plenty of I-told-you-so's to impart over the phone). If my subconscious really had tried to repress that night, then I wish it would have repressed what happened next, instead of preserving it in such perfect, step-by-step detail. I threw a punch, my first and only. I saw the look on Dad's face as he ducked out of the way, watched the cigar fall from his lips, and felt his massive fist collide with my jaw. And even as I lay sinking into the warm soft ground, and felt his size 14 oxford slamming between my ribs, I couldn't shake the wonderful-awful sensation that I was finally getting exactly what I had been looking for, that the truth had finally been revealed to me, and that not even Death, lurking among the trees, could raise me from my earthly, earthy abyss. I was a new kind of Adam, and I had created myself.

Dad backed away panting. He tucked one foot behind the other and wiped my blood off on his pant leg. He said, "Don't call me. Don't try to get in touch. I know I sound calm right now, but believe me, I'm shattered on the inside. You did that to me, son. You broke my heart into a million pieces. And for what? For what?"

I watched the Charger's taillights recede and then disappear into the night, two red pinpoints converging in the distance. The taste of blood was stuck in my mouth. So, too, was the taste of dirt. After a while, it became hard to distinguish one from the other.

• •

I had given Jennifer three days to get the other women on board, but I assumed the worst when I didn't hear from her by the end of the second day. By then I had run out of vodka, and with nothing but supermarket beer and wine to even me out, a variety of doubts cropped up to keep me awake at night. I began to wonder if they were preparing to call my bluff, if they realized that reporting them to the Ag Bureau would screw me over just as much as them. If a faction had risen up to silence Jennifer, or worse, if she had found it more pragmatic to go over to their side, then my only recourse would be to find other means of securing their cooperation, even to the point of leaving me culpable if and when the authorities got involved. There were times in the course of those two nights when I would be lying awake in the early morning hours, half-sober and bloated from the watery supermarket beer, and find myself counting heads and taking inventory, as if preparing for the terrible culling that would have to take place if the women couldn't be made to go along. But then, on the morning of the third day, the satellite phone vibrated, and I put the thought out of mind for the time being.

Jennifer's message read, *Good to go see you sunday*, and nothing more. Immediately I called Russert and laid out the specifics of the deal. He remained silent on the issue of Jennifer's double-share. In fact, he didn't say a word until after I had finished explaining the details of the contract and emphasizing how soon I would need to have the faxed copies in my hands. I imagined him sitting alone in his office with the sunlight coming in and reflecting breathlessly on how wrong he had been to underestimate me when we first met.

He said, "You've done a good job for me, Mr. Temple. You came through just like you said. All the same, I don't appreciate the communication blackout you've kept me in all this time. If you want to make deals on my behalf, you need to keep me in the loop. At this level of business, you're expected to keep the boss up to speed with your progress, even if it seems like there's nothing significant to report. Anything else is unprofessional."

I was glad he couldn't see me through the phone line; my smile must have looked pretty boyish and goofy. I asked him, "Is that what you are to me now? My boss?"

"Don't get ahead of yourself. Close up this deal and we'll take it from there."

"Yes, sir."

He had the contracts ready before the end of the same business day. I hightailed it to the nearest fax machine, which was also at the supermarket (I was beginning to see a pattern with these small valley towns). I sat in the parking lot with the Lexus idling and went over the contract line by line, serving as lawyer for myself to make sure I was getting everything I wanted. My hands were trembling as I reached the end. It was all airtight. In a matter of days, Russert would be the legal tenant of the farm in Orosi, and I would finally have enough money to get my start in life.

Understandably, I celebrated too hard through Friday night and most of Saturday; on my orders, Kylee bought out most of her associates' remaining vodka stock and brought over some of her Porterville colleagues for a two day-long rager at the Blossom Road. By the time Sunday morning arrived, I had to shower with the bathroom light off just to keep my brains from oozing down the drain. Nothing was going to keep me from my meeting with the widows, though. Had I awoken blind from alcohol poisoning, I would have searched out a doctor only after the contracts had been signed.

I was on the road before noon with my sunglasses on and a stomach full of aspirin and coffee. The roads in the valley were always horrendous when it came to dust, to say nothing of the dirt and gravel trails leading into the interiors of the parcels. By the time I reached the co-op and parked beside one of the houses, the whole lower section of the Lexus was as filthy as it had ever been. I got out and slammed the door so they could hear it; the meeting would have to begin with someone coming out to receive me. A fairly obvious power play, but good enough for the hicks, as Dad would say. I waited much longer than I expected until finally one of the girls came out onto the porch. I recognized her from the first time I came calling. She had the same contemptuous look on her face that she had been wearing then.

I said, "It's Ellie, right? Sandra's daughter?"

She slapped her palms onto the wood railing and leaned her weight against it. She said, "That's right. Sandra's girl. And Elliot's."

"Right. Nice to see you again. Can you go inside and fetch your mother? It's time for the adults to sit down and iron things out."

"I don't see any adults around here."

I showed her a friendly yet firm smile as a measure of my patience. The sun was behind the house, just a few degrees below its zenith, and even with my sunglasses on my head was beset by a nauseating ache that made the present situation all the more unacceptable. I said, "That's fine. You've had your turn at playing cute. Now go tell them I'm ready to deal."

She let go of the railing. Walking slowly toward the steps at the base of the porch, she didn't resemble Dad so much as she captured perfectly the essence of his strutting gait. How she thought she could intimidate me, only she knew. But regardless of whatever logic or illogic was driving her, she placed her hands on her hips and said, "You deal with me. Or you deal with no one. Those are the only options you're gonna get. So I suggest you fix your attitude pronto."

I laughed. Even though it worsened the pain in my skull, I laughed. "I don't have to take this. I really don't. I know I sound calm right now, but in another couple seconds I'm going to be walking through that door, whether you invite me in or not. Because it's your mother's name on the lease, not yours. She's the one I should be talking to."

"My mother tried to commit suicide two days ago." Her voice didn't crack, nor even waver, and yet I could tell all the same that it hurt her to talk about it. "She's alive, in case you were wondering. But she's in no state to negotiate with anyone. That's why you're gonna have to deal with me, or else fuck off. I'm the oldest of her three daughters. The responsibility for her share of the farm passes to me."

The more I heard from this girl, the more intrigued I became. She wasn't like her mother, or most of the valley women I had met, for that matter; she had confidence, and didn't seem to view it as a liability to be suppressed and outgrown like most country girls her age were taught. Under different circumstances, I might have been impressed. But if she thought I was going to shrink in the face of her mother's madness and her own half-cocked notions of primogeniture, then she clearly didn't realize who she was talking to.

I said, "Even if you do have the authority to speak on your mother's behalf, which is debatable, your mother's share only counts for a fifth of the total cooperative. So before any kind of agreement can be reached, I'll have to speak with the other women involved."

She shook her head humorlessly. "Wrong. This woman right here. That's all we need." She reached into her pocket to remove something, but before I could get a clear look she let go and it hit the boards with a thud and a series of short ricochets. Once it settled, I understood that something had gone terribly wrong. The satellite phone rested face-up, its screen as gray and listless as the eyes of a corpse. She appeared exceedingly proud of her accomplishment, and even struck a condescending grin to mark the occasion. "Your flunky isn't here to help you make your case. Given what she tried to do to us, pulling the wool over our eyes, while conspiring to help you drive us out, it figures that she's forfeited any right she had to a seat at the table. And since I'm the one who ran her off, I'm laying claim to her share myself."

"Well. Isn't that something? In two days' time, you've managed to go from having no say to controlling the biggest share of the operation. Maybe when you finish school, you can come work for me as an associate of some sort. Assuming you know how to use a computer."

"Whatever business we have to settle, it ends today. It ends with you ripping up your contract and walking away. But first, you're gonna give me your word that you won't tell the government or anyone else how we came by this farm. That's the assurance you're gonna give me before you leave."

"Interesting. And why should I do any of those things? Why, pray tell, shouldn't I head to Ag Bureau in Tulare and tell them everything I know?"

The screen door squealed open and a tall Hispanic boy with the wispy beginnings of a mustache stepped out onto the porch. He wore high-waisted, rodeo-style jeans and a plain red t-shirt that was at least a size too small. After a moment, I recognized him as one of Claudia's boys, the eldest one, though his name escaped me despite Ramirez's files and meeting him in person a week earlier. He said, "Because we share the same father. Because the same blood is in our veins that's in yours, and that can't count for nothing."

I said, "It counts for whatever you want it to count for. Which, in my case, is nothing."

They both looked at me for a while and then traded glances with each other. The whole scenario was Jennifer and Dale all over again: lightweight brains and lumbering brawn, conspiring together for mutual benefit, when on their own they would have been completely helpless, misfit animals waiting for natural selection to run its course. Ellie even surrendered her positional advantage by descending to the second lowest step of the small front stoop. Now we were facing each other eye to eye. She said, "I don't believe that you could stand there, knowing what we both know about our father, about our family, and tell me it doesn't mean a thing. There's no way you could be so cold."

"Why not? Because we're kin? Is that what you're supposed to be to me? My kinfolk?"

"I'm a fourteen-year-old girl with a very sick mother and two young sisters to look after. Think about that even if you don't see us as family. What'll happen to us without this place?"

"There are plenty of fourteen-year-old girls in this world who have it so much worse. You'll still be doing better than them, even without a farm."

"And you don't mind putting me in that position? You have no problem with seeing us all out on the street?"

"You sound just like him."

"Answer me. Say you could sleep at night if we wound up homeless on your account."

"Don't make this all about you. You were born and raised on one of his farms. Until he died, you never had to worry about anything. Me, I had to struggle and suffer through being that man's son, and when he died I lost the only family I had left. You talk like I'm standing here with an eviction notice in one hand and a loaded gun in the other. But if the shoe were on the other foot, if you found out after he died that all his money was tied up with me in a business on the coast, wouldn't you try to do whatever you could to get a piece of it? Wouldn't you even say that you had earned it?"

The boy came up to the edge of the porch and stood with his fists clenched at his sides. There wasn't much in the way of resemblance between him and Dad, and wouldn't have been regardless of age, weight, or race. He said, "That money won't do you any good. Not if you come by it like this."

"That's not how it works. Money, in my experience, tends to be fairly objective."

He shook his head. "God will judge you. Even if you get your way and drive us off the land, He won't let you find any happiness because of what you've done. Everything you touch will turn to shit in your hands. He'll see to that."

I watched the boy closely. There was no sarcasm to be found in his demeanor; the way he talked, it was obvious he believed what he was saying, that some paternal entity from on high was prepared to seek justice on their behalf, and on behalf of all the Temple women who continued to be hoodwinked long after Mr. Temple was gone. I couldn't help but laugh.

But he clearly didn't appreciate my levity. "What's so funny? I'm talking about divine retribution here."

I said, "I used to be like you. Back in high school, I got really into theology and western philosophy. Yes, I was that big of a nerd. I was looking for answers, and I thought I had found some writers who could lead me in the right direction. Thomas Aquinas. Kierkegaard. Saint Augustine, most of all. You ever hear of him?"

The boy adjusted his posture in a way that seemed oddly indignant. He said, "I've been raised in the Catholic Church my entire life. So, yeah, I've heard of Saint Augustine."

"Well, then you must be familiar with his concept of the city of God." I gave him an appropriate amount of time to respond, but he just stood there squinting and trying to look tough. And so I went on. "After the fall of Rome, most people, Christians and pagans alike, were baffled that God would let something like that happen. Rome had been a Christian nation for three hundred years, after all, so it didn't make sense that God would let a bunch of heathen barbarians sack the place. Saint Augustine had a different idea, though. In his view, no city or nation on earth could encompass the entirety of God's infinite grandeur. The real city of God, according to Augustine, was a spiritual place, without physical borders, abstract and immaterial. No vandals or barbarians could ever sack the city of God, and all real Christians, in his view, should pay no mind to earthly cities when building up the spiritual city is the most important thing we can do on Earth. Eventually, people started listening to him, which is one of the reasons so many intelligent men wound up sequestered in monasteries in the centuries that followed."

While the boy stood pondering the ideas I had just unloaded on him, Ellie took the opportunity to interject with a few thoughts of her own. She said, "That's some pretty deep stuff. But what are you trying to say? That we should hand over the farm and go live as nuns and monks in some far off monastery?"

"No. That's not my point at all."

"Well, then I don't understand you."

I set my hand on the railing to steady myself. The headache had subsided for the time being, but every so often a disorienting dizziness came over me, upsetting my sense of balance.

I said, "There's no city of God because there is no God. There's no retribution, no universal justice. There's only what we do with ourselves and the one life that we've been given. In that sense, only the material matters, only what you can make for yourself with the time you have left. You're an intelligent girl, Ellie. I can tell you don't go in for your brother's piety. But even you would have me forfeit my chance to make something of myself based on some vague, altruistic notion that I should care more about your sake than my own. All because your mother and my mother happened to get impregnated by the same man. I know it's not a popular outlook, and it places me in the ethical minority of just about every society that's ever existed, but I don't care. As far as I can see, there's nothing to connect me to you or anyone else on this farm. Nothing except for the transaction at hand."

Ellie's eyes turned cloudy. She said, "We share the same blood."

"Billions of people all over the world have bloodlines that intersect. That's basic human genealogy. But it doesn't make you responsible for anyone else, unless you accept the burden to begin with. Having a common ancestor, even a father, doesn't bind your soul to mine, or vice versa. To think differently is just a primitive form of religion; blood worship, the church of the genetic fallacy."

She said, "We share the same pain."

I shook my head resolutely. "No one shares my pain."

Ellie looked away. Through all my editorializing, I could see the fire inside of her beginning to dim, though her brother appeared to grow more incensed with each new word.

He said, "You're wrong. God made us to live in families for a reason. Even when there were only two people in the whole world, they lived together as one. That's the real city of God. That's what binds us together."

I edged my way closer to the steps. "Some bond. It's been fifteen hundred years since Augustine and the city of God is still nothing but a dream. It will never be built. It can't be built. And if the city of God can't be built, then the cities of men are all that matter. That's why I'm leaving here as soon as this contract I'm carrying is signed. I'm going to live a long life and make a lot of money, but first I'm going to move back to the city and build something amazing from the ground up. Finally there will be a Temple worth remembering."

Ellie wiped her eyes on the back of her hand. She said, "You'll remember me. You'll remember me and all the rest of your brothers and sisters. You'll remember this farm and what you did to us until the day you die. We'll haunt you, you fancy-ass son of a bitch. We'll haunt you while we're still breathing. I swear it."

"You're not my sister. Stop pretending."

"You're the only one pretending here. You're so warped you're even lying to yourself."

"All right, I've heard just about enough from the kids' section. It's time for me to talk to the adults now." I clutched the manila folder close to my side and tried walking past her to ascend the steps. If anything, I expected her to go for the contracts. So it caught me off-guard when she reached up and scraped her short fingernails down the center of my forehead, tearing the sunglasses from my face and leaving me momentarily bewildered. There was no pain at first, only the sudden near-blindness of the sun's unfiltered rays hitting my corneas for the first time in days. But then I felt the stinging from where her nails had broken skin. I touched my face and my fingers came away red. I whispered, "Little bitch," under my breath and lunged at her before she could do any more damage.

"What're you doing? Get off me!"

Getting her to the ground was easy; she couldn't have weighed more than a hundred and ten pounds. But once I had her there, wedged between my knee and the porch steps, she proceeded to claw and kick like a feral beast. I had to hold her by the neck just to keep her still. My hands tightened their grip until the flow of air was cut off completely.

I said, "You should have listened. There was no reason for you to make me do this."

My blood was pumping so fast I was practically seething. Particles of saliva sprayed from my lips and settled over her straining face. She was starting to turn blue when a shadow fell over us and something hard struck the back of my head. I rolled onto my back and lay gasping with Ellie beside me in the inverse position. She coughed hoarsely and held her already bruised throat. The boy came and stood over me with the rifle barrel pointed at my chest and the butt end pressed into his shoulder. I finally noticed the color of his eyes.

He said, "No one would blame me if I pulled the trigger. Not after what you did to her."

The blow to the head had left my senses scattered; I was having trouble understanding which "her" he was talking about. And as I looked up at the fearsome length of metal being aimed at me, the barrel seemed so close that I imagined I could grab hold of it and wrestle it from the boy's grip. My thoughts must have been more apparent than I realized, because he caught on almost instantly. He said, "Don't even try it," but I wasn't in the clearest headspace at the time, and his threat only heightened my feeling of resolve.

My fingers brushed the edge of the barrel before he jerked it out of reach. I expected him to fire, to put a bullet so deep inside of me that it would come out the other end through my back. But instead he executed a sort of quick rotating maneuver to bring the butt end around to the front. He struck me with enough force to shatter my nose cartilage and loosen two teeth up top. My head slumped back against the wood, blood trickling down the sides of my face. Before sleep overtook me, I felt Ellie's feet once more on the steps, and then I saw them both together, girl and boy, sister and brother, standing over me with the most fearful, critical look in their eyes. What I would have said to them, had I been able to speak, was this: that not even our father had been able to make me lose consciousness; that as far as Temples went, they were some pretty gruesome little shits.

• •

Five years is a long time to go without seeing a parent, especially when you're just a teenager. By the time I managed to track him down, I had grown into full manhood, and Dad had been out of touch with his Porterville friends for quite some time. Kylee put me in contact with one of his old associates, a shipping manager out of Paso Robles, who informed me that Dad had fallen off the map in recent years, and that he hadn't heard from him personally in the past two or three seasons.

He referred me instead to a grower in Turlock, who in turn gave me the number of a boarding house in Modesto. A woman with an almost unintelligible country twang answered and went on for ten minutes about what a gentleman he had been before finally admitting that she hadn't seen him in over a year and didn't know how to get a hold of him. It didn't frustrate me, hitting a dead end. I figured Dad probably kept tabs on the various circles he ran in, and that eventually word would reach him that someone claiming to be his son was looking for him. Sure enough, he called me up one evening on the same number I had given the guy from Turlock. Hearing his voice for the first time since our altercation, I wasn't sure if he had grown gentler in middle age, or if my memory of him was distorted by my sense of victimhood.

He said, "This call has been a long time coming, son. That's my fault as much as yours. I'd like to see you if you're willing. Thought that might have been why you were hunting me."

I counted down five seconds and said, "You're right, Dad. I do want to see you. That's part of why I came back to San Joaquin. To have a talk."

"You say you're in the valley?"

"In Porterville. At the place where you bought me my very first drink." I waited through the silence, convinced that Dad would speak again whenever he was ready to do so. But as the seconds counted down without so much as a loud breath from his end, I finally accepted the possibility that we might have been disconnected. "Dad? Hello?"

"I'm here. Just thinking. I got into an argument with the manager the last time I was down there. Afraid I may have burnt that bridge. If it's not too much trouble, would you mind coming up to San Jose tomorrow? That's where I'm living now. That's my base of operations."

I set the phone down and considered whether making such a trip was even possible given my present capabilities. San Jose was a six hour drive almost all the way back the way I had come. I was using my mother's old ride, a twelve-year-old Korean SUV with over two hundred thousand miles on the odometer. But seeing Dad was the whole point of my journey, and passing up the opportunity, whatever the hardship, was not an option. I said, "Give me the address and I'll be there sometime tomorrow afternoon. I've got a satellite phone with me, so I'll be in touch if anything comes up."

"Good, good. Let's plan on meeting up tomorrow, then."

Dad gave me directions to a bar in San Jose and a number where he said I could reach him most hours of the day. Driving north was slow, dusty, and anesthetizing right up to the moment I crossed the state line, at which point the road smoothed out and the seemingly endless fields and orchards finally gave way to the Spanish tiles and beige stucco of civilization. There was no need to call Dad on the road; the bar was fairly easy to find. In a heavily Hispanic neighborhood dominated by small shops full of lime candy and glass-bottled Pepsi, the place Dad had led me to was the only building around with tinted windows and a mounted air conditioner on the roof. I walked with the gift cradled under my arm and found Dad already seated at a table across from the bar. He looked to be drinking tequila on the rocks, or something similar that necessitated the salt and lime arranged before him. Upon seeing me, he stood and shook my hand with an affected and almost dainty grip—squeezing the lower halves of my fingers between his thumb and palm—as if he were already working to erase whatever brutish impression he thought I had of him based on the beating he gave me the last time we were together. We sat down facing each other across the table.

He looked me over and said, "I see you've finally filled out some. That's good. You were very thin the last time we were together."

An unexpected move. Right out the gate, he was criticizing my appearance as well as bringing up last time. I smiled and slid the package across the blue tiled tabletop. I said, "This is for you. It's a special reserve bourbon all the way from Kentucky. Very hard to find this far west."

Dad held the box up to the light and squinted as he read the label. He said, "That's very generous of you," which after five years of mutual silence was still the closest he could bring himself to saying, "Thank you." He set the gift on the edge of the table and took another drink from the dripping glass at his side. His hair had receded since I last saw him, bringing the bullet shape of his skull into full prominence, a long-awaited prophecy finally fulfilled. He was still imposing even in his graying years, though the strength and energy he once exuded was now offset by an obesity that brought to mind images of old Parisian men at street tables, quaffing wine and soup by the vat until their faces were as red as those of the hypertensive aristocrats of Baroque portraiture. He didn't appear to be very comfortable with his new build. For the first few seconds we were sitting together, in fact, he seemed to be holding his breath, and when he finally did exhale, it caused him to wince while holding his hand against his bloated stomach. His eyes were even watery.

I said, "You don't look so good, Dad. A bit under the weather, maybe."

He inhaled slowly through puckered lips. He said, "Think it's a hernia. Woke up yesterday with this pain in my side and it hasn't let up since."

"You should get it looked at. Might be something more serious."

"I don't trust doctors this far inland. If it's still with me tomorrow, I'll head into the city."

"I could drive you. If you need a ride."

His eyes opened wide. Whatever pain he was in had either subsided or didn't matter as much to him now. He said, "When have you ever known your father to need a ride?"

"I just thought—"

"Well think again. Better yet, go out to the back parking lot and take a look at my ride. Brand new Lexus convertible, straight off the factory line."

"Wow. You must be doing well, then."

"I don't have any complaints. And if I do, they melt away when I get behind the wheel."

"You're not worried about leaving it out there in this neighborhood?"

"I have a clamp. Old school, but still the best security available."

"Right. Well, I'm happy for you. Sounds like things are really coming along."

He nodded graciously and filled his fat face with more liquor. "And yourself? What are you up to these days? I assume you have a job of some sort. Or at least I would hope so."

I glanced at the bar behind him. The waitress had seen me come in, but she was taking her sweet time getting to my drink order. Perhaps she was already well acquainted with Dad, and thus trying to limit her face time with him. "I earned my real estate license a couple years ago. Been doing some mid-range work here and there, mostly around Hayward and Oakland. I know, the East Bay is shit, but I'm hoping to break into some higher end properties before long."

Dad smiled and patted my arm. He said, "Bigger deals will come in time. You'll see. Right now, the important thing is that you're staying hungry and alert. You've got ambition. That's good. I was afraid, years ago I was afraid you were never going to find a sense of purpose. The way you talked the last time we saw each other, all that stuff about God, it had me worried you were going to be a daydreamer forever. Glad to see you've finally made up your mind about wanting something out of life."

"I didn't really have a choice, Dad. Having to fend for yourself forces you to make those kinds of decisions."

His smile disappeared. He stared into his glass of tequila and shifted his sitting posture. Either the pain was on the upswing or the discomfort caused by my response was manifesting itself physically. "No one said you had to wait all this time to contact me. Unless you think I'm so petty as to hold a grudge for—"

"Dad. Stop. You're the one who keeps bringing up the past. If it were up to me, we'd agree to put that awful night behind us and concentrate on the moment at hand. Doesn't that sound like a better course of action to you?"

"It does. It really does."

"Good. So here's what I'm thinking. I've been on the road all morning and I need a drink. And I'm guessing this place wasn't designed to keep up with the likes of us. So I say we take this primo bourbon back to your place and see where the day takes us from there."

Before I had even finished speaking, I knew Dad's interest was piqued. He arched an eyebrow and shook the ice in his otherwise empty glass. "Where do you imagine it will take us?"

"I don't know. But I'll tell you one thing. I've got the number of some ladies on the peninsula who put your valley girls to shame."

He didn't laugh or make randy comments like you might expect a man to do in such a situation. He simply took out his wallet and placed a folded bill on the table next to his glass. Between his weight and the constant pain he was failing to hide, getting up from his seat proved noticeably difficult for him. He pressed both hands flat against the table and pushed himself up with such strained force I worried the legs might give out. I wondered if he could even handle being with a woman in the condition he was in, or if he was merely determined to prove his virility to me as I had once been forced to prove mine.

He stood breathing heavily with both hands at his lower back. Lines of sweat glistened across his bald head. He said, "All right. Let's get moving."

Growing up in one of the more affluent parts of the Bay Area, I had seen plenty of luxury cars when I was young, but nothing quite so luxurious as the German convertible Dad somehow had acquired. He drove with his seat back as far as it would go and still his stomach nearly engulfed the steering wheel. I tried to picture him driving alone with the top down, his remaining hair tousled by the wind, the very picture of graceless middle age striving and fighting against the dying of the light. I didn't have much time to think, though, before we arrived at a tract of small condos with the same drab, weather-faded look that betrayed most US-era properties in the region. Dad huffed and panted his way up the short staircase. The symptoms of his illness were becoming increasingly unpleasant to witness; walking behind him on the steps, I could smell the sickly, bilious farts seeping silently out of him, and had to breathe through my mouth to keep from gagging. When we got to the door, he couldn't find his keys in either of his front pockets. He looked back at the staircase with an expression of pure misery before remembering he had stuck them in his back pocket. I followed him inside.

He flipped the light switch and said, "Generally I prefer a very minimalist arrangement. Just a bed, bath, and mailbox to come home to. Too many complications in your day to day life will keep you from focusing your energies on what matters. You'll learn that in due time."

"Minimalist" was a good word to describe the condo, though "dingy" and "paltry" would have suited it better. Whether it had been built before disbandment or not long after it, the whole atmosphere and character of the place, right down to the smell of the air, seemed old and decrepit, like the sort of bombed-out shell of an apartment where you could imagine war refugees cowering to escape the violence outside. The main living area had a single sofa chair with a cushion so compressed it couldn't have offered more than psychological protection from the springs underneath. Beyond that, there were tables and lamp stands situated at various points along the walls, very much like the furnishings of your standard roadside motel room. Through a space between the stove and vent hood, I could just make out a sink and countertop on which rested a dish rack loaded with plates that probably never found their way into the cabinets above. Of course it didn't strike me as odd to find Dad inhabiting such a place; in the grand narrative I had composed for him, he was every bit as much a monster as the troll from the nursery fable, and so it wouldn't have been too difficult to envision him living in squalor under a bridge while his money sat idle in an account or deposit box. I went to the kitchen and found two clean glasses at the bottom of the rack.

Taking the flask from my pocket, I said, "I'll stick with vodka for now, but I'm eager to see what you think of the bourbon. The guy at the shop said it was a rare find even for them. They only had a few bottles left in stock."

Dad collapsed onto the sofa chair and snorted skeptically. "He works on commission. Of course he's going to say that."

I unscrewed the cap on the bottle and eyeballed at least two shots over the clouded white ice cubes from his freezer tray. He took a small sip to begin with, smacking his lips together in consideration. Then he raised the glass again and knocked back more than half of what remained. I watched it flow into him. He leaned back in the creaking chair and sighed bracingly. He said, "I wouldn't be surprised if you over-paid. But for what it's worth, it is a very nice label. Better than most of the swill you find these days."

"Glad you think so. Drink up."

I poured some vodka into the second glass and sat on a corner of the square coffee table. Across from me, Dad was already getting sleepy-eyed, or at least the energizing discomfort he had been suffering through all day had transitioned to a seemingly painless lethargy that appeared to suit him just fine. He was even smiling slightly, positioned as he was with his head tilted back, balancing the glass on his stomach between laced fingers. I tried to think of any other time in my life when I had seen him genuinely contented and relaxed, but nothing came to mind. In my memories of him, which seemed so much more real than the sick old man before me, nothing could break the current of hostility that permeated everything he said and did; not even that night at the whorehouse, not even all the whiskey and fatherly pride his money could buy.

I said, "By the way. I don't know what this means to you, but Mom passed away four months ago. She'd been fighting cancer for a while, and it just proved to be too much for her. Thought you should know."

Dad raised his head slowly. The frown he formed his lips into was less jarring to me than his smile, but there was a forcedness to it that felt particularly disrespectful, as though he still couldn't bring himself to be honest with me, even if doing so would have meant admitting that my mother's death didn't bother him. He said, "I'm sorry to hear that. She was a good woman, Rachel. You were fortunate to have a mother who put your well-being above everything else."

I raised my glass. "Cheers."

Again I watched him drink. Again he seemed to grow more relaxed and groggy. He said, "Of course the real test of a woman's character is how she treats her father, and her husband after him. That's one feature of the modern world that's taken an incalculable toll on the foundations of society, the notion that a woman or girl is independent from the man who looks after her. Years ago, some misguided fools got it into their heads that the man-haters were right, that the innate differences between the sexes are just superficial, and that women can take care of themselves. Well, I ask you, how many women were able to go without a man's protection immediately following disbandment? And how many girls who didn't have a man's guidance succumbed to degradation in those years? Well, let me tell you, opinions changed for the better once the Republic was founded and normalcy returned to civilian life. Suddenly the time-honored truths passed down from the noble lords of old weren't so superficial."

Dad tilted forward in a way that suggested he was going to stand, but instead he leaned the bulk of his girth on one armrest and spread his legs out indecently. Drops of whiskey trickled from the corners of his mouth. The air conditioner must have been operating at full blast, but still his face was sweaty. He looked like a newborn baby, bald and pudgy and dripping with amnia. His mood was even unpredictable.

"Jesus fuck. When I think of all the bullshit that passes for popular wisdom, all the poisonous ideas that have been carried over from American times, I get so frustrated I can hardly stand to remain alive. If the mass of people were only capable of recognizing, if more than one or two percent of the population had any rational faculties whatsoever, then maybe I could tolerate their company more than I do. All my life, for as long as I can remember, I've had to fight their stupidity, and it's always been an uphill battle. When I was a boy in the US, it was a very patriotic time. People used to talk about freedom like it was the most important thing in life. But I always knew they were full of shit. I knew from a young age that if you were to give them what they were asking for, of the ones that survived, ninety-nine point nine percent would come to curse their freedom in time. They would beg for the chain before long. But would they admit it? Would they ever learn to accept that the ones in a position above them were there for a reason? Hell, no. They would tear it all down before that. Their father, their husband, their employer, their God. They would snarl like animals and bite their masters' hands rather than confess their own weakness. And those of us who were born stronger? What can we do except grit our teeth and try to bear the insults? That's the burden I've been carrying my whole life. That's the burden I still carry. Christ."

This time he really did stand up, straining with both hands against the armrests as he slowly emerged from the sunken compression in the sofa chair. Staggering a little bit more with each step he took, he found his way to the rest of the bourbon. He could barely keep the bottle steady, and ended up with more on the counter than in his glass. He lost his balance turning and had to brace himself against the beam.

"Sometimes I wish I could feel the way they do, the stupid, happy people of the world. Just once I'd like to know what it's like to be free of this weight. I think about my father and how happy he was every day of his life. He was so simple he didn't even realize how mediocre he was. He thought because he knew a lot about science that he was an intelligent man. He had his wife and his job and a family of his own, and that was all he ever needed. I always knew I never wanted to be like him. More than that, I knew I never could, be like him. I never felt any shame or guilt because of my abilities. But as I get older, it's so exhausting, living like this day after day. I've tired myself out just talking about it."

He set his glass down and backed away from the counter. At the rate he was deteriorating, I knew if I didn't get him off his feet now, pretty soon he would collapse of his own accord, and that once he fell he would be immovable. I snuck up and held him by the shoulders.

I said, "You're not well, Dad. We need to get you to bed. We'll visit the doctor in the morning." Throwing my arm behind his back, I led him step by step to the bedroom. It was almost like dancing in a way. The cheap box-spring mattress squealed sharply under his weight as he settled onto the bed. As soon as he was positioned halfway comfortably, he shut his eyes and fell into a deep, semi-comatose sleep. I pinched his cheek to make sure. "Dad. I've got something important I need to tell you."

I waited for a response, standing over him and watching for any disruption in the rhythm of his breathing. When it was clear he wasn't waking up anytime soon, I set about searching the shabby little room for any spare quilts and blankets that could be used to constrain him. Fortunately, the master bedroom was as slovenly kept as the front room was sparse, and all it took was a few quick tugs to bring the bed sheet out from under his leg; it had long ago receded to the bottom left corner, leaving the rest of the mattress exposed. From there, it was simply a matter of locating a pair of scissors and cutting the sheet into strips that could be tied securely around his wrists and ankles. I dove into the task with an energy and sense of purpose that, under different circumstances, I'm sure would have made the old man proud.

• •

I once heard an atheist talk about space dust. It was during my final year of high school, when guest speakers would come in all the time to lecture us about college and opportunities for the future. One day, I believe it was in the early fall, an astrophysicist came to give a short spiel about whatever UC campus he was representing, and toward the end of his presentation he started veering off onto tangents (he was an older scientist, already retired from academic work, and far too soft-spoken and frail to hold the attention of three hundred exhausted seniors for very long). One of the things I remember him talking about, though, was space dust.

As he put it, "I'm not a spiritual person. That is, I don't believe in a divine creator. But I do believe in a common link between all carbon-based life in the universe. The carbon that's in your body right now, it's existed in one form or another since the aftermath of the Big Bang over fourteen billion years ago. It hasn't changed since then, at least on the atomic scale. Maybe, at one point in time, the particles that make up who you are existed as cosmic dust floating out in space. Perhaps one of you sitting in this room today shares the same carbon that once formed a hair follicle on the head of Julius Caesar or a skin cell on the face of Marilyn Monroe. In this sense, we are all connected to one another on the most basic level of existence. We're all descended from the same dust from outer space."

Between the Augustinian phase I was going through at the time and my general loathing for student assemblies, it's not surprising that I hated listening to the old scientist rhapsodize about the meaning and origins of life. Too materialist. Too much muddling of science and philosophy. That's the verdict my seventeen-year-old self arrived at, and years later, after my perspective had changed, I could look back with a hint of nostalgia on how misguided I was then, while simultaneously finding new reasons to tear down the learned astronomer's premises from a more enlightened vantage point. For even in a universe without God, the astrophysicist was still searching for ancestors among the comets. In place of the blood, clay, or celestial spermatozoa the theologians looked to as evidence of our shared beginnings, the atheist substituted iridescent dust drifting aimlessly through the Milky Way. That simply wouldn't do as far as I was concerned. To my young and newly godless mind, there could be no freedom and progress until we as a species divorced ourselves from any mystical notions of a common, elemental denominator. We can only move forward when we stop looking to dirt for answers.

For the man who called himself my father, there was no freedom or progress to be had, not until he broke down and gave me what I wanted. He slept fifteen hours straight and awoke screaming in pain and vomiting uncontrollably onto his chest and mattress. He railed against his bonds until his ankles were bruised and the loose headboard had left a ceiling-high crack in the drywall. It was all a matter of waiting on my part. I had suspected I might have to employ arcane stress positions to get him to talk, but the pain of his own body proved torturous enough to suit my purposes. By the time the sunlight broke between the closed blinds of the small bedroom window, he was slipping in and out of consciousness, gagging constantly on his own bile as his ghostly pallor gave the pearls of sweat on his forehead an almost brown or golden hue, like a thin broth. He writhed constantly, extending his abdomen out as far as it would go, as if to distance himself from his enraged entrails as much as possible.

I said, "You're in bad shape, Temple. If I had to take a guess, I'd say it's either your appendix or your liver, but in either case you should have seen a doctor some time ago. I can help you get the medical attention you need. But first, you need to tell me where you keep the money you've saved up over all these years. You need to point me to your checkbook or banking statement, something that will let me get my hands on what I'm entitled to. Which, I'll tell you right now, is a pretty sizeable amount by my reckoning. And I'd say you're not in any position to haggle given the state you're in. So why don't you spare yourself the prolonged agony and tell me where the money is? That's your only way out of this."

Dad's eyes rolled back behind his brow. I picked the bucket up from the carpet and splashed some ice water in his face. Partially digested globs of food clung to his cheeks and to the matted furls of his beard. He mumbled "hospital" and his head slumped down against his collarbone. I doused him again.

"Don't try to pretend like you don't have anything saved up. You've been living alone, working nonstop for years. You couldn't have spent it all on liquor and whores."

"Hos . . . hospital."

It occurred to me that the only thing keeping him from passing out entirely was the pain itself. In this way, pain became my greatest ally, the arbitrator coaxing him along in a language I could only half-speak at best. Dad, of course, was perfectly fluent in pain; he had caused me plenty of it (emotional, physical, and spiritual) and now his toxified system was using his own vernacular against him. And still there were moments during his suffering when he appeared almost peaceful, as the sick sometimes do, I've heard, when the fever dreams take over and the reality of their illness is briefly obscured. But then his gag reflex started up again and the force of his dry-heaving knocked him back into cognizance. He looked around the room and saw me standing beside the bed. He tried shutting his eyes to me again. Worried he might not reemerge this time, I decided to take more active steps toward attaining my goal. I plunged my hand into the water and struck him across the face with an open palm.

I said, "Listen. There's only one way I'm leaving San Jose today, and that's with a large sum of money in my pocket. So either you tell me where you keep your bank book or deposit box key, or I'll start looking for them myself. It can't be too hard to find something in this cracker box. But you won't like it if I have to go looking. Because once I find it, I just might be inclined to leave you tied up here on your own without anyone to help you. Think about it. Strapped to a bed, rotting away from the inside. Imagine that and then tell me it wouldn't be preferable to pay a ransom instead."

As he listened, Dad stretched his neck out so that the point of his head was nearly brushing the headboard. He hocked a wad of phlegm into his mouth and spat at me with so little forward momentum that the loogie arced almost instantly and landed on his own sick-covered chest. It was a bit of petty vindictiveness on my part, I know, but I reached down and took his pillow away. His head fell flat against the exposed mattress, and as I began tearing the room apart from corner to corner and top to bottom, I thought I heard him whimpering softly.

"You know Kylee told me all about the bridges you burned down in Porterville. Turning a knife on a sixteen-year-old girl fresh off the bus. Makes me wonder if there's any evil you wouldn't sink to given enough time." He had stopped fighting against his constraints; he had stopped rustling altogether, in fact. Crouching above the dresser drawers, I glanced up briefly to see that he was still breathing. There was nothing I could have done, of course, if his breath had given out, but the longer he remained confined, the more gratifying it became to feel myself in control of such matters. "In case you were wondering, I told Kylee all about my plan before coming up here. She wished me good luck; compared to what you deserve, she said, being drugged and robbed is getting off easy. That's the sort of close friend I have in her. Been a better source of support to me than you ever have."

Though I was looking everywhere around the room except back at Dad, I listened closely for sounds of distress from where he lay. The thought of him feeling acute shame and rage as well as pain was blissful to me at that moment; otherwise, I never would have gone so far as to label Kylee a "source of support."

I said, "I wonder if you would be so obvious as to keep your important documents hidden in the closet."

The groan he let out just then told me my intuition was exactly right. I threw open the door of the small closet and proceeded to dump plastic and nylon-wrapped suits onto the floor three, four, and five at a time. I had never seen so many clothes crammed into such a tight space. Over the years he must have spent a small fortune on his wardrobe, and now he was so fat he probably couldn't have fit into any of his old suits without spending a second fortune to have them let out. Suddenly I noticed a shelf up top with a plastic container that appeared to be precisely what I was looking for. I tore off the lid and right away discovered a plain white envelope resting on a stack of folded papers. I counted the money inside; a few hundred dollars, and nothing more.

"Where's the rest of it? There has to be more than this." I dumped the papers out over the pile of suits. One of the first things that caught my eye was an old American Social Security card, a badly creased and faded artifact the likes of which I had only seen on historical websites. "Who's Elias Francis Rabedeaux? Is that your real name? Is that the name of our family?"

No response from the old fraud, nothing but the ongoing sounds of sickness. Faced with one illuminating piece of evidence, I decided to go through the rest of the papers one by one and see what other information revealed itself in the process. While his identification cards were almost all pre-Republic and in generally poor condition, the more recent documents (financial and property records from at least four different counties) were all but pristine. And the story they told was deafening. Endeavor by endeavor, failure by failure, they illustrated the chronological landscape over which, in the course of twenty years, Dad had waged his losing war against the forces of poverty and mediocrity; an online travel agency out of Santa Clara, a winery that never made it past the investment stage, a seafood import business with operatives on both sides of the Pacific. All these ideas and more he had tried to turn into successful businesses, and without exception they had imploded on him, fallen into the red, failed to get off the ground, or otherwise disintegrated from sheer incompetence. I held the papers, the proof of his life's failure, out in front of me. I held the papers in my hands as a stinging pain grew behind my eyes. Then I tossed them all into the air and watched them float and fall over the bed and his massive body like so many birds falling dead upon the sea.

I said, "Is this where it all went? Is this what you sunk all your money into, you fat, pathetic hypocrite?"

The great entrepreneur had no words by which to vent his outrage, the first time I could recall such a thing ever happening. All that remained of the contents of the storage box was a roll of rather official-looking documents that differed from the others in that they were scanned copies instead of originals. I unfolded one of them and immediately noticed the name "Dawn Temple" typed in block letters across the page. I was going to ask him if this was some aunt he had never told me about, but then I realized the page I was reading was actually a marriage certificate, and that attached to it by a staple in the upper left corner was the lease agreement to an agricultural parcel way out in central San Joaquin.

"Why didn't you tell me that you got remarried? Unless she was very ugly, I would think you'd want to parade your new wife in front of me. Isn't that the type of man you are?"

His breathing had changed since I started going through his personal files. His whole manner, in fact, seemed oddly subdued, as if he had put the pain out of mind for the time being, replacing it with something more pertinent or troubling.

I looked at the rest of the pages. At first I thought they were all photocopies of the same two documents, the marriage license and the lease, until I looked closer and saw that each of the certificates had been issued by a different county, and that they each had a different date and wife listed beneath his signature. Five certificates, five wives in total, each with a different parcel of land on which to lay the foundation of the marriage. It was almost funny to me at first, the thought that he had failed at six marriages and five government farms on top of all his business failures, but from the start I could tell that something wasn't quite right. It didn't feel like a discrepancy exactly, but more like an absence or omission of something critical. And then it hit me: there were no divorce certificates, no evidence that the leases had ever been cancelled. He hadn't been failing at marriage; he had been capitalizing on it. These documents weren't proof of his failures; they were the deeds to his fiefdom. Once again I felt my hands go numb as electric needles danced across my spine. My tongue itself seemed paralyzed inside my mouth, but somehow I managed to make words.

I said, "Five wives. You have five wives. That's where your money went, isn't it? That's what you've been doing all this time. Buying land for your broodmares to graze on."

He puffed air onto his soiled mattress. He would not look at me.

"Let me ask you one more thing. How many children do you have? In total. How many sons and daughters do you have besides me?" I jammed two fingers into his side, where I thought the appendix was, and waited calmly for his screaming to dissipate. "How many children do you have? How many of us have you brought into this mess?"

I raised my fingers again and made sure that he could see them. He struggled briefly against his straps, and then broke down. "Twelve. I have twelve children. And you."

The feeling in my hands returned, at least enough so that I could take hold of the pillow and press it over his face. It's an unpleasant business, suffocating a human being. It's not like in the movies; even when immobilized, the victim can still thrash his head in such a way that, together with the sweat, water, and vomit on his cheeks, makes it extremely difficult to form a tight seal over his mouth and nose. I had such a hard time, in fact, that he was able to fire off some final words as the pillow slipped. "Filth. You're filth." That was the last thing he said, the final insult to cap off a perfectly malicious life. I got up on top of the bed with my knees dug into the mattress and pressed the whole weight of my body against him so that eventually his thrashing changed to twitching which in turn lessened by degrees until he finally stopped moving all together. And even then I remained fixed in that position far longer than reasonable caution required, scrunched up against the side of the headboard, enveloping his entire face with my body, like a fetus attached to the mouth. By the time I uncurled myself and took the pillow away, more than twelve minutes had passed. Sometime during the struggle, as the fire of his life prepared to flicker out, the whites of his eyes had turned red from all the burst blood vessels, and whatever power or mystery those eyes held for me when he was alive, it flickered out as well.

ANTHONY

Father. My father. What did I do? What did I ever do to cause you such shame? Is it in me, or is it me? The heart of me?

• • •

My mother only drank when taking Holy Communion, or when the pain of the moment became too much to handle on her own. Either way, I think she liked the ceremony, the ritual of it, priest and incense with one, stemmed glass and candles with the other. She only drank alone, and always in the dark, the wax light glowing against the dark of the bottle, and the dark of the room always on the outer edge, always waiting. The night word reached us of Dad's death, she put my brothers and sister to bed early and hid away in her bedroom with a jug of cooking wine, which was the only wine we had in the house. Around midnight I looked in to make sure she hadn't gone to sleep with the candles burning. I saw her lying there in the dark with glowing tears falling down her face and the jug of wine on the nightstand. She slipped her finger through the small glass handle and swung the jug over her lap. She pressed the cork into her palm and pried the cork loose and refilled her glass and shoved the cork back in. She raised her hand and beckoned me to come closer. I dropped to my knees beside the bed. It was one of the few times in my life when I saw her without makeup. In the dim light, only one half of her face was visible.

Mijo, she said. What I'm about to tell you, you must promise to keep to yourself. Your brothers mustn't find out until I figure out how to explain it to them. And there are other things I'm going to tell you, deep and shameful secrets, things I've never told anyone, not even your father. No one must know these things, mijo. Not your brothers, not anyone. Promise me, mijo. Promise before God that you won't tell a soul.

She kept calling me mijo and I didn't know why. Spanish wasn't spoken in our house, not even while Dad was away. I promise, I said. I promise to God I won't.

There are things about my past I've hid from you until now, because I was ashamed, or because they were too painful to speak of. I was born in California, back when it was an American state, but my parents came to this country from Mexico, escaping the violence that had destroyed their families and so many others like them. Before I was even born, boy cousins on both my mother's and father's sides had been killed in the fighting down south. The only way to escape the savagery of the cartels was to run, and so that's what my parents did. They came here, to the valley. I went to school in Orange Cove just a few miles away. But they were faithless people, my mother and father. All their belief, all their faith in God, had been buried in pieces alongside their murdered loved ones, sacrificed on the altar of an Aztec pretender clothed in the red and blue of the blessed Madonna. I grew up attending mass only on holidays, and without ever hearing the Bible read aloud in our house. I'm not telling you this to make excuses for myself, but so you will understand where I came from and why it was easy for me to make the mistakes I made when I was young.

You're seventeen years old now. Practically a man. In my heart, I still see you as a little boy, but when I was your age I was already pregnant and determined to spend my life with the man I loved. That man was not your father. I hope you won't think less of me for admitting this. So many girls my age were already having babies, and when I fell for a boy from school, who had graduated two years ahead of me, I felt like I was an adult who could make my own choices. Your grandmother tried to convince me to have an abortion, but I was in love, and I thought I was ready to handle being a mother. And so I gave birth, in the final year of American history, to a baby boy, your brother, who I named Oscar, after the grandfather you never met. There was no way I could have known what troubles lay ahead or what tragedies were in store for us. I was only a girl. My pride told me I was ready to handle the responsibility of caring for another life, but God Himself told me I wasn't. And He told me in the cruelest way possible.

Your brother was the best thing in my life in those days. His father went out with friends and got drunk, but still I kept faith in our little unwed family. He cheated on me with other girls, and brought disease into our house, but even then I couldn't make myself leave. It wasn't until the very bad years that followed, when everyone was suffering and your grandparents decided to take their chances back in Mexico, that I realized we were all doomed from the start. At fifteen months, Oscar was taken from us, dead from measles along with so many other little ones. If he had been born a few years earlier, he could have received a vaccination. But all the doctors were leaving the valley by then, and anyway, there was no way we could have paid for it on our own. My sins, mijo. I blamed myself for your little brother's death, as I blame myself now for failing to have him baptized. I hope you know I say a prayer for him every day. Same as with all of you.

I should have seen then that God wanted me to turn to the correct path, but I was still young and foolish, and the pain of losing a child is worse than anything you can imagine. As Jonah tried to escape God's command, I tried to escape the pain of a grief so terrible it stayed with me even when I was asleep. I started drinking all the time. Wine, beer, whatever I could get my hands on. When that didn't work, I started smoking weed, and eventually the man who sold it gave me my first taste of methamphetamine. That was all it took, just a taste. Like the fruit of forbidden knowledge. From there, things got so out of control so fast that even Oscar's father deserted me. I was alone for years, working one awful job after another just to feed my addiction. There were times when I prostituted myself, mijo. I'm sorry if that's difficult for you to hear. Selling her body is one of the lowest things a woman can do, but I can talk about it without guilt now, because I know I've been forgiven. But at the time I thought I was the most wretched creature in existence. I even thought about killing myself, I was so lost. It's only by the grace of God that I'm here at all. He saved me from the nightmare of my own mind. That's what the mind is, a nightmare, and to live day after day inside a mind as tortured as mine was a hell worse than anything death seemed to offer. I can say without exaggeration that, if I hadn't found salvation when I did, I would have succumbed to despair a long time ago, mijo, and you and your brothers and your sister never would have been born. So you see, it was all worth it in the end. It was all a part of His plan. Even marrying your father, and all the pain and loneliness I've suffered over the years, even that was worth it because it gave me my children. I know what you're thinking, but before you say anything, let me explain.

I was working as a waitress at a diner in Coalinga when I first met him. I'd been clean just over a year and most of the young men I knew through church were working as laborers for the farms in the area. They were rough and ordinary men who only wanted a wife because they had never learned to cook and clean for themselves. But your father was different. He was educated. He was successful. When I saw the car he was driving and how expensive his clothes looked, I figured he must be someone important. And when he took an interest in me, when he asked me out on a date, it made me feel like the girl in a movie, who catches the eye of a rich man who takes her away to a better life. It felt like my sins had finally been forgiven and good things were starting to happen for me again.

But it all started to feel very different once we got married and moved out here to run a farm. Faithless as they were, your grandparents were devoted to each other. I don't think I ever saw them spend a night apart. That was the example they set for me of married life, of how a husband and wife should be together. Then I get here and, as soon as the farm's up and running, your father announces that he's going away, and that I can only expect to have him home again two or three times a year. Business, mijo. That's the reason he gave for why he was away all the time. To make more money for us, to find the best prices for our crops, and to provide us with a better way of life. Even then it sounded suspicious to me, but I accepted my burden the same as if I had married a traveling soldier or migrant worker. I told myself it was the way it was done, that my parents had been an exception to the norm. But in my heart I knew better. I knew he was keeping something from me. What it was, if I'm to be honest, I admit I didn't really want to know. It had to be something bad, and I'd already had more than enough badness to last me the rest of my life. All I wanted was peace and security and a home to call my own, and if that meant being alone for months at a time, then so be it. I thought I could learn to accept it.

Having children changes everything, though. You no longer think of your own needs alone, or even first. One by one, I found myself with three boys to take care of and no man in the house to help me bring them up. A boy needs a father in his life to teach him what it means to be a man. I could never do it on my own, mijo, for you or any of your brothers. It's just not how God made us. That's why it made me happy when you started spending time with the men of the farm, and when you became interested in hunting and being out of doors. These are good things for a boy to spend his time learning. It upset me that your father wasn't here to help you learn, that he never had time to give to us except when he was passing through, and that even then it was always about business. The business of the farm, the business of keeping an eye on his sons, the business of making me pregnant. That's all that brought your father home to us year after year. It got to the point where I would lash out at him sometimes when he was here. I was careful to hide it from you and your brothers, but there were times when I would beat my fists against his chest and curse him for leaving us alone for so long. I wasn't strong enough to hurt him, of course, and so he never really got angry. He used to laugh at me, in fact, and hold me by the wrists to watch me struggle. That's another way your father was different from other men—only words could ever really hurt him.

There was a night some years back, mijo, when I was pregnant with Karina. You remember how worried we were then. We were all expecting him to come in January, but he made us wait a month because he said he had important business on the coast. On top of the pregnancy hormones, that was the final straw. I waited until you and the boys were asleep and asked him to follow me out to the packing shed. It was cold and empty that time of year, so I knew no one would walk in one us. I didn't yell so much that time, I had carried the anger inside of me for so long. I told him if he didn't make an effort to be home more often, if he didn't show through his actions that he still cared for us, then sometime when he was away I would pack up the house and take you and your brothers far away from here. I promised I would find another, more loving man to be with. For all he knew, I said, I had already been with other men who were better lovers than him. I said that last part just to be cruel, just to make him angry, and it worked. It worked too well. Before I understood what was happening, he was coming at me through the dark, and the next thing I knew he had me by the wrists again, and I was lying with my back pressed to the cold, hard ground. I was seven months pregnant, and still he forced me to the ground. I hope you know I wouldn't lie about something like that, mijo. I swear to God that's what he did. Then he held his face over mine, with his hot breath beating down, and he said that if I ever tried to leave him he would find me. He would find me and he would take you and your brothers away. He said he knew lawyers and judges all through the valley, and that getting full custody would be no trouble for him. Not after he told them about my past.

And then he told me, mijo, and I'll never forget the look in his eyes as he spoke, he told me that if he ever had real reason to suspect I'd been with another man, and that one of my children wasn't his, he would find out about it. And then he would kill me with his own two hands. And then he would kill the child.

In the dead silence and the dead darkness of the room, Mom raised the glass of wine to her lips and drank until the glass was empty and then set the glass on the nightstand beside the jug. She lay breathing and holding my hand. Why are you telling me this? I asked. I was begging her to make sense of it for me, because my own brain was all but petrified from all I had heard, and because even with a clear head I doubted I could piece it together by myself.

I know I said some shocking things just now. That was so you would understand me better and know where I'm coming from, and what I've been dealing with all these years. Your father wasn't the man you thought he was. He wasn't even who I thought he was either. The woman who called this afternoon, who gave us the terrible news, that woman was his wife, mijo. His first wife.

Alarm bells and papal condemnations rang in my ears. Dad was divorced?

She drew her lips inside her mouth and shook her head. No, Anthony. He was still married to that woman, the same as he was to me, and he had three other wives on top of that. Your father was an arrogant sinner, like pharaoh in Egypt, or the pagan emperors of Rome. He died with five wives, five farms, and so many children I'm still trying to find out the exact number. You have brothers and sisters you've never met. Some of them have light skin and blond hair. You even have a sister who's named after your father. Elliot. How is that a girl's name?

Neither one of us tried to answer the question, it was just one of so many that seemed to hold no answer and could only vex us with its infernal mystery. I took the wine jug up by the handle and filled Mom's glass to the brim. She took a drink and looked down at me from the vantage point of where she lay. I didn't have to ask permission. She pressed the glass to my lips and tilted a small drink down my throat. I didn't care for the flavor, but I did feel a bit calmer.

What do you need from me? What can I do to help?

She slid down into the covers so that we were facing each other eye to eye underneath the candlelight. Pray with me, mijo, she said. Pray for our souls, and for the souls of all your brothers and sisters. Including the ones you haven't met.

I shook my head. I don't know them, I said. They might not even be Catholic.

It doesn't matter. Their mothers are all like me tonight, depressed and weeping over their glasses of wine. I'm sure of it. So will you pray for us? Can you do that, please?

Yes. I can do that.

We bent our heads over the wine-stained sheets and began to whisper silently in the dark. I don't know when the last of the candle burnt out, but by the time we opened our eyes again, it was like passing from one darkness into another, from the uncertainty within to the one without, with only her reassuring voice to make me believe it could all somehow be overcome.

I walk through a field of earth, unsure of my own footing. Slogging through layers of compost sown into the dry topsoil. Summer sun on my forehead, horse-flies on the wing. They go for the ears, nostrils, mouth, dark places always, loving the darkness, like the sun's own excrement, clinging to the crevices where intruders are most unwelcome. The priest said we are all excrement but for divine grace, the body a temple of mud and dung, the soul encased inside like a saintly relic, too fragile to be touched. What carpenter or mason could build such a flawed structure and call it his own? I am alive in the heat, unstoppable. Forgive me for being invigorated by unclean things. Forgive the rifle strap, forgive the kill. No hunting to be done, only killing, performed with the sort of pathetic ecstasy I should have outgrown long ago. Ground squirrels dashing from burrow to burrow, massacred in a puff of dust. Sparrows exploding in brown fragments across a bone-blue sky. A Sunday afternoon. God forgive me. Empty five rounds and masturbate in the brush behind an irrigation pump. Jizz and excrement, two parts of a depraved whole. Only sweat for lubricant. Do not look at me.

• • •

Ellie's bruises were no joke. Four finger-sized marks all around the sides of her neck. It was two days before the swelling went down and she could talk like a normal person again. While she was recuperating, I liked to sit down with her at the kitchen table and watch her eat the chicken tortilla soup Katie had made special for her. She would scoop a bit of sour cream onto the end of the spoon and stir it slowly into the hot orange broth. Then she would raise the spoon to her lips and blow on it and slurp the broth into her mouth without giving any thought to proper table manners. No one was going to scold her for that now. By the third day she was feeling well enough to try out a peanut butter sandwich. She tore it into small pieces and consumed it bit by bit like a European on TV snacking on bread and olive oil. Grape jelly clung to her fingers, lending them a purple hue like the ones imprinted on her throat.

You don't have to talk if you're not up to it, I said. But you know I've been waiting all week to talk about it, and sooner or later we're going to have to talk about it.

You don't have to tell me, she said. Her voice was so hoarse it made my heart ache, remembering what happened to her on the porch steps. I've been wracking my brains in silence, she said, trying to figure out what I would say when the time came to decide on a plan.

I was wondering what sort of plan you would come up with.

I didn't. That's the problem. I've worked it over in my head a thousand times, and any way you look at it, we're screwed. We're holding a mad dog by the scruff of the neck, and the only thing dumber than holding on to it might be letting it go.

I don't know if you've noticed, but it looks like my mom and the others are sitting this one out. After what happened with Jennifer, it seems they're putting all their faith in us now. We're the ones who will have to decide what to do next.

You think I don't know it? Jesus, Dawn still hasn't recovered from walking in on Mama in the bathroom, and Katie's been so depressed I wonder if I shouldn't be keeping an eye on her as well. Even Will and Logan are more anxious than usual. None of them know what to do.

I don't see how they can leave such a huge responsibility to us alone.

Whether we knew it or not, we were taking on that responsibility the minute we decided to confront him ourselves. We're in the mess we're in now because we failed to meet the challenge head-on. That can never happen again. We can't let it.

I think we handled ourselves pretty well all things considered.

No. We let him get into our heads and provoke us. We both did. And now we're paying for it. Big time.

He's the one who should be paying for it. For what he did to you. For what he was trying to do to the family.

I know where you're going with this, and I'm only going to tell you once—put it out of your mind completely. Your moment to play the white knight was over after you knocked him off of me. Anything more and you'd just be jerking off your own ego. And it's already pretty well jerked.

Ellie smiled and looked down at the remains of her sandwich. She had stripped away all the bread contained within the crust, and now she decided to break the crust up into square sections and arrange the sections around the edge of the plate like some sort of fancy finger food and then take them up one by one and finish off each one with a few quick bites. The way she teased and talked down to me, it was a wonder I ever missed talking to her at all. For a while there, when I was still getting used to having her around, I thought there must be something wrong with her, that she was disturbed like her mother, or maybe even a little autistic, to where she couldn't control the things she said. It took me a while to realize, though, that she was fully aware of how she came across, and that she could even see herself as others saw her, and that she just didn't care. Bossy and obnoxious, sarcastic and blunt. Adjectives didn't mean anything to her, or at least not enough to make her hide her light. She was so bright she could shine right through you and reveal the words written in lemon juice across your paper soul. And while most people, in their selfishness, would have tried to exploit the gift for their own benefit, she was always comforting and listening to other people, and even looked down on those like me whose noble gestures were sometimes guided by a desire to prove our own worth. I often wondered what plan God had in store for her, and why he would bestow so much insight on a non-believer.

Is this what having responsibility means? That I'm powerless to do anything?

She smiled again. Not exactly, she said. There's still one thing you can do.

What's that?

Sandwich.

What about it?

Make one. With lots of peanut butter.

You're feeling better now. Make your own.

Not for me. For him.

Him? Make a sandwich for him?

Sure. When was the last time he ate?

Last night. Mom gave me some of the leftover chili to feed him.

He has to eat again eventually.

Is that what we are now? His room service?

No. We're his captors, and even prisoners are entitled to three square meals a day. Especially when they're being held illegally. We need to keep him comfortable until we figure out what to do with him in the long run.

He's a drunk. He doesn't give a crap about food.

Then we need to show him that we care about his health even if he doesn't.

I don't care about his health. He could curl up and die as far as I'm concerned.

Don't think about him, then. Think about the family and what it means for us to defuse this situation.

You still think we can persuade him to give up his claim?

I don't know. I don't know what to think. All I know is there's something wrong with him. I saw it in his eyes when he was on top of me. He's torn up inside, just like the rest of us. And if he's just like the rest of us, then there's still a chance he might deal.

You're giving him too much credit. You heard the way he talks. He's not like us. He's an arrogant sinner from the big city. When he looks at us all he sees are beaners and rednecks, fresh meat for him to sink his teeth into.

Ellie moved her head slowly from side to side. I noticed her wince as the still-swollen muscles in her neck grew taut. You might be right, she said. For now, though, give him something else to sink his teeth into. Make him a sandwich, and hurry it up.

I pushed my chair out from the table. I started to stand but froze halfway and looked back across the table to where she sat. One of these days, I said, I'm gonna figure out why I let you tell me what to do so often.

She laughed. Isn't it obvious? You love having a woman tell you what to do. You'd be a complete mess without it.

I shot her an evil look on my way to the kitchen. The bread was still out and I pulled two thin slices from the paper wrapper and slapped them both down on the counter. Sometime when I was in grade school, the local supermarkets stopped carrying the sweetened, factory-made peanut butter that came in plastic jars, and from then on all we could get was a gooey domestic brand with a layer of oil that rose to the top each time it started to settle. I stuck a knife in the glass jar and stirred the oil and butter into a more or less consistent paste and spread the paste over the top of each slice of bread. There was something about that type of peanut butter that felt indecent to me, like we were never meant to disturb its natural condition. I shook the grape jelly from its congealed state and watched it ooze forth and settle in a large glob in the center of one of the slices. I stuck the other slice on top and pressed it under the palm of my hand until jelly burst through the seams of the crust. Wrapping the finished PB&J in a dish towel, I turned and headed down the hall to the back bedroom. There were plenty of clean towels in the drawer, but I opted instead for the soiled one hanging on the refrigerator door.

The room at the far back of the house was barely big enough to fit a twin bed. In our earliest days on the farm, when everyone and his sister was fighting for living space, Dawn had volunteered to sleep out on the living room sofa, but Mom and Sandra convinced her to take the little room at the back, which was practically an over-sized closet, and too secluded for any of the kids to be trusted with. Now, with Jennifer gone, Dawn had taken up the spare bedroom in the house across the way, leaving her former room to serve as a makeshift holding cell for our hostage. I listened at the door before opening it. Nothing. Not even a rustling of bed sheets. I turned the knob and looked inside and saw him sitting up on the bed in the same shirt and pants he'd been wearing when he arrived in our driveway. The sheets and blankets were still tucked in under the corners of the mattress, which meant he'd either slept on top of the covers or not slept at all. The chain was wrapped three times around his ankle. There was a padlock to hold one end to his foot and another to secure the opposite end to the brass head-rail. In the hours before he regained consciousness, I'd combed the property from east to west trying to scrounge up something to ensure he couldn't escape. It was between this and an old iron crate that had been left behind by a previous tenant. It looked like it had once been used to transport pigs and other livestock, and as far as I was concerned, it was still an option.

I unfolded the towel and set the sandwich on top of the covers. Made you something to eat, I said. He didn't answer, and he didn't look at me. He had picked out a spot on the plaster wall that he liked to stare at, and he wasn't taking his eyes away anytime soon from looks of it. The peanut butter's pretty thick, I said. You want a glass of milk?

He kept his back to me as he shook his head. Vodka, he said.

We don't have any vodka in the house. It's milk or water, take your pick.

Vodka.

Fine. Have it your way.

I was about to turn and head back into the hall when I noticed the bumps on the back of his head. He'd gotten it worse than Ellie, my rifle butt had made sure of that. But now that I saw him sitting as he was, with two purple notches rising up out of the mesh of his unwashed hair, I started to worry about how we would handle a corpse on the property if it ever came down to it. From what I'd heard about people with concussions, it was maybe a good thing he hadn't slept the past two nights.

We're not trying to make your life miserable, I said. We're just trying to protect ourselves from whatever evil you're trying to bring down on us. What would you do if you were in our position? Would you let yourself go and trust that it would all turn out okay?

I waited to hear what he had to say, because, to be honest, I was really curious to know. When he finally spoke, there was no sarcasm in his voice as far as I could tell. If I were you, he said, I would walk out into the orchard on a clear day and put a bullet in my head. That's about the best fate you or any of your illiterate family could hope for.

He turned to look at me, probably hoping to take some small pleasure in whatever expression he expected me to have on my face. But as his captor, I wouldn't allow him the satisfaction. I tried keeping as calm as possible, and shook my head like an adult humoring a child's disobedience.

Then I suppose by your logic, I said, the same fate would be best for you. You are family, after all.

He looked at me through the dark circles that bordered his eyes. The front of his head had gotten it even worse than the back, with his broken nose setting badly and swelling up so that he couldn't breath without emitting a faint whistle. He turned again and went back to staring at the wall.

That's your logic, not mine, he said. If it helps you, though, to think of me as a brother, then by all means, go ahead. I suppose you need something to take pride in, if not yourself.

You're wrong, I said. Having you as a brother doesn't make me feel proud at all. If anything, the way you've behaved around here, threatening women and hurting young girls, it only gives me reason to be ashamed. What do you think about that?

He shrugged. You're Catholic, he said. You're bound to find some reason to feel shame.

I twisted the dish towel in my hands until the little bit of remaining moisture had been wrung out. All right, I said. Try this one, then. If anyone in this family is at risk of getting his head blown off, it's you. I've got the rifle, the aim, and the will to do it. The only thing stopping me is the moral conundrum it puts me in. *Thou shalt not kill* means something to me even if it doesn't for you. But you keep pressing me and I might just find myself overcome by temptation. I don't want that, though, and I imagine you don't want it either. So how about you try to meet me halfway and work on being civil toward me while you're here? You think you can do that? Does that sound reasonable?

He laid back suddenly across the bed and rested his bruised head beside the sandwich. Vodka, he said, and closed his eyes.

Fine, be like that. See where it gets you.

He still had his face to the wall as I slammed the door and left him alone once again in his improvised jail cell. I hadn't taken two steps toward the kitchen before the regret started to sink in and I could see clearly what Ellie had meant. It was too easy for him to get to me. I'd have to learn to keep a cool head if I was going to keep working at him, and if the peaceful resolution we hoped for was ever going to be a real possibility.

I sleep every night in a hot room, seven, eight months out of the year. Sweating into the sheets. Turn the pillow, find the cool side. Every window open and no breeze to be felt. No reprieve in the nighttime, no relief. Crickets in the brush patches, lights of cars, strange screams from the labor camps, like pagan howls. My heart is deceitful and my body is a gullible sap. This hand doesn't know what's right and wrong, or it would submit to being hacked off. Above all, dreams are ungodly things, shadows of sins waiting to be committed, maggots feeding on an already rotten brain. Feel them harden and hatch to flies, vomit acid on the childish parts of you, until there is no innocence or ignorance left to hide behind, and you can smell your own wretchedness through the dark, rank and chlorinous in the heat of the room. At night he stalks you for miles across an open terrain, shoulders hard and red from the late day sun, a serpent-skinned Lucifer to ply you with food and drink, and reveal to you the true knowledge about yourself, although it's too painful and terrible to bear. You wrestle with him all night and through to the break of dawn. Feel the torn sinews of muscle contract deep into your thigh. You wrestle, and you fail to understand. You wrestle, alone and agonized, in the early morning dark. You wrestle until your own breath disgusts you, swamp gas settling low over the moist bedding. None of it matters when morning comes. Just another day until the next worms hatch, until it all starts over anew.

• • •

I was skinny, but I was strong. I had big hands, a fighter's hands. That's what the PE teacher said. On the school jogging track, in the heat of the summer, and in the freezing mist of the winter, he would have us sprint fifty and one hundred and two hundred yards side by side and measure our performances against one another, and pull the champion out from the pack and shower praise on him, on me, and point out the hard places on my calves and arms where the new muscles stood out, and make me feel like real manhood was within my grasp, and that all life demanded was continued suffering and pain to get me there, to make me great like I imagined I could be. It wasn't enough just to be a fighter. I had to be something more. I wanted to be a soldier. Chris had been a soldier. I think Dad would have been proud to see me a soldier. A soldier knows what he's meant for and carries out his duties without hesitation. Resolve. That's what he has. That's what I always needed. That's what Dad said, anyway.

When I was fourteen he showed up out of the blue one day and asked Mom what was for dinner. He had put on weight since the last time we saw him, making him seem more giant to me than he already was. When he reached across the table for a piece of bread, you'd have sworn he planned to crush the basket in his palm and devour the whole thing, wicker and all, in one massive chomp. Nobody could eat like Dad could. The rest of us were burnt out on the bland meals that Mom prepared daily in the kitchen that always smelled of burger grease and aerosol. But Dad ate with the same gusto regardless of whether it was Mom's cooking or Chinese takeout. At our table his appetite was always healthy, and as a rule we knew to stay quiet until after he'd finished his first serving, and to leave at least one quarter of every dish at the table for him to take or leave at his discretion. Fourteen years old and I was already over six feet tall, and I was hungry as hell all the time, and still I couldn't take an extra spoonful of chili without permission. Not when he was at the head of the table.

Eventually he killed a belch under his breath and looked up from his demolished first helping. So, he said. What's going on around here? What's new with everybody?

He turned his head and zeroed in on me before anyone else had a chance to speak. I could tell right then that he knew. Somehow he knew. I'd been concealing my guilt from the moment he pulled up to the house, and now, by some secret means of intuition, he had smelled me out for the liar I was. Mom tried to preempt what she must have seen coming.

Dad, she said. Anthony's been—

I don't believe I was asking you.

My brothers' eyes shot up from the table. Like no man I'd ever seen, Dad could silence a room without ever raising his voice. Mom sunk back into her chair and rested a hand on her stomach. My new sister or brother was due any day now, and whatever strength she had to resist him was probably eaten up by the same fatigue that drove her to take five minute naps half a dozen times throughout the day. Dad kept his eyes on me until I finally broke down and made eye contact in return.

I got an interesting call the other day, he said. You wouldn't know this, but I made it clear a long time ago to the school district that they're supposed to get in touch with me directly if any problems ever arise concerning you and your brothers. It's my right as a father, after all. To know what's going on inside my own house. And since I assumed correctly that your mother couldn't be trusted to keep me in the loop, I had to find other methods of staying informed. That was rather prudent thinking on my part, given the circumstances. Wouldn't you agree?

Dad, he's just a boy. This is what boys—

Believe me, you'll know when I'm ready to hear from you. Until then, kindly keep your damn mouth shut.

Mom lowered her head and stirred the congealed chili on her plate. Mark started to whimper as fat tears rolled down his face. Seizing her moment to escape, Mom got up and carried him and Sebastian to the back bedroom, leaving Dad and me alone at the table. I didn't blame her for that desertion. The first thing I did whenever Dad was scolding her was take the boys outside. Once the first plumes of smoke appear on the volcano, you have to get to a safe distance before it erupts. Even if that means leaving someone behind.

Well, now, Dad said. I believe you have something to tell me. So quit dancing around it.

I'm sorry. I didn't mean—

Until now, no one in my family has ever been suspended from school. I never was. Neither of your grandparents ever were. Do you know what type of person gets suspended? Delinquents. Deadbeats. The type of people who can never hold on to anything, just like the trash you see working out in the orchards for pennies on the hour. Is that your future? Is that what you have planned for yourself after all you've been given? After all I've given you?

It's not. I swear it's not. I'm sorry. What happened was—

I'm not interested in your carefully crafted explanations. Your principal already told me exactly how it went down. I had to squeeze it out of him over the phone, but I got the full picture. I don't know which is more shameful, that you got suspended, or that you couldn't even hold your own in a one-on-one fight against a boy a grade below you. You made an ass of yourself and you didn't even have it in you to stand your ground. That's what I call a lack of resolve.

Dad pushed his plate away. I said nothing, staring down under the table at my worn and dust-covered tennis shoes. I had to wonder what version of events the principal had given him, if he had stuck to the simple facts of who hit who and when, or if he had explained about the confrontation that preceded the fight. Did Dad know what a creep the other boy was, and how he had spent half the lunch period harassing girls on the yard, snapping their bra straps under their shirts until they ran crying to the restroom? Would he have been proud to know that, of all the boys who'd seen him carrying on like that, I was the only one who stood up and told him to stop? Or was all that rendered meaningless on account of I had lost the fight? Two days later and my side was still sore from where he kept punching me. Short, fierce jabs to the kidney, one after another. Of course he would be psycho enough to read up on the human body, to learn all the weaknesses of our anatomy just so he could put his knowledge to use in a schoolyard bout. I'd barely managed to land a punch across his shoulder when he slid left and started in on my side, seizing my shirt collar with his free hand to keep me from backing off. He even knew to pivot between blows so I couldn't work my way around him. I never really had a chance. And anyway, it wasn't long before the alarm sounded and the monitors were swarming in around us.

There's one other thing I'd like to know, Dad said. Your principal told me this boy has a history of being picked on, and that the other boys tease him all the time because of his weight. He wouldn't tell me much else about him. But I want to know—was he taller than you? Was he?

I closed my eyes and breathed in deep. There were times I hated being burdened with height. All through elementary and middle school, teachers and coaches were always sizing me up and commenting on how fast I was growing and making assumptions about my athletic prowess, and then acting disappointed when I failed to develop as a basketball or volleyball player. It was true I was always in the top row of every class picture I'd been in as far back as kindergarten. But adults forget how toughness gets started in the heart of a child, and how easily a tall boy can turn soft if he's not vigilant, and how meanwhile the short boys are all turning into Mexican dogs, just waiting to sink their teeth into the neck of the first tall thing that crosses them. And then the tall ones have to make the choice to become tough, and to keep the toughness in their hearts all the time, and reflect on it day by day like the faithful reflect on their religion.

I'm not hearing a response, Dad said. You will answer me, though. Even if we have to sit here together all night.

He wasn't, I said. He wasn't taller than me.

He was shorter than you?

Yes.

You lost a fight against a boy who was younger, fatter, and shorter than you?

Yes.

I could hear Dad's breath passing in and out of his nostrils. He seemed calm. He seemed calm even as he pushed his chair out from the table and stood and pulled the jangling keys from his pocket. I think it's time we went for a drive, he said.

It had been more than a year since I'd ridden in a car with Dad. It was a Sunday afternoon and he drove all of us to a Chinese restaurant on the far side of Visalia. Sebastian and I were in the backseat while Mom sat up front with Mark on her lap, trying to keep him quiet enough not to irritate Dad. The car he was driving then seemed small to me for some reason, or maybe it was the feeling of having the whole family packed together in the same vehicle for the first time in forever. In any case, this time he had me sit in the front seat right next to him. No where to go to escape his gaze. True, he kept his eyes on the road the whole time, but it still felt like he was watching me, keeping me in suspense over what he was thinking and where we were going and what he was going to do to me when we got there.

We drove through town and out of it again and then turned onto the fresh black road that stretched for miles through dusty nothingness until dead-ending right in front of the county ag bureau and a few other government buildings. Dad took us about half the distance to the bureau before pulling into the parking lot of a general medicine clinic with the blue and green emblem of the national health insurance emblazoned on the main wall facing the road. Dad parked in the most deserted corner of the lot and shut off the engine. He motioned for me to get out with him.

I'm a responsible man, he said. I don't shirk my obligations, least of all when it comes to my own flesh and blood. But that's just the thing. Blood is blood. That's all there is. It's what binds us together, and without it, all that's left are empty words and disappointment. That's why we're going to find out right here and now whether your failures are really my own, or if some treacherous slut has been making a fool out of me for fifteen years.

He popped the trunk and reached down deep inside. The nylon bag he took out was about the size of a beer can with a thin zipper running the full length of one side from seam to seam. He unzipped the bag and removed a clear plastic tube with a cap on one end and a strip of masking tape holding the cap in place. I peered into the tube and saw that it contained nothing but a plain cotton swab attached to a wooden handle that was almost as long as the tube itself. Dad held the strange container in front of my face and shook it from side to side.

Do you know how a paternity test works? he asked.

Instead of answering him, I pressed my lips together as tight as I could, like I was trying to form an impenetrable seal across my face.

It's very simple. I'm going to use this swab to collect saliva from the inside of your cheek. That's the DNA sample. The staff in there already has my DNA, and they're going to run some tests to see if we're a match.

It takes about two days for the results to come in. I'll wait at the house with you and your mother until then. If, at the end of two days, the tests come back negative, if they show that I'm not and never have been your father, then I'll know who it is who really deserves to be punished. I'll finally know who to blame.

Tears came to my eyes without my realizing. It was too late to try to force them down, so I let them flow freely down my face. I thought about Mom alone in the house with my brothers, walking through the kitchen with bare feet and straining through the burden of her condition, and all the while trying to get Sebastian and Mark to settle down and give her a break. I didn't know much about her life or the kind of woman she was before she met Dad. But I knew she was a God-fearing woman, and that she wouldn't lie to me about where I came from, or about whose blood it was that every second of the day was coursing through my heart and flesh. I dropped to my knees right there in the parking lot.

I'm your son, I said. I know I am. I have to be.

He tore the cap off the cylinder and pinched the bare end of the swab between his huge fingers. You may be right, he said. But it's time we know for certain. Now open your mouth.

I was crying so hard I could hardly breathe, but somehow I still managed to talk. Please don't. I'm certain. I'm already certain you're my father.

You can't know for sure. You weren't even born. Now open up.

As I spoke, I tried to shrink my mouth to a point no wider than a needle, in case he tried to get the swab into me by force, which seemed to be the direction he was headed. I have your eyes, I said. That proves it. My eyes are the same as the ones you're looking at me with.

He stepped back and looked at me like he'd never taken the time to notice the color of my eyes before. Anyone can have blue eyes, he said. That doesn't prove anything.

I feel it, though. I know that I'm a part of you. Mom wouldn't betray you like that. She wouldn't break a Commandment.

Dad shook his head and smiled mercilessly, turning his wrist so that the swab swirled like a magic wand in the hand of a birthday party magician. They say that sometimes our blood can work through us without us even realizing it, he said. Cellular memory. That's what they call it. Seems to me that if you were really my son it would be so much more difficult for you to do things that embarrass the family name. So maybe you were never meant to carry my name. Maybe that's what you're trying to tell me and you don't even know it.

I clutched his pant legs in my fists. My knees were already sore from kneeling on the asphalt, but at that moment I wouldn't have stood for anything in Heaven or Earth unless he ordered me to. I'm your son, I said, though I could barely speak through the grip of the invisible hand on my throat. I am your son. I made a mistake. I'm sorry. I'm sorry. Please forgive me. Forgive me.

I looked up at him again and saw that his face was blank above the protruding rim of his beard. He held the swab suspended above me and I didn't move and didn't try to get away.

You've hurt me a great deal, he said. I hope you realize that. You hurt your father with how you handled yourself. You're too much of a hothead.

A low breeze swept in over the lot, drying some of the tears on my face. I know, I said. I'm sorry. I don't know why I get angry so easy. I've tried to keep it in check. I've prayed to God for patience and strength. Nothing works. It's like there's this part of me that's impossible to figure out no matter how hard I try.

No one told you to go and make yourself complicated, he said. You're a country boy. A farm boy. You should be carefree and easy-going.

I know. I'm sorry.

Call me sir. It's a sign of respect.

I'd never called anyone sir or ma'am in my life except sarcastically, when me and my friends were joking around. Just the sound of it felt gaudy and old-fashioned.

Do you realize how embarrassed I was to get a call like that from your school?

I do.

You do what?

I do, sir.

Do you promise never to put me in a position like that again?

I do, sir.

Do you promise that, if you ever get in another fight, you'll do it away from school?

I do, sir.

And do you swear that, no matter who it is next time, no matter how much bigger or older than you he is, you won't back down until the fight is finished?

I do, sir.

Good. Now get up. Your mother's going to be worried.

We drove back the same way we came. On the way through town he stopped at a drive-thru and bought me a chocolate milkshake in a tall paper cup. Don't breath a word of this to your mother or brothers, he said. Tell them we sat outside drinking milkshakes and had a long talk about responsibility. Don't even mention the paternity test. I'll know it if you do.

The milkshake had turned soupy by the time we got home. I'd held it in my hand the whole way, but couldn't bring myself to drink it.

I imagine myself in prison, in a room of iron and stone. I see my captor's pale face. I ask what crime I've committed and I don't receive an answer but I don't fight against the prison walls because I know in my heart I'm guilty in one way or another. I was born guilty, and every day I've been alive I've only incriminated myself further. My sickness is my guilt. My guilt is my sickness. What healthy person would have dreams such as these? What dreams such as these would come to a healthy person? When I open my eyes for the first time in the morning, there's a moment of blissful amnesia when I forget that I am who I am. And then it all comes back to me, the flesh and substance of reality, reminding me as well as I can be reminded that I've never been true to the word of God Almighty, that I've lied in confession, lied in conversation, lied in my day to day actions, and died already, spiritually, through my inaction. Who is there to hear my plea? Not the parish priest, that orange-haired man with his American accent and the logic of Rome buzzing inside his skull. Not the monsignor, old relic of the old way, discredited now by two popes in succession. What if no one is there to hear my broken cry? What if no one cares to be burdened with it? Is it damnation, or is it release, this feeling of being abandoned? Who am I, if not the child that was never wanted deeply?

• • •

Chris came to the farm one spring as part of a group of hired men fresh up from the state camp in Cutler. He had worked as a foreman for half a dozen farms around Dinuba, and with two of our regular foremen skipping out before the first grapes started to swell on the vine, he was brought on at the last minute to tackle the work of two men and be responsible for twice the load they'd carried. It was tough work even for a seasoned hand, and not much more money to compensate it, but if Chris was unhappy with the arrangement, he never complained about it in front of Mom or me. We never heard him complain about anything, in fact. Besides a few of the younger guys who'd grown up in the camps and in the fields and on the road, he was the only white man I'd ever known who didn't seem to think the work of the farm was beneath him, who didn't glare at my brothers and me on our way to school like they were wondering what sort of topsy-turvy world it was that saw Mexicans in the big house and white men working in the field. And after I found out about his military record, about how he'd fought in an actual American Army regiment in the wars before disbandment, there was nothing Mom or anyone else could do to keep me from trailing after him every chance I got.

He was good about it, too, always having a dumb and bratty kid like me underfoot. Sometimes in the summer he'd even let me sit beside him on the fence while he was taking his lunch break. I never saw him with any food other than the standard sack lunch the people at the state camp sent the laborers off with every day before dawn. It was always the same—cold meat and cheese wrapped in a cold tortilla, a packet of potato chips, a hard-boiled egg, and a piece of overripe fruit left over from the previous season. He'd sit atop a fence post with his heels on the board and devour first the egg and then the orange and let the shells of both fall onto the loose ground beneath him. I'd watch him through the corner of my eye. I could tell he was all alone just from the lack of variation in his lunches. It made me excited, and it made me sad, imagining what he'd done—or what had been done to him— to leave him with no one who cared for him. Even the most disagreeable pickers still arrived in the mornings with snacks and cakes and greasy tamales prepared by family members waiting for them back at the camp. Even those who had no one to begin with, the orphans and outcasts and runaway fathers, still managed after a time to be adopted out of necessity into some such group of traveling misfits. A man with Chris's talents would've never found himself alone. Not unless he wanted it that way.

One afternoon I got gutsy and decided to see for myself what was lying underneath it all. I made like he was one of the eggs from the state camp kitchen—one crack at the base of the shell and you could peel the rest away piece by piece.

Did you spend a lot of time on farms like this when you were my age? Only reason I ask is cause you seem real comfortable out here in the vineyard.

Chris stared out past the tree line with his eyebrows pinched together and a shine of sweat across his forehead. No one grows up feeling comfortable around the vines, he said. God help anyone who starts acting relaxed with this crop. That's when the bugs swarm in and pick you right down to the stem.

I nodded at the careful wisdom of his remark. I wanted to be like that when I grew up, to be so settled and sure of myself that my opinions rang out with the music of perfect infallibility. Did they have a lot of grapevines where you grew up?

I never saw a vineyard in my life until I was already a man, he said. I grew up back east, where the snows fall a foot thick in the winter. You ever seen snow up close?

The real answer to his question wasn't something I had to think about. After living my whole life in the valley, snow was nothing to me but a word, a mirage that painted distant mountaintops on a clear day in winter and vanished from sight and thought the rest of the time. There was no reason for me to lie, and I didn't understand why I did. My Dad took me to see the snow one time, I said. He took all of us. We made snowmen and raced each other on skis and snowboards. It was a fun day.

Chris wasn't the sort of guy who needed to look right at you to have a conversation. Most of the times we talked, in fact, he tended to scan the terrain in front of him with my words falling in his ear as I spoke facing it. This time, though, he turned and looked at me like something about the tale I was spinning didn't quite add up. Which it didn't. I turned from his gaze and looked off across the field to the shaded area under the ash tree where most of the pickers liked to eat lunch. It was always the same problem for me, the same old Catholic dilemma. I was honest just enough to be bad at lying, and I lied just enough to get caught.

Did you see a lot of snow overseas? In the war?

He shook his head. No, he said. No snow, no rain, no relief of any kind. Nothing but sand and heat and flames rising up from the land. Falling from the sky.

Why were you over there?

Well, he said. They told us it was to protect the country from terrorist attacks. But really it was to show that we were still capable of getting something done. A lot of other countries were watching us close near the end. We did a lot of bad things just to prove we still could.

And then the states disbanded anyway.

That's right. I was lucky. Some of the guys who got left behind on foreign bases had to pay their own airfare to get back to their families. Some never made it. And some didn't bother trying. Wherever they were when the news hit, they decided to make a fresh start there. Who knows? If things had turned out different, I might have changed my name to Abdullah.

I don't know why anyone would come here if they didn't have to.

That made it twice in one conversation that he turned to look at me straight on. I smiled and laughed so that my question would seem sarcastic in retrospect, even though, to be honest, I had meant every word. It made no sense to me that someone would leave the east, even a disorganized and disbanded east, and come to the most boring corner of the world to pick fruit for state-subsidized subsistence wages. To him I must've seemed like a spoiled little shit, disparaging all the blessings I'd received even as the man in front of me was relying on the ag bureau to keep his stomach full throughout the day. But Chris didn't try to scold or correct me. He just took a match and a crumpled cigarette from his shirt pocket and struck the match on the post and took a slow drag as the bluish smoke unfurled through the air.

I wasn't going to stick around to see the shit-show unfold, he said. Once the Army stopped cutting paychecks to the soldiers on the ground, I knew it wouldn't be long before everything fell apart. I went AWOL from a V.A. hospital in Texas and lived in twenty different places in as many years. Mexico, Central America, sorts of places a man with security training could make money easy without having to answer too many questions. But I couldn't keep it up. Not at my age. So now I'm just trying to work my way north one job at a time.

I looked at him with my mouth partly open and my eyes partly closed. AWOL, I said. You left the Army without permission.

Without leave, he said. But yeah, I did. I'm a deserter. I deserted the American Army. Along with some five hundred thousand others.

Okay. I get it.

But how do you feel about it? It's okay. You can tell me the truth. I won't get mad.

I guess, I guess it's all right. Like you said, they stopped paying you a wage.

That's right. And if I'd stayed any longer, I'd have been there when they finally had to cut out the chow as well.

I get that. It's just. I don't know. I don't know if I could ever run away from something after I'd made a promise to it.

He looked at me close and breathed the smoke from his mouth back in through his nose. What about your family? he asked. Sounds to me like you've got plans to run away from here the first chance you get. Won't they feel like you broke a promise then?

I don't want to run away from them, I said. It's this place. I want to get as far away from it as I can.

This place isn't so bad. I've seen plenty worse.

Doesn't matter. I was born here and I've spent all my life here so far. So I don't want to grow old and die here. I want to live somewhere different.

Different is a point of view. It all depends on where you're standing and where you started off. This valley was different to me when I first came here a couple years ago. And if you were to see the place where I grew up, you'd say it was different enough to suit your needs, but after a time you'd see it's just the same product in different packaging. There's plenty a man can do to improve his situation, but not if he's always looking around the bend for the next thing that's new and different. That's what I think anyway.

No, I get it, I said. *There's nothing new under the sun.*

He shook his head and smiled like I was cute for playing the wise old sage at the ripe age of fourteen and a half. It's true I was full of shit, trying to sound smart with words taken straight from the monsignor's mouth. There's nothing new under the sun. That was one of his favorite verses, and the more he repeated it the more willing I was to believe that even my own self was a plagiarism of some earlier version from long ago. Every year on my birthday I grew more anxious about who I was becoming. If there really was nothing new in the whole course and history of the world, then boys like me were probably a dime a dozen in the grand design. But then why was it so hard to find someone who spoke my language?

As I was contemplating my own weirdness, Chris took the last drag off his cigarette and carefully twisted the flame out against the post and flicked the butt into the dirt far from the dry grass that bordered the fence line. Let's assume you do make it out of the valley one day, he said. How do you expect to make a living once you're out there?

I don't know, I said. I haven't thought that far ahead.

Well, what are you good at?

Not much, really. I tried going out for sports at school, but I didn't have any skills.

Skills come with time and practice. Right now is the time for you to decide what you're interested in. So what interests you? I take it farming doesn't exactly do it for you.

I gave out a small fake laugh. Not even, I said. That's part of why I want to leave so bad, cause there's nothing to do around here.

I see you out walking around sometimes in the late afternoon. Over by the packing house. What do you do over there all by yourself?

Nothing. I don't do anything.

The more Chris pressed me for answers, the more his questions froze me, until finally I was sitting off the edge of the fence rail with my mouth hung open like a mounted bass on a fisherman's wall, too embarrassed to admit how deep my weirdness really ran. Every farm boy and girl in the valley had some private habit they indulged in alone, out in the orchards and fields where no one was watching. Some streaked and others jerked it. Others daydreamed, and made hidden fortresses out of the trees, and lost themselves in hidden fantasies that were too loud or disconcerting to risk exploring inside the house. As for me, there were things I knew children were capable of doing that could raise adult eyebrows immediately, and I prayed that Chris wasn't like other adults, cause at the rate we were going, I was bound to reveal my secrets to him in one way or another.

I like to burn ants with a magnifying glass, I said. I know it's stupid and gross and I shouldn't be doing it at my age. But like I said, there's not much to do around here, especially in the summer. Figure I might as well put the burning sun to good use. But please don't tell my mom. She wouldn't approve.

Chris nodded slowly, looking down at his own dangling feet and the dry curdled dirt beneath his heels. More than a month since any rain had fallen and the earth still held the shape of its last heavy swelling. Long memory it had, the poor dry sand-soil of our country. You ever kill any larger animals? he asked. Anything that walks on four legs instead of six?

God, no, I said. My thighs squirmed against the fence rail. Torturing animals, especially pets, was one of the sure-fire ways for a farm boy to land himself in trouble with the teachers and administrators at school. Just talking about it, even jokingly, was sometimes enough to get him sentenced to counseling, to weekly sessions with a district headshrinker that were longer and more humbling than any parish confession. And even supposing you made it out unexpelled, no one would look at you the same again. You'd live out the rest of your time in school alone and friendless, eating lunch with the retards on the retard bench. I'm no psycho, I said. I never hurt any cats or dogs. I swear.

Chris gave me another look like he thought I was being funny. I'm not talking about that, he said. I mean real hunting, with a rifle. I'm asking if your father ever took you out and taught you how to shoot.

I blinked and lowered my head and knocked my shoes against the boards to dislodge the stuck-on dirt. I could picture Dad at home in July with the sunlight absorbing into the dark fabric of his suit as he strolled leisurely between the rows of sagging vines, thumbs through his belt loops, strange smile stretched out over his face. Every one of our grapes was destined for the raisin box, to spend the hottest months of the year shriveling on burlap mats on the ground while fruit flies risked poisoning for the chance to taste the warm sweet juices inside. But for the few weeks each summer when Dad was around, before the drying commenced, he liked to play the part of the winery baron, to run his hands over the grapes and feel the yeast clinging to his fingers. Sometimes, when he thought no one was around, he would raise his heavy arms over his head and shout some triumphant phrase in French or Italian, I didn't know which.

He wanted to teach me shooting when I was younger, I lied. But Mom wouldn't let him. She said I was too young, and it was too dangerous.

Understandable, Chris said. But do you think she'd let you learn now that you're older?

I don't know. Maybe.

Chris smiled. I keep a couple of .22s in storage up at the camp, he said. If the misses says it's all right, I'd be happy to teach you how to use one of them in the afternoons and evenings. The neighbors' orchards are deserted then. We won't be a bother to anyone.

While my head maybe sprang up a little faster than I would've liked, I still did a good job hiding just how exciting the prospect was for me. Yeah, sure, I said. That could be cool.

Okay, then, Chris said. I'll talk to your mother this evening.

Sounds good.

He nodded and fished through his pocket for another cigarette and another a match. Sometimes in life there are moments that are so liberating you're almost repelled by the new sensations they carry. Still I said a prayer of thanks under my breath. I knew in my heart that Jesus might not approve of hunting for sport, that he was a shepherd and not a butcher, and he laid down his life for his flock. But I wanted to learn. I wanted to hunt. I wanted a new kind of communion with a different kind of blood.

Who am I, if not my father's son? What am I, if not my brother's keeper? Brother's keeper. Keeper and captor. Poor confused prisoner. Poor little

Oscar, dead before I was even alive. Little brown body covered in red sores. Sores. Bubonic plague. Brown body, Black Death. Father Ramsey used to show us the medieval pictures in his theology book. Hooded figures with long proboscises walking side by side with the image of death. Unclothed Santa Muerte, sexless before fields of the ulcerous and dying. Total breakdown of society, custom and decency abandoned. One family member falls ill and the rest band together to help. Half the family and the sick are sectioned off by the healthy, two halves living in mutual quarantine side by side under the same roof. Bread tossed through windows into rooms whose doors are never unlocked, loved ones waiting with dark eyes and guilt-ridden hearts for the moment the food stops vanishing. Hear the bells of the death carts making their rounds through fetid streets. Would you kiss him one last time in parting? Could you bear to throw her face-down upon the stack? They believed the air had turned foul and betrayed them and looked to leeches to thin out their blood. They believed it was sin that had brought the scourge upon them, and laid whips upon their backs and shards of glass beneath their feet and crowned themselves with thorns to suffer as He had suffered. Blood was always the answer, until it became the problem. Blood of the Redeemer turned spiteful overnight, Old Testament voices echoing amid hoarse and congested cries. Blood of the family rendered meaningless as all stared down the same cataclysm, all alone, all fending for their own sake. Got to get away. See him running now, escaping to the country. Histories forgotten, names invented out of nothing. What's that? Oh, yes, Mister Cooper. John Cooper. Why, no, I don't know nothing about the troubles going on down south. From the north originally.

Sins of the modern world piling up around us, like dark-age corpses in a lye-caked pit. Mother abandons her husband. Father neglects his families. Grandparents desert their homeland and desert their troubled daughter and desert their adopted country for the homeland they deserted before. No principles anymore. No faith in blood of any kind, divine or otherwise. Jennifer had faith in blood. Can't fault her there. Only words to keep her in our corner, shrugged off as soon as the shit hit the fan. Excrement in the fan. Shit-caked walls. Only words to keep any of us together. Broken vows, promises unkept. No shame going AWOL as the nation takes its last breath. Not my nation, though. One had to burn for the other to rise. Phoenix from the ashes, Arizonians camping outside our borders. Patrolman thinks himself slick if he can sneak a shot through the fence links to thin out the herd. A real badass, vanguard of the Republic, defeating evil through murder one sunspotted grandma at a time. I could be the real deal, though. I could fight in a real war. I could endure and keep my post and stay standing while others fled. The good shepherd lays down his life for his sheep. A whole valley full of them. Beautiful death, virtues extolled, glorified forever by God and by Caesar. And yet I feel my own knees buckle. And yet I feel my own heart sink. The hired hand will flee when the wolf approaches. Godless Chinese or ghoulish Russian. What would they say if they saw me standing at the gate, under the Bear Flag, with my brown skin wavering in the fickle light of distant fires? Would they burst out laughing? Yes, they very well might. Where is your blood? the Han will ask. Where is your blood? the Cossack will ask. Here, here, I will say. See, it is only half of me, but it is real. What, that half? they'll reply, faces grinning under the shade of red and white banners. The father who lied to you, who from the moment of your birth tried to tie you to the land like an illiterate peasant? For that blood you will die? For that you will risk everything?

Yes, yes, I will cry, and turn away sobbing. God help me, yes. I want to suffer and I want to sacrifice. I can't be alone.

Where is the city we were promised? How do we begin to build?

• • •

After recuperating in darkness for the better part of two weeks, Sandra finally came out to rejoin the rest of the family right as the summer harvest was about to commence. Her appetite had returned in short jumps over the course of her seclusion, with the biggest jump, from liquid to solid food, giving us the most anxiety along the way. Whatever expired medicine she had taken in her moment of weakness, none of us had any idea what the long-term damage might be and whether her system would ever fully recover. Dawn stayed close by her side all through her recovery, just as she had with Beth some months before. She was the one who figured that calcium would help to repair her stomach lining, and who drove into town each morning to make sure we had plenty of fresh milk on hand. And when Sandra at last agreed to come out from her bedroom, it was Dawn who held her arm on the slow walk down the hallway.

Now they were at the kitchen table with a half-eaten cheddar cheese sandwich beside them on a plate. The other half of the sandwich was working its way through Sandra's uneasy digestive tract while Dawn stood behind her with a pair of scissors, cutting her long mess of hair down to a cooler, more comfortable summer coif. Ellie was by my side at the gas range. We stood and leaned our palms on the counter and waited for the leftover Sloppy Joe meat to finish reheating in the pan. A week of free room and board and our prisoner still hadn't softened up. He kept his back to me whenever I entered the room. He sneered and demanded vodka and saw every kindness we showed him for the desperate bribe that it was. Even Ellie, with all her liberal reservations about violence, seemed almost ready to give the go ahead for execution. Though she never had to worry about pulling the trigger. We all knew who that task would fall on.

Every minute he stays here puts all of us at risk, she said, stirring the bubbling meat in the pan. The foremen are already suspicious, what with Dale walking off the job without a word. Won't be long till they start getting nervous about whatever's going on up here at the house. Then we'll be lucky if we can find a pack of blind junkies to lead the harvest.

I shook my head and sighed and watched her split a couple of cheap supermarket hamburger buns in half and arrange them on the paper plates resting beside the range. She stirred the steaming meat mixture one last time and scooped a heavy spoonful onto the flat bottom half of each bun. The Sloppy Joes were her own doing, part of her continued effort to make things easier for our mothers in the wake of everything that was going on. For three days the house had been filled with the smells of ketchup, cumin, and chili powder. Ellie smacked the top bun onto the congealing meat and cut the sandwich in half with a butcher's knife and laid the knife on the counter over a paper napkin. She managed to take a bite without slathering the corners of her mouth with sauce. I wished my brothers knew that trick.

There's no middle way between it, I said. If he can't be reformed, he has to be dealt with. Trouble is, my heart isn't in it the way it was a few days ago. If you'd told me then we'd have to give him the Old Yeller treatment, I'd have jumped at the chance. But now I don't know. It's funny. You bring a person meals and tend to their needs and you start to feel responsible for them, no matter how big a bastard they are. Makes me wonder how the guards at San Quentin used to manage it back in the day. Wish I could pick one of their brains right about now.

Ellie scratched at a mosquito bite behind her armpit. With the heat rising more and more each day, she'd started going around the house in some of my old t-shirts with the sleeves cut off clean at the seam. We'd grown familiar enough with each other to share such things in common, and to where I didn't think twice about seeing her bra straps running free in the breeze.

I wish there was a way to get through to him, she said. I don't like to believe it about a person, least of all someone with the same blood as me. I don't like to believe someone could be so cruel and heartless. But then I think about how it's Elliot's blood running in our veins, and I wonder if we aren't just a herd of black sheep all flocked together. You've got to admit, he's more like him than we are.

Is that supposed to make me feel better?

It should. I wouldn't want to be like either of them.

That's what I mean. You can't kill a man unless there's distance between you. The longer I spend acting like his maid, the harder it'll be for me to put him down.

It shouldn't have to come to that. But we're damned if we do and damned if we don't.

You don't know how right you are, I said. I've been studying on it these past weeks, and what I found isn't too encouraging. The Bible takes a hard stand against fratricide. Men who kill their brothers wind up marked and exiled. Entire races cursed for the sins of one ancestor.

Ellie set her Sloppy Joe down on the plate and looked at me with raised eyebrows. Glad you found something to keep your spirits up through all this, she said. But we need a practical solution. The Bible's not going to help us here.

She smiled a smart little smile and continued chewing through the mouthful of meat lodged in her cheek. Blasphemous as she was, I suppressed the tongue-lashing I would have given her just a few weeks before. To that end, I suppose I owed her for planting the seed of the solution in my mind.

How many wine bottles do we have left in the pantry?

Ellie shrugged. Beats me, she said. Go ask the two drunks. They're bound to know.

Come on. That's not fair. Your mother drinks more than mine.

Yeah. But that's saying a lot and you know it.

All right, fine. I'll go see for myself.

What are you going to do?

I'm going to do what I should have thought to do a long time ago. Do me a favor and fix another sandwich. I'll be right back.

While Ellie ladled some of the dripping meat onto the remaining bun, I went around the house collecting everything I would need for the mission at hand. I started in the pantry. Of the nine compartments built into the big cardboard box, only four still contained full bottles of wine. A few odd bottles were arranged on the shelf beside the box, but I reasoned they appeared even more questionable than the cheapo Mexican stuff our mothers purchased in bulk. Nothing from the local vineyards was ever worth a damn, though sometimes a passable Chilean brand went on sale down at the supermarket. In school the ag science teachers taught us all about the Napa region and the unsurpassed quality of California reds, but once you got to the age of sneaking drinks for yourself when no one was around, you realized that hardly a soul east of the Diablos had ever really tasted the wine of our country. I grabbed one of the bottles from Sonora and blew the dust and dirt off the label and carried the bottle by the neck to my bedroom.

The Bible was resting closed on the four-inch space of wood frame between the headboard and the mattress. An old edition of the New American Standard Bible that had outlasted America itself, the book was battered and yellowed with a stripe of filth down the side from where my unclean fingers had gripped the pages. Stained much darker since Dad died. The cover was deeply cracked, like my ankles in August, when the sun blazed and there was no moisture left in the air or ground. I flipped to the New Testament and skimmed the pages until I landed on the passage I was looking for. Marking the page with my thumb, I carried the Bible and the wine to the kitchen and collected the sandwich and the rest of my supplies. I came down the hall balancing the paper plate on my forearm like a waiter. The prisoner lay curled up on the edge of the bed with his back to the door and the loose chain wrapped around his calves. I set the plate, bottle, and glass on the dresser and took the heavy corkscrew from my pocket. He didn't acknowledge me at all until the cork popped out. Then he turned his head.

Is that what I think it is?

Three meals a day for days on end and this was the first time he'd spoken before I did. Tilting the stemmed glass to an angle, I poured the deep red wine against the side of the bowl and watched it rise up halfway to the rim. It's not vodka, I said. But it should help to get that monkey off your back.

I set the bottle on the bookcase and held the glass out for him to accept. He looked at the offering with his hands pressed flat against the bed. I raised the glass to my lips and took a sip and made sure he saw me swallow.

See, I said. It's fine. Go ahead and drink.

He reached out and seized the glass with both hands. It couldn't have been more than five seconds before the glass was empty again and he sat gasping and eyeing the rest of the bottle. Another, he said.

I took the Bible out of my back pocket and opened it to the passage I had chosen. He saw what book it was and shook his head. You can have another one in a little while, I said. First, there's something I want to read to you. You said you were a believer once, but that you had lost your faith. So I'm here to bring you back into the fold. Right now you're probably thinking I'm wasting my time. Maybe you even feel sorry for me. Well, brother, I feel sorry for you too. Cause whether you'll admit it or not, you were a prisoner long before you showed up at our door. You're a prisoner of your own sin and arrogance. But I know someone who can set you free. Someone you used to know before you started down the path of darkness.

It pleased me for the most part to hear how I sounded. Seemed like I was doing at least as good a job as any of the priests or missionaries they talked about in church, the ones out there in the world spreading the Word to the desolate places far from Christendom. At the same time, I understood it didn't matter how I felt about my ministerial abilities, that the only thing that would save either of us was how he felt. And to be fair, he did look at me for a long time with what appeared to be thoughtful consideration. Then he burst out laughing.

Go ahead and laugh, I said. We both know there was a time when you weren't too high and mighty to believe. There was a time when faith still meant something to you.

He drained the last transparent drops from the bottom of the glass, keeping his eyes on me all the while. If you knew what it took for me to stop believing, he said, you wouldn't have much faith either. In God or anything.

You're wrong. Faith isn't about being free from pain. It's about being strong enough to handle pain when it comes.

Right. That's why you're extorting me with a bottle of cheap Shiraz. Because faith is so attractive on its own.

I gave you one glass because I knew you wouldn't listen to a word

I said without it. And I'll give you another if you agree to listen some more.

He slid his feet off the covers and sat forward on the edge of the bed. The chain went lax, settling in small coils across the floor. Go on, then, he said. Tell me the good news. Show me what I've been missing.

I set my finger on the page and began to read.

He entered Jericho and was passing through. And there was a man called by the name of Zaccheus. He was a chief tax collector and he was rich. Zaccheus was trying to see who Jesus was, and was unable because of the crowd, for he was small in stature. So he ran on ahead and climbed up into a sycamore tree in order to see Him, for He was about to pass through that way. When Jesus came to the place, He looked up and said to him, Zaccheus, hurry and come down, for today I must stay at your house. And he hurried and came down and received Him gladly. When they saw it, they all began to grumble, saying He has gone to be the guest of a man who is a sinner. Zaccheus stopped and said to the Lord, Behold, Lord, half of my possessions I will give to the poor, and if I have defrauded anyone of anything, I will give him back four times as much. And Jesus said to him, Today salvation has come to this house, because he, too, is a son of Abraham. For the Son of Man has come to seek and to save that which is lost.

I closed the book and looked up at the prisoner's blank face. He was holding the empty glass out in front of him, ready to accept a refill the moment it was offered.

You understand why I chose this passage? I asked. Course you do. You're a smart guy. The message should be clear to you. Zaccheus was a sinner and a cheat, but Jesus gave him the chance to redeem himself. But first Zaccheus had to prove that salvation meant more to him than money. He had to humble himself, and offer retribution, before he could truly be saved.

The prisoner nodded. Indeed, he said. And I suppose in your reading of the story, I'm the sinner. I'm Zaccheus, and you're one of the people I've tried to cheat.

I took up the bottle and started to pour. This time I gave him three-quarters of a full glass, more or less, and watched him empty it all the faster. How would you have me read it instead?

Well. For starters, I'd say you should look at your own house before you presume to judge me. How much attention did you pay to this story before I showed up? Did you ever read it and wonder what Jesus thinks of you and your family living here in a house while your pickers are forced to stay in the state camp down the road? Sounds to me like you should sell the land to Russert and give the money to the poor folks around here. Or do you only bother with the Bible when it suits your own needs?

You don't know what you're talking about. We're not rich. Even when Dad was alive, we were just barely getting by from year to year.

Am I supposed to feel sorry for you? Is that what you expect from me? When you've got me chained up like a rabid dog?

I expect a little gratitude. For the wine, at least.

Right. Gratitude is the first step. First you do these small favors for me until I feel indebted to you. Then you work your Catholic guilt over me until I start sympathizing with you. Before long, I'll be saying grace at the dinner table with the rest of the so-called family, and you'll have a case of Stockholm Syndrome on your hands so classic you could publish an article about me in a leading psychiatric journal.

That's way out of line.

Sure. Deny it. As if you didn't realize the significance of what you were doing, bringing wine and a Bible in here and preaching to me about redemption.

I thought it might do your soul some good to be reminded of the word of God. If I'd known you were going to be so paranoid about it, I wouldn't have bothered.

The good of my soul. Is that what the story was supposed to make me think about?

So what if it was? It's not like you couldn't learn a thing or two from Zaccheus. Don't you see something of yourself in him?

The prisoner laughed. Hardly, he said. I should think an entrepreneur like me would have very little in common with a tax collector.

He raised his glass for another refill. I looked at the glass and held my breath and let the breath out slowly. I'd sworn I wasn't going to let him provoke me this time, even if it meant turning the other cheek as he took massive shit all over the Scriptures. All over me and my faith. I grabbed the bottle by the neck and stuck it right into the milky white palm of his other hand. Pour it yourself, I said, and retreated back down the hallway.

Ellie was seated at the kitchen table with her mother, scraping bits of meat and sauce from her plate with a steel spoon. She looked at me as I sat down. Since the attack, the bruises on her neck had faded to a shade of yellowish brown that at times seemed to blend together with the color of her hair, making them less painful for me to look at.

How'd the sermon go, padre? she asked. I was listening outside the door. I heard you preaching to him.

I folded my arms over the table. In the seat beside me, Sandra was quietly patching a rip in one of Gracie's nightgowns. She appeared comfortable with a needle and thread, though it still made me uneasy seeing her up and about after what she'd tried to do, let alone with a sharp object in her hand. He's a hard case, I said. I tried everything I could to be civil to him, but it's like he's searching out ways to be difficult. Like the only joy he can find is in antagonizing me.

What did you expect? You must have known he wasn't going to drop to his knees and repent after one Bible lesson. You could have read him the whole book cover to cover and it still wouldn't have done any good. His heart's frozen against it.

So is yours. Maybe you should try talking to him.

Oh, no. If I go in there and lose my temper, there's a chance one of us might not make it out alive. You saw the way I was when we took Jennifer down. I can handle some things with a cool head, and other things I can't. I really can't.

I know. I remember.

She nodded and proceeded to take the paper plate up by the rim and lick the remaining sauce like a cat lapping up the last bits of food in its bowl. That whole business with Jennifer felt like an episode from the distant past, even though it had occurred only a day before our tussle on the porch steps. Ellie had stayed up all night by her mother's side, and by the next morning she was stumbling from room to room in a state of hostile anxiety, snapping at everyone and anything and making the whole household nervous along with her. Looking back on it, she was bound to let loose on somebody that week, so I was glad it happened to the person on the farm who deserved it most. It was Beth who brought her betrayal to our attention, who found the phone and smuggled it from one house to the other so we could inspect it firsthand.

There's only one number saved on it, she'd said, and the area code is from somewhere on the coast.

There are times when the people in your family surprise you, when their response to a situation defies everything you've come to expect from them, though not necessarily in a bad way. For me, that moment came when Ellie stood and rose up out of the ashes of her mother's depression and went marching across the yard to bring war down upon the heads of Jennifer and her two trembling brats. It's almost comical, seeing a hundred-pound girl pulling a grown woman out the door by her hair. Almost. Until you hear the shrieks of the older woman, and the wailing of her kids and parents beside her, and you have to run up and restrain your sister from doing something she might regret. The rest of the family, meanwhile, had already gathered outside, ready to judge the situation for themselves according to who was really in the right.

Who are you going to believe? Jennifer asked, circling round with her arms outstretched. This girl's crazy! She's an unstable lunatic just like her mother!

She tried to sew discord among us, right up to the end. But the weight of evidence against her was damning. Will and Logan moved her personal belongings out from the house while me and Ellie stood guard over the seething, indignant Judas. They took care not to damage the kids' stuff, but as for Jennifer's expensive wardrobe, they showed no concern, dumping one pile of clothes after another into the trunk of her car, unfolded and unstowed. With as long as it took to send them on their way, our combined rage had all but fizzled out by the end, leaving only guilt and uncertainty to take its place. The look on her kids' faces was the hardest thing to bear. All of history contained within those two pouting mugs. Someday they would think back on what had happened that day like exiled aristocrats dreaming of the old country, remembering us only as the vicious rebels who had driven them from their homes, while our little brothers and sisters, in turn, would be brought up with stories about how their self-proclaimed betters had once tried to swindle them. An entire branch of the family tree, hacked off in one clean stroke. And their crime was still less severe than what the prisoner was guilty of.

I guess I'll have to keep handling him on my own, I said. Though I'd feel a lot better if we could reach an understanding about what needs to be done. One way or another, we've got to end this soon, before it gets any more out of hand.

Ellie leaned an elbow on the table and propped her head up with her hand. Agreed, she said. But if reason won't work, and faith won't either, then we're not left with a whole lot of options. I don't like to say it, but it might be better if we don't give ourselves too much time to think on it, or we might become so paralyzed with doubt that we never reach a decision.

I could take care of it. Even now, I believe I could make myself do it, for the good of family. But I need to know if you can handle it. Knowing I did something like that for you.

She looked across the table at her mother, who was working so contentedly at her stitching you'd have sworn she had earplugs in. She didn't, though, and probably wouldn't have used them no matter what grim subjects we discussed. All those years married to Dad, she must've learned to drown out what she didn't want to hear. Same as the rest of them.

I wouldn't starve myself out of guilt, if that's what you mean, Ellie said. All the same, though, I'd like to avoid it if there's a way. You said it yourself, bad things happen to people who go down that path. Karma has a way of balancing the scales.

Karma is a pagan lie. It's not something we need to worry about.

As Ellie stood up from the table, I thought at first that she was going to carry her soiled plate to the trash bin. It wasn't until she'd been standing a few seconds that I noticed the look on her face and turned to see what she was seeing, though I was in no way prepared for what was there when I saw it. Dawn stood trembling under the aura of the florescent kitchen light, soft tears falling down her face. The prisoner stood directly behind her, one arm across her waist, the other pressing the sharp point of the corkscrew into her jugular. The chain trailed behind him back into the hallway. He must've used the corkscrew to pry one of the bars on the bed rail loose. Sandra dropped her sewing to the floor. I stood and stepped forward and spread my arms out to signal her and Ellie to keep back.

Not another step, he said. Where is it? Where are you keeping it?

Keeping what?

The car. The one I drove here. Where are you hiding it?

Who says we're hiding it?

Right. Like you'd really keep a Lexus out front for all the pickers to see.

I closed my eyes and opened them again. I breathed out slowly. The butcher knife was resting on the counter not five feet behind them, its blade held in a scabbard of sauce and hard white grease. I felt like the sheriff from one of the shows we liked to watch, talking calmly to the armed madman when all I wanted was to get a clear shot. It's in a supermarket parking lot, I said. Few miles up the road. It's safe there. We just checked on it this morning.

Lot of good it does me there, he said.

His dark eyes were always shifty, but now they were zipping around like two trapped squirrels searching for a path to freedom, and growing more desperate as they failed to find one. Dawn, on the other hand, appeared the model hostage. In spite of her tears, the rest of her face was marked by the most serene, albeit vacant, stillness. Clearly she was somewhere far away, deep inside that hidden place girls and women go to when they can't control what happens to their bodies and things get too awful to handle.

All right, he said. Here's what you're going to do. You're going to bring me the satellite phone I had on me when I first arrived. You have exactly one minute to find it before I start drawing blood. One minute. You hear me?

I got it, I said, and I moved to pass through the rest of the kitchen and into the hallway. But then he took several steps back, pulling Dawn's limp body along with him.

No. Not you. You. He gestured to Ellie with the tip of his chin. You get it, he said. Sixty seconds, starting now.

Ellie stood still, watching him, before the ticking of the clock began to weigh on her and she rushed off down the hall with her bare toes scraping the carpet. The prisoner moved himself and Dawn to the side of the kitchen, putting more space between them and the counter. If I could find a way to get a hold of the knife, I was sure that overpowering him would be easy. He may have been older than me, and crazy to boot, but he was still a soft-ass from the city, and two weeks tied to a bed hadn't made him any harder. The problem, of course, was Dawn, and how close I could hope to get before he made good on his threat. As it was, the point of the corkscrew was pressed in tight against her windpipe, in such a way that it wouldn't have taken more than a knee-jerk flinch on his part to break the skin. Slowly I raised my hands above my head.

You're not going to do this, I said. You're not going to hurt her.

He smiled. I warned you about underestimating me, he said. Your sister has thirty seconds and then the whore gets skewered.

Don't call her that.

You mean you don't know? This girl was a regular old harlot before Dad lifted her up. Spent more time on her knees than a Catholic convert.

I kept my eyes on him, if only to keep from giving myself away by glancing at the knife. All this time I could've guessed what Dawn's past was like even without being told. It never bothered me, really, in the same way I refused to let Mom's past bother me, shameful as it was. Ellie once accused me of using the pain of the women around me to serve my own vanity. She may have been right. But now all I could think of was finding a way to free Dawn from the grasp of the vengeful madman in front of me. The point of the corkscrew had moved slightly, revealing a wine-red mark on the flesh where it once had rested. I was so tense I didn't notice Sandra approaching from behind me.

Please, she said. Her voice was more than a whisper but less than anything else. You don't have to do this. Whatever problems we have, it's not worth hurting an innocent person.

Innocent? He asked the question without sarcasm, as if the mere fact that she'd use the word was baffling and fascinating to him. No, he said. She's not innocent. You all knew I was chained up back there. Someone has to pay, one way or another.

The shot rang out so suddenly, me and Sandra both jumped back and bumped our thighs against the side of the table. His collapse was immediate—he didn't even have time to react until he was already on the floor. His screams filled the kitchen as Ellie came in from the hallway. She discharged the empty shell and planted the butt of the rifle squarely on the linoleum and kicked the corkscrew to the corner. Then she turned to Dawn.

Are you all right?

Dawn was shaking in Sandra's arms. Now that the danger had passed, the realization of just how close it had come seemed to be hitting her all at once. I can't, she said. I can't stand it. I won't be threatened like this. Not here.

You won't be, Ellie said. Not ever again. She looked at me, then, to see how I was doing. It's embarassing to admit, but my mouth was hanging open. She nodded to the space on the floor where the prisoner lay writhing. See what the damage is, she said.

I grabbed the knife off the counter and used it to cut away the section of pant leg where the bullet had gone through. More blood than I had ever seen was pouring from the wound. Tears streamed down the prisoner's face as he completed his final transition from villain to victim.

Help me, he said. I'm dying. Dear God, I'm really dying.

You're not dying, I said. The bullet tore through the side of your calf. It's not pretty, but it's a flesh and muscle wound.

I won't say it wasn't a let-down, and in fact I think he could hear the disappointment in my voice as I gave the diagnosis. Pretty soon most of the extended Temple family was crowding into our kitchen at the same time. Ellie, Beth, and Katie all worked at comforting Dawn while Sandra kept watch over the little ones in the living room. Logan helped me fashion a tourniquet of sorts out of dish towels and a leather belt and together with Will we managed to get the prisoner onto his feet and lead him back down the hall to his room. Mom scowled as he hobbled by. Desgracia, she said. It was the first time I'd heard her use the word.

The prisoner was bawling so uncontrollably it seemed doubtful to me that it could've all come from the pain in his leg. Maybe this was the worst thing that ever happened to him, I don't know. Since arriving at the farm he'd been struck in the face, bashed over the head, and chained to a rail like an animal. But something about the loss of blood really triggered something in him. He was shivering as we laid him out on the bed.

Go get some hot water and the first aid kit, I said. We'll do the best we can to clean it up.

A few squirts of iodine and a bandage roll later and the wound was sterile enough to leave unattended. I almost forget to refasten the chain to the bed, not that it would have made much difference. We took his bloodied bed sheets and left him whimpering in solitude.

Get some rest, I said at the door. I'll be back later with dinner.

Will and Logan gave me strange looks on the way back up the hall. I didn't blame them. Though they trusted me with the responsibility of a situation neither of them wanted to be saddled with, their patience had been shallow since Ellie's bruises first appeared. Now the well was all but dry.

There's a lot of space out there in the orchards, Logan said.

Yep, Will said. Hundred and twenty acres. Whole lot of space.

Space enough to where you could lose something out there and never find it again.

Lose it under the soil and it's gone for good.

Bury it deep enough and it's like it never existed.

Ain't that the truth.

Yep.

I nodded along with their insinuations, but refused to commit myself to anything aloud. Back in the kitchen, Beth and Sandra were mopping up the blood, leaving damp bright streaks of red across the linoleum. I took Ellie's arm and led her away from the group of women and secured us a private space to talk in the pantry. She still had the rifle with her, propped up at her side with her hand around the barrel, keeping it steady. Months ago, when we were still getting to know each other, I would've teased her and called her a lesbian and demanded that she give it back to me right away. Now I could've given a rat's ass about any of it. My priorities had finally been put in order.

Is he really going to make it? she asked.

The wound's shallow but it's wide, I said. It's liable to get infected. He'll need stitches for it to heal properly.

Yeah, but he's not getting any. There's no point in trying to find a doctor. Not now.

Ellie nodded. You're right, she said. There's no going back from it. No way we could ever feel safe with him around.

I'm glad you feel that way, I said. And I understand why you couldn't do it yourself.

Believe me. I would've if I could. But I was afraid of hitting Dawn by mistake. His leg was the only part of him that was open. Otherwise I'd have dropped him right then and there. Never thought I'd be able to do it. But seeing Dawn like that erased all doubt from my mind. We've got to take care of this before he destroys us all. You were right. You were right all along.

Gratifying as it was to hear her praise me in earnest, instead of with her usual sarcastic double-edge, I couldn't bring myself to enjoy any of it. No, I said. I was never anything but talk. If I'd been able to handle the meaning of the thing, I'd have done it when I had the chance.

Don't blame yourself for that. There was nothing you could do. He was too quick.

I had the shot. I had him on his back with the barrel on his chest. But he took a good look at me and knew I'd never go through with it. He knew I was scared shitless about what it would mean for my soul.

Let's not pretend like we know how he thinks. We've been burned twice already.

I need you to do me a favor.

Of course. Anything.

I need you to give me a couple more days with him. Before I carry it out.

What for?

I'm going to keep reading to him from the Bible. I'm going to try to save him before I set his spirit loose.

Christ. What's the point if you're just going to kill him?

Everything. That's the point. If I'm going to take a life, then I have to know I gave him a fair chance to be redeemed. Or else I'll wonder about it forever, and it'll tear me up inside.

She looked at me with her lips slightly parted and her tongue drawing compulsive circles over the roof of her mouth. If she tried to keep the rifle away from me, then she'd have to be the one to take care of the problem, and then before long her own thoughts would get to her, and she'd be the one in need of saving. That was my figuring, anyway, as she pondered my request, moving her cold eyes over me, like doubting Thomas looking for nail marks.

I don't understand you, she said. You're my brother, but I don't understand you.

I know, I said. But I'm asking you, as a brother, even though you don't understand me, to trust that this is something I have to do.

All right. I can do that. Work your magic, padre. See if you can make a miracle happen.

There's only one person who can make miracles happen, I said. And right now I'm hoping he loves Mexicans.

We each came out of the pantry carrying a bottle of wine in one hand and a pair of glass Mason jars in the other. Whatever qualms the widows had about us drinking were rendered moot by our introduction to the world of violence. We passed the afternoon sipping wine from jars right beside our mothers. No one said much of anything on any topic. We drank wine and stared at the walls and tried to ignore the groans of pain echoing softly from the far end of the hall.

And I have seen my father drunk and uncovered, the pale immensity of him turning pink in the heat of the sun. And I have tried to turn my head away and be respectful and ignore the wine soaking into his whiskered chin. My brothers will never know the shame and fear our father could cause in a child's tender heart. To them he is already a shade and a memory, who can do no more harm to anyone. Absence makes the heart grow fonder, and there's no greater absence than death. But to me he will always be close, terribly close, close and not forgotten. No, never that. And I have felt his breath on my neck from time to time when I'm alone. And I have heard his voice in the high narrow halls of our house, in places he never walked except that I walked there and he walks with me. Always with me. But if I am cursed then every part of me is cursed. My family is cursed and my nation, too, and even he, the curser, will feel the burden of his cursing words in time. A snake eating its own tail, a bear killing its cubs to keep the sow in heat. And I have been desperate in body and heart. And I have fallen for the fickle and depraved.

• • •

Chris taught me about killing before he taught me about shooting. The first time we went out into the orchards, he only brought one rifle. We walked along the edge of the fence posts and out past the end of the property line and onto the neighbor's parcel. A brown hawk glided high overhead, rising effortlessly on the slope of the wind. Chris planted the rifle butt against his shoulder and dislodged the safety and fired a single shot into the air. The hawk seemed to shrink inside itself before rolling over and falling already dead through the barrier of leaves and creaking branches that separated sky from earth. Chris reset the safety and looked at me.

You think you could do that yourself?

I nodded.

All right then, he said. But we're going to start you off on glass bottles, work your way up to targets that move and breathe.

A bird doesn't look that hard to hit.

It's not, if all you want to do is take it down. But I'm going to show you how to go for the clean kill each time, and that starts with practicing your aim.

The clean kill?

He pressed two fingers to the base of his throat. Through the neck, he said. That way you won't have to deal with having a wounded animal on your hands. It's less important for birds, but a bigger animal can make a real mess if you don't put it down clean on the first shot. You get what I'm saying?

I nodded again.

All right then. I've got some bottles here in my pack. You count off twenty paces in that direction while I set them up. And try to keep each step the same distance.

He followed his own advice, positioning each bottle in the center of the post so they were all spread out evenly along the top of the fence. I would've recognized Mom's brands of wine anywhere, but it didn't stop me from firing when I was ordered to shoot. The first two shots sailed high, but then Chris adjusted the sight for me and afterward I hit four in a row, three dead-center through the labels. He brought out more bottles and had me try it again from fifty and a hundred paces, instructing me all the while about holding my grip steady and the difference between squeezing and pulling. On the final series I hit two bottles through the base and knocked another off its post without breaking it. Chris seemed pleased with the quick progress I was making. He reached over and touched my shoulder and squeezed it gently.

It'll take more practice for you to really get comfortable with it, he said. But you're on track to become one hell of a marksman, I can already tell.

I hope so, I said. Can we come out here again tomorrow?

If you like. But do me a favor. Don't tell your mother about the bottles I got out of her recycling bin. I know she likes to turn them in for the deposit.

Don't worry. I won't say anything.

Thanks. You're a good man. Proud of you.

He smiled and took a cigarette from his shirt pocket and lit it with a match. He took one drag and held it out for me to accept. No harm in it, he said. Long as you don't make it a habit.

I held the burning cylinder between my fingers and breathed smoke into my lungs for the first time. I tried not to cough, but I couldn't help it. As much as Dad enjoyed his cigars, he was never around enough for me to get used to them. I took a second drag, this time without inhaling, and passed the rest back to Chris. Thanks, I said. Wasn't as bad as I thought it would be.

Chris smiled. Nothing ever is, he said.

He swung the rifle over his shoulder and started leading us back out the way we came. Now I had two secrets to share with him. I liked that, having a secret to hold onto with an adult. Sometimes it felt like everything I did was under the scrutiny of the older generation. If not Dad himself, then Mom, the teachers, the administrators, the priests, and all the clerks and busybodies in between. So having someone older around who knew how to do things, and was eager to teach them to me, and who confided in me like I was a grown man myself—it meant a lot to me. Maybe more than the shooting itself.

Next time we'll try out some live targets, he said as we crossed back into the vineyard. You really impressed me today with how fast you caught on.

Thanks, I said. It felt good hitting the mark.

Always does, son. Always does.

The orchards became our private hunting ground, a poor man's country club where the only leisure activity available involved pitting our skills and brains against the survival instincts of whatever smaller creatures came before us. Squirrels, gophers, hawks, even the occasional lanky brush rabbit. All that fell within our sights were taken down, through the neck, a clean kill to rid our lands, or at least the neighbor's lands, of whatever minor nuisance the animals were capable of provoking. The first time I saw a coyote in the distance, slapping its flat paws on the gravel with its snout low to the ground, the rifle almost leapt out of my hands, I was so excited. From the shady blind of overgrowth I was in, I turned the bolt and drove a bullet straight into the chamber. But Chris stopped me before I could discharge the safety and send the bullet on ahead to do its work.

You don't have it, he said, lowering the barrel with his outstretched hand. From this distance all you could do is wing it. Best case scenario it'll take off running, and then bleed out a mile down the road. You don't want it that way. Trust me.

I set my eyes on the dirt beneath us. Without having to see, I knew my opportunity had come and gone, that the coyote had scampered back behind the safety of the tree cover, oafishly unaware of how close it came to being fired upon.

What if I don't get another chance like this? To catch a coyote in the open?

Then you don't get another chance, he said. That'll happen more than once in life. The best you can do is make peace with the loss and try to hold out hope for something better.

Is that what you did after you deserted the Army? You hoped for something better?

He looked at me with a mix of anger and surprise, which made sense, I suppose, given how rarely I resorted to talking back to him. I wanted that coyote, damn it, and now it was gone, and in my resentment I forgot myself, and how easy it would've been for him to pack up the rifles and tell me never again. But instead he looked off into the distance at whatever point on the horizon he liked to fixate upon. The rings under his eyes were red and dry and scaled with dust from so many hours in the vineyard. He licked his lips and began to speak without turning.

There was no hope left in those days, he said. For a while we lived like animals. We took whatever we wanted, and measured the right and wrong of a situation by how strong we were compared to the other party. Some still live that way even now. You give up on the little things, the little rules you set for yourself, and you'll forget the big ones too in time. That's why we go for the clean kill. Because it's a short walk down the road to savagery.

He put his hand to his nose and smelled the stink of tobacco on his fingers. I couldn't tell, from where I sat, whether he was talking to me like I was a child or full-grown man. All I knew was that I had spoiled the mood somehow, as I was bound to do, and now the guilt of a hundred glaring priests was bearing down on me at once without Chris even having to look me in the eye. His words were enough.

I could do some wicked things, I said. If I wasn't careful, I could be a pretty bad guy.

I expected him to laugh at me for talking tough, but instead he nodded his head and leaned in closer under the shade of the dry grass thicket. So could I, he said. Ain't we a pair?

When I looked out again at the strip of clearing, the coyote was nowhere to be seen, and the sun was beginning its final blazing descent into the Pacific a whole world away. As if beholden to some similar, cosmic time piece, Chris stood and came out from behind the thicket with the rifle perched sideways across his forearms. He started walking away, not back toward the vineyard the way we came in, but farther out into the border edges that our neighbor's parcel shared with two others just like it. I followed. I wiped the dirt from my pantlegs and jogged after him and kept the pace alongside him all the way to the end of the trail. My legs were half-asleep from crouching so long. I didn't let it show.

You want to check out the orchard across the road?

He kept on walking at the same pace. Some other time, he said. Just got one thing left to do before we head back. Won't take but a minute.

We walked through a gap in the tree line and out through the other end and walked down a dirt trail bordered on both sides by the deep-cut and hardened tread lines of two massive truck tires. At the end of the trail, we came upon the concrete bank of a waterway that had been dug out and paved long before I was born. All over the valley, the old American irrigation ditches lay dry except for a few repurposed channels the new authorities saw no point in letting go to waste. Two feet of black water flowed hurriedly along the floor of the ditch, driven onward by some change in elevation too imperceptible for human eyes to detect. Chris sat on the edge of the bank and tore his boots off one after the other and lay them upsidedown against his pack. His socks were soiled brown and sported gaping holes on both heels.

You going for a swim?

Chris started to undo his shirt buttons. I'm washing up, he said. Suggest you do the same if you plan to sit at your mother's dinner table.

He had a point and I knew it. By any civilized standard, we were filthy beyond tolerance. All afternoon the sweat on our skins had sealed the drifting dust in our pores and built up a muddy residue behind our ears and in our ass cracks. Laying his shirt over the concrete, Chris revealed a chest covered in sweat-matted hair and two thick biceps split in half by what the white boys called a farmer's tan. Tattoo across his right pectoral, insignia of some forgotten unit of an army of a nation that no longer existed.

Got some soap in my bag, he said. Reach in and get it, will ya?

I bent down and unzipped the pack and removed a crumpled zip-loc baggie containing the eroded slivers of two soap cakes. When I stood up again, Chris had his pants off and was taking his first steps into the water below. His pale thighs clenched at the coldness of it, but he knelt down all the same and splashed some over his face and shoulders. Then he turned and looked at me, naked as the day he was made, and motioned for me to join him.

We got to make this fast, he said. Your mother's liable to start worrying.

I held the baggie between my teeth and pulled off my shoes and socks. The heat of the ground against my bare soles was all the moti-vation I needed to get in. And once I was standing with the icy water racing past my legs, I didn't think about what we looked like, standing together as we were, like a couple of Edenites basking in our own igno-rance. I let out my breath and opened the baggie. Chris reached in and grabbed one of the slivers and started soaping himself. He laughed as I turned my back to him.

It's nothing I ain't seen before, he said. Quit fooling around and get to work. We both smell like ass, whether you notice or not. Wouldn't feel right bringing you home in such a state. Your mother would never forgive me.

I backed away from the edge and turned and bent down to wet the soap. As I started in on my chest and armpits, I tried to keep my eyes on the water and its dizzying current and undertow. Sprigs of yellow grass growing up through cracks in the cement floor, bending with the flow of the water without yielding root. But gradually the sounds of Chris' lathering drew my gaze until finally we stood facing each other, suds and scum leaking down our legs, with the high sun already bringing out the color in places that normally never saw its light. While I had barely begun to peel away the layer of grime on my own body, Chris was work-ing himself over with the soap like he hadn't had a real good scrub in months. He left no spot untreated, starting from the ridge of his freck-led shoulders and moving down across his stomach and into the hairy pockets of his inner groin. It was the first time I'd seen anyone besides my brothers bathing, and even more exhilarating than the sight of him was the awareness that he was watching me too.

It's okay, he said. We're not breaking any rules out here. We're just a couple of soldiers in the bush, doing the best we can. Am I right?

Yeah. You're right.

Good. Now don't forget the back of your neck. Lot of dirt builds up there.

When we'd finished rinsing off, we climbed back up to the bank and sat there for a while drying in the sun and not saying much. We slipped our clothes and shoes back on and started walking back toward the vineyard with wet dirt sloshing inside of our socks. It took me a while to get over the feeling that I was in trouble of some sprt, that despite the soap and water I was somehow even dirtier now than before. I couldn't help but think of Dad standing over me with the swab in his hand, and what he would've said if he could've seen me there in the ditch. Or what Mom would've said for that matter. Or Father Ramsey. I'd always known, in one way or another, that I wasn't the natural goody-goody the nuns and teachers doted on, that any goodness I hoped to exemplify would have to be done in spite of my nature and not because of it. But still, I always tried to keep my sinful tendencies in-check, and if from time to time I wandered off into the orchards, it was always on my own. No one had ever seen that side of me till now.

Chris must've known something was up, cause he slowed his pace and set his hand between my shoulder blades. You impressed me with how you handled yourself today, he said. You got more sense than a lot of the hunters I've known. And they were grown men.

Thanks. I hope to keep getting better.

I know you do. That's why I want you to have my spare rifle.

I stopped walking and turned to look at him. What do you mean you want me to have it?

Chris smiled. I mean it's yours, he said. It's a pain in the ass keeping them both hidden from the camp managers, and all I really need is the one anyway. I'd rather it go to somebody who'll get some use out of it. And it looks like that somebody's you.

I don't know what to say.

Shit, say yes. That .22 was made before disbandment. I'd have killed to have a weapon like that when I was your age.

I looked down at the rifle and turned it over in my hands and felt a new sense of wonder about it simply because it was now my own. For my last four birthdays, Dad had gotten me the same thing—shoes. They weren't fancy or unique or engineered for sports, they were just plain black sneakers for day to day use. But far more important than the shoes themselves was the fact that they were new. How many of your classmates have new shoes every year? he asked after the second pair. How many boys around here can feel proud of the things their parents give them to wear? Of course he had never been to my school in person or seen any of my classmates in the flesh. If he had, he would've known that every family in the valley bought their kids new shoes once a year for the same reason he thought it was important to do so. Now, after four years of walking with my father alongside me, of feeling his callousness with each step I took, it was amazing to be given a gift that actually made me happy, regardless of the circumstances that had preceded the giving.

This is the best present I've ever gotten, I said. I'm going to hold on to it forever.

That's good to hear, Chris said. But hey, do me a favor. If your mother asks, tell her I loaned it to you for practice. It's not registered, and I'm afraid she might not want it in the house if she found out.

You want me to lie to her again?

No, just keep it open-ended. Tell her what she wants to hear. You get me?

Yeah. I get you.

He started walking again. Good, he said. Now let's pick up the pace. Getting late.

I kept the rifle in my closet, at the bottom of a duffle bag full of old clothes that were too small for me but not yet big enough for Sebastian.

I took it out from time to time when I was alone, to clean and polish the barrel, or just to look at it and admire the deadly simplicity of its design. And of course I took it out in the afternoon to go hunting with Chris, to follow him in search of whatever prey we could find, which never seemed to grow beyond small birds and brush critters no matter how skilled I became at tracking.

I looked for the coyote. Every time we were out there, on the edge of the clearing where I first saw him, or in the stone fruit labyrinth across the road, I fixed my gaze far into the distance, just in case he might show. But he never did. It got to where I questioned whether I'd actually seen him it all. He had come into my mind and laid his bony tracks and then disappeared without yielding a second chance. I didn't know what I'd do if I ever got him, if I'd try to have him stuffed like some wealthy sports-man, or if I'd simply stand over him a while reflecting on what I'd done and then leave the hairy carcass to rot. With hunting or with anything else, I never thought about what I'd do after the prize had been won. I knew there were some Christians who thought often about heaven and the glory that awaited them when they got there. But I could only focus on the journey, and all the pitfalls that awaited me along the way.

We continued bathing together in the irrigation ditch. Either Mom never put two and two together, and never questioned my wet hair and cleanliness at the end of the day, or she figured there was noth-ing strange about two men washing together and didn't think to say anything. Not that there was anything strange about it, in that sense. Another couple of years and I'd be showering with up to fifteen boys at a time in the locker room after wrestling practice. Somehow, though, no matter how comfortable we became around each other, there was an uneasiness between Chris and me. It always felt like he was egging me on, pushing me to strip away even more layers until he could see me for what I really was.

One time we were in the water with a fresh bar of soap, luxuri-ating in the amount of lather it produced. The sun was so bright that every time I closed my eyes and opened them again the world seemed tinted blue like I was seeing it through colored glass. I noticed Chris had stopped scrubbing and was looking at me with his hands on his chest.

You're starting high school soon, yeah?

In the fall.

You got a girlfriend in your class?

I shook my head. No. I've never had one.

Right, he said. But I bet you still get a little taste now and then.

I'm a Christian.

Does that mean your junk don't work?

It means I haven't done anything. With anyone.

Chris smiled. You got a nice cock for your age, he said. You're saying no girl's ever touched it or put it in her mouth? You're saying you wouldn't want her to?

He looked at me as I stood, my arms and shoulders drying quickly in the burning light. For the first time since the first time, I turned so he couldn't see. I could hear him laughing behind me.

It's okay, he said. No shame here.

There were other incidents after that where Chris overstepped his bounds or spoke too crudely and made me feel dirty inside my own skin. I learned to do a better job of laughing it off, of making like I enjoyed the vulgarity he inflicted on me the way fat kids at school pretended not to mind the jokes played at their expense. We still went out hunting at least three times a week, so much that halfway through the summer Chris had to buy another bar of soap. Then, one Saturday in August, we packed a cooler full of sandwiches and drinks and headed out farther than we ever had before, out beyond the boundary of the main parcel tract and into the bare country on the outskirts of Reedley. We dropped a few crows we found perched on telephone lines, but no larger prey revealed itself. Toward midday we stopped and rested beside an abandoned irrigation pump and ate two avocado sandwiches apiece. Chris lit a cigarette and put his boots up on one of the pipes. He was in a relaxed mood. He shooed a mosquito off his thumb and watched it fly away and didn't wait to see if it returned.

Now that you know the basics of how to handle a weapon, he said, you can learn to hunt pretty much anything. Someday you should try your hand at hunting deer. Probably come away with a pretty nice buck.

I'd like to, I said. Been thinking about it since we first started practicing.

Should ask your father next time he's in town. He might know some rich folks who'd let you use their property up in the mountains.

I took a drink of water from the canteen and wiped my lips and sat with my head low between my shoulders. He's not much for the mountains, I said. But Mom might let us go camping sometime in the winter, when there's snow in the hills. You should try asking her.

Chris took his feet off the pipe. He stood and dusted off his pant legs. You're going to have to start making your own plans, he said. I'm heading out at the end of the month.

I rose to my feet slowly and came up close beside him. I could smell the cigarette smoke in his hair and on his skin and I could see the way he was trying to avoid looking me in the eye. Where are you going? I asked. What happened?

Nothing's happened, he said. Season's over. Job's finished. It's time to move on.

You're a foreman, I said. Mom should've talked to you about staying on through the winter. She should've asked for your help in seeing us through the cold months.

She did. She invited me to stay on straight through to next year's harvest. But I turned her down. I got enough saved up now to start the next leg of my journey. No sense sticking around here longer than I have to and making things complicated.

I looked at him with the beginnings of tears in my eyes. What did it mean to be complicated if our time in the orchards had been simple?

You've got no reason to be like this, I said. How can you just wander from one place to the next, changing the lives of the people you touch, and then leave without a second thought? How can you live like that?

That's how it is on the road, he said. You stay in a place for a while and make friends while you're there. Then you pick up and leave and maybe you see them again and maybe you don't. It's nothing personal. It's just the way it is. You get used to it. Trust me, you'll remember me more fondly after I'm gone. The heart appreciates distance. It's a forgetful little muscle.

He kicked the lid on the cooler shut and picked the cooler up by its handle. Suddenly it hit me that the hunt was over, that he was packing up to leave, and that this would be the last hunt we ever went on together.

You told me to stay at home, I said. You told me I had it good here, and I should think twice before leaving. Did you believe that? Did you ever mean any of the things you said?

You're my boss's son, he said. You really think I'm going to encourage you to run off?

No, I said. But you did other things with me you weren't supposed to do.

He set his hands at his sides and looked at me. Yeah, he said, and you did things you weren't supposed to do either.

I could tell on you. I could tell Mom about it.

Yeah. And I could tell her about the rifle.

I can't go back. Not now. How can I go back to the way things were? How I used to be?

You'll find a way, he said. You think it wasn't hard for me after the war? You think I never looked inside myself and felt completely alone? At least you have faith. I lost any faith I had a long time ago. And you've got your own rifle now. I won't deprive you of that. So buck up. It's not the end of the world.

He turned and started walking with the cooler swinging at his side. I followed after him, but didn't try to close the gap between us. Not the end of the world. Spoken only like someone of that generation could, the ones who awoke one morning to find the world they knew gone and still had to decide what to do about breakfast. I kept the rifle in the closet and told Mom he took it with him when he left. What he really took from me, I never told a soul.

How do we begin to build? How do we start over again when the blood inside our veins is tainted with betrayal? Poisoned by tragedy. Pain of trauma inherited through cellular memory. Indians knew it, heathens though they were. Cain and Abel never saw the garden, but they felt the sting of disobedience in their hearts, and knew it from their parents' stories. Probably why Cain couldn't work the soil worth a damn. Too much to live up too, too many expectations. Only the free can find favor in the fruits of their labor, and there's no freedom for a child burdened by a parent's broken dream. What must it have been like to grow up in that house, to hear of a world without pain where no one ever died and nakedness was a thing without a word and so it wasn't a thing at all? Father Ramsey used to talk about lost tribes in South America, about heathens in Africa who've never been blessed to hear the Word of God. Anecdotes of a world we'd never see filtered through the American accent of a middle-aged virgin. Some clueless boy would ask, Wouldn't it be better if they never heard the Word at all? At least then they'd be more likely to end up in Purgatory instead of receiving eternal damnation. And the old priest would bat his weary eyes and reply, Everyone deserves the opportunity to receive salvation. What good would it do sparing them the Word if it wound up costing them the chance to enter paradise? That was his answer to Adam's children. That was what we had to content ourselves with when our parents told us old stories about life in the garden.

I try to imagine what life was like back then. I tend to see it as full of contradictions, as a world where everyone was rich and happy and also addicted to crack. Tom Hanks and Eddie Murphy fighting terrorists in space while obese children starved to death. Dad never talked about that world. It was old and sad and complicated, and so it didn't concern me whatsoever. Mom talked about the mistakes they made back then, that whole generation living it up like the party would never end, dumb sluts popping champagne corks on the deck of a sinking ship.

Should've seen the sort of things we wore in public in those days, she'd say, shaking her head. You'd be ashamed of your mother if you could've seen her then.

Ashamed? Is that what you wanted? Is that what all this was for? Why do I have to learn from your mistakes, when I may have been one myself? Your pain and your shame are in my blood, they are my pain and my shame, too, but that's not all I feel. Here's what I've seen and what I know and what I remember. I was eight years old and it was January. Worst frost on record. Dad was gone, off wherever it was that he went. For three days the power was out and there was no butane left in the gas tank and the foremen were under emergency lockdown at the state camp. You'd dress me in sweaters each night at bedtime and pile me with extra blankets to keep the cold of morning from creeping in. You'd wake at dawn with the electric alarm broken and walk out into the vineyard with a hatchet stuck through the pocket of your mended winter coat. And by the time I awoke you'd have already hacked and gathered the grapewood and built a fire in the living room hearth and boiled water over the range to make the oatmeal and hot cocoa for my breakfast. That was you. That was your love. And on the fourth day, after the fuel truck came, I opened my eyes in the morning and missed the smell of woodsmoke in the house.

Was it blood that made you stay by me when all others went away? Was blood the only thing? Child, born of blood and agony, proof of maternity laid bare for all to see as soon as the head begins to crown. No swabs needed, no tests required. Is that why I was dear to you? Is that why he never had faith? I've tried... I've tried to be better than I am. That world you lost, the one that took my brother... I've tried to live up to all the good things you've told me about it, and shut out the wicked things as you shut out your past. But I'm not a fresh start for anyone. I was never such pure clean clay. My name was written somewhere before I was born, and blood won't help me with the task ahead. If I build, I build on a foundation of tears.

. . .

For two days and two fitful nights I stayed by the prisoner's side. For two days I tried reading to him from Scripture, alternating between various passages but coming back time and again to the part about Lazarus rising from the dead. The longer I delayed, the more unreachable he became. Unreachable and incoherent. I tried my best to keep his wound clean. Each morning I rinsed the area with warm water and iodine and applied fresh bandages to the cut. But still the wound began to fester. By the third morning he was running a fever so high he couldn't even sit up to take soup. From then on all he could do was lie on his back and suck ice cubes and empty his stomach irregularly into a tin bucket on the floor by his bed. The chain had already been pointless for some time, but now it just seemed absurd. The only way he was going anywhere was if someone carried him off. And if God wasn't going to step in and do it, then I knew exactly who the responsibility would fall to. Chris was right. The clean kill is best. A dying animal is nothing you want to have on your hands.

By day four I was almost as agitated as him. Katie had sent the pickers and foremen away indefinitely and the whole farm was at a standstill waiting to see what we did next. What I did. Ellie seemed especially worried, and had taken to bringing me soup in the back room just as I'd done for the prisoner up till then. I was skipping meals and she knew it, but most of all I think she wanted to keep an eye on me, and to see how close I was to declaring his soul lost. Truth was I didn't feel capable of holding out another night the way I was going. Not unless I wanted to aspire to martyrdom at such a young age. But all through the afternoon I kept reading to him from the Bible, unsure of whether he could understand me, and hearing in my voice an absence of conviction that troubled me more than anything except the killing left to be done.

Then Jesus raised His eyes, I said. And He said, Father, I thank You that You have heard Me. I knew that You always hear Me, but because of the people standing around I said it, so that they may believe that You sent Me.

He let out a groan and rolled onto his side with his hand clutching his stomach. It was more of a torture now than anything, keeping him alive. But still I hesitated, because I was afraid, and because I'd learned enough from my own readings of Scripture to know what marks may be branded on those who take up arms against their brothers. And he was my brother. That was the shit of it. That was what I couldn't get past. God help those who failed as their brother's keeper. I took the blanket from the corner of the bed and laid it over him and knelt by the corner of the bed where his head was resting.

Do you want some wine? Would that make you feel better?

He stirred slightly at the mention of it and then rolled onto his back with his face curled in disgust. Vodka, he said. Enough to put me out.

I'm sorry. We still don't have any vodka. It's hard to come by in these parts.

Doesn't matter, he said. Just stop looking at me.

What?

You heard me. I can feel your eyes on me every second of the day. Just stop it, please.

I shook my head and looked down at the carpet. You need to see a doctor, I said. You've needed one for a long time. I've been ungenerous with you until now. Just say you'll forget about us, about the farm, and I'll drive you into town myself. We can tell the people at the clinic it was a motorcycle accident. They won't make a stink about it. And you'll get the help you need.

He coughed violently into the bed sheets, his throat muscles convulsing with each strong hack. He shuddered and caught his breath and afterward he lay in such gentle stasis I was afraid he'd finally passed out. There's only one way out for me, he said. You know it as well as I do. So take your little farm boy gun and finish me off. Unless you haven't got the balls.

I stepped back and watched him from as much distance as the size of the room would allow. I'll do it, I said. I'll put you to rest. But on one condition. Confess your sins to me right now. Let me give you over to the other side with a conscience free of guilt.

The sounds of a dying man are troubling, but none more so than the sounds of his laughter. His body couldn't handle the stress of it, and after a few big chuckles he was back coughing into his sheets. Are you a priest now? he asked. Are you equipped to deliver last rites?

He was too smart for me, damn him. He knew I wasn't ordained to do anything more than offer him false comfort before the end. Any talk to the contrary was just Protestant optimism at its most weightless. I'm not equipped to do anything, I said. But who's to say what God hears and what he doesn't? If you unburden your soul to me now, before the end, I have to believe it would count for something. All this time you've been without God's love, you must've thought at least once about what you would do when you were on your deathbed, if you were called upon to repent.

Of course not, he said. I never imagined I'd be anywhere near a believer when it happened. I hoped to die alone, with a small empire to my name, leaving behind a jealous public, and a few close friends to scatter my ashes into the Golden Gate.

We'll bury you in the orchard and say a prayer over your grave, I said. That's the best we can do. I'm sorry, but you haven't left us many options. But you can still guard your soul against the doom of eternal damnation. You believed in it once. Why not now, here at the end?

He seemed to grow tender at the sound of my words. His eyes stayed shut for a good long while. Then he opened them again and cleared his throat and looked at me in a way he hadn't since the afternoon he first came to us, when he was the very picture of importance, and all his ugliness was still waiting to be revealed.

I'm not who I was when I was your age, he said with sweat shining across his forehead. I've done things you couldn't imagine. I know things that would leave you shattered.

I closed my Bible and crept closer to the side of the bed. My hands were shaking from a lack of sleep and from nervousness and from the sudden excitement of what he might say next. You sound ready, I said. You sound like you're ready to confess.

You're not a priest.

No, but I'm still your brother. We're brothers by blood, and brothers in Christ. That's about as good as we could hope for without having an actual priest around.

He wouldn't look me in the eye. Actually, he appeared to shift his body away, as well as he could in his weakened condition, anytime I fixed my gaze on him too long. You're not my brother, he said. Who fucked whose mother and who planted what seed don't mean anything in the grand scheme of things.

He was still talking smart, but I could tell the fever was draining his resistance. There was a careful desperation in the way he spoke, like a drunk man talking slowly to avoid slurring his words. Our father wasn't perfect, I said. But he was still our father. That's a truth bigger than anything we can hope to change. The same is true for us. We're still brothers. Blood is blood. The Lord decided it was so before any of us were made.

I killed our father. What does your God have to say about that?

I looked at him and smiled. You're trying to bait me, I said. But it won't work.

It's true, he said. I killed him. He was sick and I killed him. I pressed a pillow over his face until he stopped breathing.

Why are you saying this?

It's what you wanted. I just gave you my last confession.

That's not possible. He died of appendicitis. The doctors said so.

The doctors didn't look close enough. His appendix burst, but that's not what killed him. I tied him down and suffocated him with his own pillow. I did it. Me. Not God.

You weren't there. You couldn't have.

I was. I was there when his life gave out. I felt it leave him. Big man that he was, it was like feeling the air go out of an inflated cushion.

My eyes went cloudy. I took a step back and put my hand on the bookcase to steady myself. All the sleepless nights in that room had made it seem bigger than it was. But once I was against the wall, seeing the room in its entirety, I suddenly felt more claustrophobic than I had in my entire life. Even the smell of the place, that stifling smell of sickness and stale air, seemed to close off the space around me. I leaned over and swallowed the saliva rising up from the back of my tongue.

How could you do that? Your own father.

Don't pretend it's a mystery, he said. You knew him. You know what he was like.

It doesn't matter. You were his son. That's like the worst thing a person can do. I can't even think of anyone in the Bible who did something so evil.

Try a different religion, then. Look at the Greeks. That's how Zeus got his big break.

I used the edge of the bookcase to increase my forward momentum so that when I lunged forward it came as quite a jolt to his system. He started coughing again, but I wouldn't give him a chance to breathe. I was crouching over him with my face just a few inches above his.

Tell me, I said. Tell me how you could do it. What was it for?

Money, he said. I wanted money to start a new life. So I tracked him down and tried to squeeze some money out of him. But there was nothing there. He was broke except for the farms. So I killed him and went looking for what I was owed. That's how I ended up here.

I felt my hands closing in around his hot damp face. He was either too weak to resist me or he thought he deserved this. Or he didn't think he deserved it and he liked feeling unjustly persecuted. Whatever the case, I gripped his skull like I was preparing to crush it.

That was it? Money was the only reason?

He laughed. No, not really, he said. I'm smart and determined. If money was all I wanted, I could have gotten it some other way, and more easily too.

Then why? Why did you do it?

What's the use in talking to you? I couldn't make you understand why I stopped believing in God. How am I supposed to make you understand why I killed our father?

You're saying there's a connection between the two?

I guess. Although I never hated God as much as that.

You said you didn't believe in God.

I know. That's the trap I'm in. If you want to stop believing in God, then you really have to stop believing. You can't kill God, because once you kill something, you believe in it forever.

I don't understand.

That's all right. I never expected you to.

He turned his face away and closed his eyes. The shudder that ran through his neck and shoulders seemed to intensify the longer I stared at him. I would have done anything, he said. All my life I tried to get beyond you. I would have done anything just to be able to leave you behind.

Who are you talking to?

Don't look at me. For Christ's sake, just leave me in peace.

Who do you think I am?

Don't look at me. Don't look at me.

I could tell from the rising and falling of his chest that he was still with us. My rage seemed to rise and fall along with his breathing, replaced in the falling moments by a numbness that made the idea of what I had to do next seem a lot more bearable. He was the first confessed murderer I had ever met, and he said that belief and death went hand in hand. It would take me a long time to unravel what he meant, but for now there was nothing left for me to think about, except that I was finally ready to start believing in him.

Ellie was waiting in the hallway, just a few steps outside the door. I didn't ask how long she'd been there or what she wanted. I let her speak first.

Listen, she said. We've got a problem.

Where's the rifle?

In your room.

Bring it here. And make sure it's loaded.

Seriously? Now you're ready?

I don't have the time or energy to explain just this moment. Go get the rifle and bring it here, along with all the sheets and linens we can spare. Then get the little brothers and sisters out of the house. Your mother and Dawn too. They don't need to see it when we carry him out. We'll need Will and Logan's help for that now that I think of it.

That'd be a fine plan if you'd decided on it yesterday. But now we've got another situation to deal with.

Jesus. What now?

Come here.

She was practically on tiptoes leading me down the hallway. When we reached the end she poked her head around the wall and beckoned me to look as well. From the vantage point we were in I could just barely make out the form of someone, a man, sitting at the table with one leg crossed over the other. We stepped back from the wall and leaned in close enough to whisper.

He says he's a private investigator from the coast, Ellie said. He wouldn't say who sent him, but he says he's looking for our brother Elliot.

So tell him we don't know what he's talking about.

I tried that. He won't buy it. It's like he already knows we have him.

How could he know?

Maybe one of the pickers said something in town.

Or maybe he's trying to intimidate us cause we're kids.

Either way, I want you to find out how much he really knows and what he wants from us. We'll have a better idea what to do after we get a read on him.

What're you going to do in the meantime?

I'm going to get the rifle. I'll be right here, waiting and listening. You need backup, just give me a sign.

You like carrying that rifle around. I can tell.

Shut up and get in there.

I went into the kitchen and took a seat at the table. I was already sitting down before I got a clear look at the man who had surprised us with his unexpected appearance. Even more surprising, to me, was the fact that he was a Mexican, and a dark one at that. He was dressed like an old-fashioned vaquero, with his shirt collar done up in a bolo and detailed patterns pressed into the sides of his leather boots. He rested his hat on the table and brushed his fingers against the side of the band. His face wasn't as sun-worn and cragged as the faces of the some of the old-timers I knew, though in truth he didn't look quite as old as his clothes suggested. Somehow I never imagined a creature like him existing on the coast. In the back of my mind I must've known there were Mexicans in that part of the country, but I always pictured them as a pale and spiritless breed of charlatans, the kind of bit-part actors who could pass as white, Mexican, or Armenian whenever the situation suited them. This guy didn't strike me as that sort of animal, though. He tapped a paper cup in his hand and raised it to his mouth and filled it with juice from his packed lip.

Hello, he said. My name's Bob Ramirez. I'm a private investigator based out of Santa Cruz County. Although I do visit the valley on occasion when work requires it.

Is this one of those occasions?

Indeed it is. And your name is?

Anthony Temple.

Anthony Temple. All right, Anthony. Here's the thing. Four days ago I was in Delano, where I had a long conversation with Jennifer Temple regarding the whereabouts of Elliot Temple Jr., who's been missing for nearly a month now. She's been having a rough go of it lately. You know life on the road isn't easy for anyone, but especially for a single woman with two young children and her parents to look after.

What happened to Dale? Why isn't he helping her out?

Let's just say when the chips were down he proved to be less reliable than she thought.

Good. She can rot for all I care.

I thought you might say that, considering the circumstances by which you parted ways.

What did she tell you about that?

Everything. She told me everything, at least up to the point where she was expelled from the farm. She told me she and Elliot were conspiring to cheat you and yours out of a fair deal. She said Elliot was planning on coming back here the day he disappeared.

I don't know anything about that.

Before you start denying anything, listen to what I have to say. This isn't a shakedown. I'm not here as anything but a mediator. All I want is to see this situation resolved peaceably with each side getting what it's owed.

I'm sorry, Mr. Ramirez, but I have a hard time believing that. And an even harder time believing a peaceful solution is possible at this point.

I can understand that. That's why all I'm asking is for you to hear me out.

He reached into his jacket and produced a folded stack of papers and set it on the table beside his hat. The papers unfolded and lay still on the table. He looked at the papers and then at me and then he nodded unsmiling.

I've just come from the Russert Growers Company, he said. Mr. Russert's reconsidered his position and is willing to offer you all a new deal separate from the one that was originally proposed. He's upped his price and devised a contract that divides everything up equally between the five original Temple women. That includes Jennifer. But, of course, it leaves out Junior, and it leaves out me. No one gets anything from this deal except those that had a stake in it to begin with. All he ever wanted was the land, and he doesn't much care who serves as intermediary. Take a look. It's all official.

I took the stack of papers off the table and read through it as best I could, deciphering the legal jargon in my own limited way until I more or less understood. Ramirez was telling the truth, so it seemed. Russert was offering us a plum package for control of the co-op lease, enough so that each family could start over, if we wanted to, on some better stake of land, or go in together again and come out richer than we'd ever imagined. That was the gist I got from it, at least, though it wasn't enough to reassure me. A private investigator was little better than a lawyer in my book, and so he might know all manner of ways to cheat the little guy when it came down to brass taxes.

Suppose we don't care whether the deal is fair or not, I said. Suppose we still don't want to sell regardless of whatever Mr. Russert's offering us. What would you say to that?

Ramirez shrugged. I'd say this farm is nothing but a millstone, he said. Elliot's been wrong about a lot of things, but that doesn't make him wrong about the way the wind's blowing. Once Vandeman gets his bill passed in Congress, there won't be a parcel farmer in the country who can afford to hold onto his land. Russert's offering you all a chance to escape before the market opens up and the big boys come in to pick the bones of this valley clean. And he's offering you a fair shake this time, with no middlemen to siphon money off the top. One lump sum divided five ways between the remaining co-op wives and Jennifer. You'll all finally have enough money to make your own stand in this world without relying on your father or the government to look out for you. And you won't have to watch your back for Jennifer anymore. She's agreed to take an equal share of the deal, no more no less. All she wants now is to be able to support her kids and look after her parents.

He held his open palm in front of his chest, like everything was on the table now, laid out plain to see. The whole time he was speaking I'd been sitting with my head turned down and to the side, staring at the dark soles of his boots, mulling it over.

You make a strong case, Mr. Ramirez, I said. I wish I could believe it's as good as it sounds. But I like to think I've dealt with enough horseshit in my life to know when somebody's trying to con me. A professional man like you, going out of his way to do this for us, and not asking for a cent in return? It makes about as much sense as a Hubbard bible, which is to say it doesn't make any sense at all. So either Mr. Russert is trying to fool us both, or you're trying to take advantage of a household run by folks a whole lot younger and less experienced than yourself. Either way, it's a shameful business you're involved in. Shameful and see-through.

Ramirez gave me a solemn nod and emptied his lip once again into the cup, which had begun to wilt and turn brown around the edges. I'd be lying if I said I didn't feel shame for some of the work I've done, he said. Truth is, shame is part of what brought me here.

How's that?

Well, son. Little over a month ago, I was parked outside the tree line of this property with a high-powered listening device zeroed in on your house. Little while before that I was in the state record's office digging up everything I could find about your mother and your sister's mother and everything else about your family that was available. I did it because your brother Elliot was paying me to do it. That's how I first got involved with this debacle, cause he wanted me to scope out the place and find out as much as I could about you all.

That's a bold thing to admit in this house, Mr. Ramirez, I said. We've been to hell and back the past month on account of what that man tried to pull. And you helped him bring that evil down on us. You need to realize that. You need to realize what you put us through.

I do, son. I really do.

Ramirez took his hat up from off the table and fanned himself with it, which seemed an odd thing to do considering it was a mild day and not particularly warm inside the house at all. Then he set the hat back down and uncrossed his legs and leaned forward with his hands on his knees and his eyes fixed on me like all the worth of heaven and creation depended on the words he had to say next.

I'm here to barter for that young man's life, he said. That's the only reason I'm here. Time came when I knew he was headed for trouble, but by the time I worked it out to do something about it, he was already a missing person. I'm trying to make up for that now. Been trying to this whole past month. That's what led me here. That's why I went to see Russert and hammered out a better deal for you all. Because I'm wrapped up in this mess in a way I'm not proud of, and if that boy dies on account of it, there's no way I'd be able to escape feeling responsible. Do you get me? Am I making sense to you?

I shook my head. It didn't make sense to me, any of it. There was either something he wasn't telling me, or he had worked himself up over nothing. Does he owe you money? I asked. Is that the real reason you're chasing him down?

He let out a tired sigh. No, sir, he said. He already paid me what was owed for the work. This doesn't have anything to do with that.

Are you in love with him?

He looked at me puzzled and laughed softly without breaking the seal of his lips. I am not, he said. I don't go in for that way myself.

Is he in love you, then?

I doubt it. Last time we spoke he pretty much said he wanted nothing more to do with me.

Then why? Why go through the trouble? You're not related to him.

No, sir. I figure I'm just about the only person on this farm who isn't related to someone else here by blood or marriage.

Then I'll ask again. Why put yourself out like this? Why bother over the likes of him?

Ramirez leaned back in his chair. He wasn't a fat man, but his chest rose high with each breath, like he couldn't get enough air to satisfy him. He stood and walked to the window and looked out through the blinds at the sun-swept land he was trying to convince us to sell. He was still squinting when he turned back around.

I don't have to talk to you, he said. Your name isn't on the lease. The only reason I'm pleading with you right now is because your sister sent you in here, and so I figure that means you're the one who decides what happens to Elliot. Am I right in thinking that?

You're free to think whatever you want. Doesn't matter to me.

Right. Well, let me tell you something, warden. I'm an old man. I've been all around this country from one border to another since before it was a country at all. I've killed men and had men try to kill me, and through it all I've managed to avoid messy entanglements. That was the closest thing I had to a code for a long time. Don't get attached. Trust nobody. That sort of philosophy might suit a man well in a time of war, but it doesn't lead to a very rewarding life afterwards. If you can even call it a life at all.

He took his seat back up at the table. His stomach rested high over his belt, making his whole upper half appear stiff and compressed. If he was uncomfortable, he didn't show it.

You were a soldier?

He spat into his cup and nodded. I was never in any army, he said. But I served as a sort of soldier nonetheless. My war was here, in California.

What war was that?

The war that made this country into a nation.

I don't know that one.

You wouldn't. They don't teach about it in school. It's not the sort of founding myth they want to advertise.

You're talking about the early days of the Republic.

I was spilling blood for this country before anyone thought of the Republic, he said. Nowadays people try to forget what a shitshow it was back then. After the US fell, years passed where California was just as lost and divided as the rest of the former states. San Francisco and L.A. were like Athens and Sparta, fighting to control as much of the land between them as possible, with Sacramento in the middle trying to hold it all together. Rich men in those days weren't picky about who they depended on so long as we could get the job done. Student activists, Unionists, local secession movements. I killed a lot of people to protect the interests of a few, including some who really didn't deserve it. They just got mixed up with powers greater than themselves.

I could hear the tone of his voice, and it seemed like he was sincere in his regret, but at the same time all I could think about was how badass it must've been for him to live like that from day to day, not knowing whether his next assignment would be his last, or if he would ever again have a country to call his own. The Israelites, too, were a violent bunch in the time of old Canaan, back when they had to carve out every inch of their promised land from the flesh of their enemies. Suppose that's how a lot of nations get started, in blood and terror, rewriting their stories as they go along, leaving out the grizzly bits for the sake of posterity.

That's all very interesting, Mr. Ramirez, I said. Seriously. I could listen to your war stories for days, but I'm not sure how it fits with what we've got going on here.

I'm getting to that, he said. First I wanted you to understand where I'm coming from. Sometimes that's all a person can do to make themselves heard.

All right. Go on then.

He looked around the room like he was worried about someone listening in. To be fair, Ellie was listening from her blind behind the wall, but I had a feeling he knew she was there already and didn't mind if she heard what he had to say. A lot of what he was telling me, in fact, seemed like it was spoken to the family as a whole.

That boy you've got locked up in there, he said. He's a spoiled brat. Worse than that, he's a brat who's had to struggle and suffer some compared to the friends he grew up with, and so that makes him think he's tougher than he really is. The whole time I was on the case for him, he looked at me like I had never existed separate from the job he was paying me to do, and like I would cease to exist in this world once the job was finished. The rest of the time he treated me like a dumb beaner, like all the things I'd seen and done in my life didn't matter cause I wasn't carrying a slip of paper from a university.

Know what you mean, I said. He has that way of looking at people.

So now it was out. He knew we had him. I watched his face for changes, holding my breath. He didn't blink, though. Just tapped his finger against the side of the cup and continued from where he left off.

There's boys like him all over the country. On the coast mainly, but in the capital also. Boys whose families were well-off before disbandment and whose parents used the crisis to cement their position as aristocrats. They grew up in the shadows of the sea walls, with phones in their pockets and gates around their neighborhoods, believing they've faced real hardship because their parents make them study all the time. I worked for those boys. I killed for them. I lost my faith in God and man in part because of them. So if anyone has a reason to despise them, and what they represent, it's me.

And here you are trying to get me to set one of them free. You're asking me to forgive him for all that he's done. For all that he is.

Yes. I am.

Why?

Several reasons.

Name one.

Well. For starters, I decided he doesn't deserve to die.

I laughed. You deciding on something doesn't make it right.

No, but it's good enough for me.

You just said you don't have any faith in people.

That's right.

But you've decided this person is worth trying to keep alive.

Yes. I have.

You don't have faith in God either. You're not a Christian.

I'm not.

So how can you say who deserves to live and who doesn't?

Because I decided on it.

That's no kind of answer.

You're wrong. It's the most important kind.

You're not related to him. Not by blood.

I've already told you I'm not.

And there's no higher power you answer to either.

Not in the way you mean.

Then what do you care if he lives or dies?

Because I decided on my own to look out for him, or at least to save him from himself. That's important, the deciding part. Anyone can do the right thing when they believe they have to, because of family or because of faith. But when you make the choice to help someone else, even when there are no ties binding you together, you make the choice to step up and act more decently than most of the people who have ever lived or ever will. And then your life is your own canvas, and you become freer in the doing than you ever would have been if you'd held yourself back. You stop trying to live up to something and you start trying to live.

This is who you spend your time helping? A boy who's already had more privilege than me and all of my brothers and sisters put together?

Ramirez cleared his throat. He looked at me and looked at the contract and warped his mouth into a pained grimace that frankly startled me. If we're going to have any kind of country at all, he said, we can't go around killing everyone who deserves it. There's too much blame to go around. The whole of California would be a mass grave before the end.

You didn't always think so, I said. All that time you were killing for the rich and powerful, you must've thought at least some of them deserved it.

I did. There were some bad ones for sure.

And some good ones also? Ones who didn't deserve it?

I said so before.

Right. So how do you decide to kill all those people and then turn around years later and tell me I haven't got the right to do what I need to do?

I didn't decide. Not really, anyway. If I did make a decision, it was that following orders was a good enough excuse to get me by.

You were older than me then? You were older than me when you started to kill?

Yes. I was already grown.

But you expect me to be more mature than that. You expect me to turn the other cheek for no reason other than because it's the right thing to do.

He shook his head. I don't expect you to do anything unless you want to, he said. But I will say that you won't like it. You won't like living with yourself if you harm that boy. We all have to live with the decisions we make, even when we tell ourselves there was no other choice. Can you do that, son? Can you live to be as old as me and still feel regret in your heart for what you did when you were seventeen? Your brother did some awful things, and so did your father, but you don't have to be like them. You can choose to be better.

Ramirez set his spit cup on the table and crossed his leg back over his knee. He was waiting for me to decide on how I could be better, but all I could think of was how much better he was at looking after Elliot than my father was at looking after me. He didn't have to be here. He didn't have to be working so hard and saying these things to try to get through to me. At church we learned about faith and duty. Honor thy father and thy mother, be your brother's keeper until you just can't keep him any longer. To see somebody go to such lengths over somebody he barely knew, and without the weight of heaven on his shoulders for incentive, was something I'd never had to puzzle out before. It gave me a strange feeling down inside, like a sadness over something I knew I'd lost but couldn't remember having.

Ellie, I said. Could you come in here, please?

Ramirez turned and watched Ellie appear from behind the wall with the rifle hanging low at her side. The safety was still on. She'd heard the same things I had.

Is Mr. Ramirez going to be taking the prisoner with him? she asked.

It's not for us to decide by ourselves, I said. I need you to find our moms and the others and get them in here for a vote.

Ellie nodded. She handed me the rifle and smiled at me and left the kitchen at a quickening pace.

Come on, I said. You can see him now.

Ramirez followed me down the hallway. There were no sounds from the other side of the door. I kept both hands on the rifle with the safety on and my finger on the button.

He's in bad shape right now, I said. There was an incident a few days ago that he started, and it could've turned out a lot worse. You'll want to get him to a doctor right away.

I'm sure you handled him the best you could, he said. You mind if we have a moment alone?

Go ahead. I'll be out here if you need me.

From where I was standing, just outside the door, I could've heard everything they said, except they didn't seem to be saying anything. My worries swelled and solidified and seemed to be confirmed when he came out again and I saw the look on his face.

What happened?

Ramirez put his hand to his forehead and held it there. I was too late, he said. Now I'll have to live with it forever.

He's really gone?

See for yourself.

Ramirez stepped back from the doorway to make enough space for me to pass. The musty odor hit me in a single wave, followed by the shock of realizing what had happened in the room in the short time since I left it. The prisoner was mounted to the foot of the bed with his mouth open and saliva leaking down his chin. Seeing how he'd managed to carry it out, it was clear it had been a slow and terrible way to go. First he had to wrap the chain around the posts of the bedrail until it was as taut as possible. Then he must've crawled up onto the top of the rail and swung his feet over to the other side. As weak and feverish as he was, every step along the way had to be an ordeal. No energy left once he was dangling, though there were still scuffs in the carpet from his free foot's thrashing. On account of the chain, one of his legs was twisted back, suspended in air. It made him look like a marionette, like a grotesque Pinocchio who chose to die rather than remain an imitation of a living boy. I walked back out of the room and closed the door and stood in the hallway facing Ramirez. His head was down.

I'm sorry I didn't get here sooner, he said. I might have been able to reach him.

Don't be sorry, I said. Whatever hell he's in now can't be worse than he hell he brought with him.

I tried to seem calm, but my head was spinning as we marched back down the hallway. When I finally took my eyes off the floor, I saw that Ellie, Mom, and the rest of the women were all seated in the kitchen, just as it had been weeks before when our lost brother first revealed himself to us. I looked around from one side of the table to the other, studying the individual faces of my family. Katie stood up from her seat. She was holding the new contract.

Are you men about ready to start talking business?

Father. My father. What did you do? What pearls did you lay before the swine who betrayed you? What pearls did you withhold from me? What blinded you from seeing me? The real me?

• • •

I only did half of what I promised. I buried him in the orchard with the evening sun blazing red across the sky. Will and Logan, me and Ellie, together we carried him out of the house wrapped in a sheet and dug him a final resting place in the soft earth between two rows of nectarine trees. We chose the younger trees so the roots wouldn't take him right away. We dug deep so the coyotes and wild dogs couldn't get at him. We covered him and smoothed out the soil and stood around the plot with our heads bowed. But I didn't say a word to commemorate him or guide his soul in passing. No one else spoke either. He wouldn't have wanted prayers, and it didn't seem to matter one way or another. He was dead now, another branch of the family severed and gone forever. Whatever sins or secrets he took with him couldn't trouble us, and those he left behind were already being washed away in the frenzied business of planning our next maneuver.

Ramirez left that same evening and couriered the contract to Russert on our behalf. A money order arrived two days later with four-fifths of the sales price all together in a lump sum. Mom had never had so much cash on hand at one time. None of us had. In our final nights at the farm, around the kitchen table where so much else had happened, we sat together and talked in measured voices about the Vandeman Act, about the direction the country was headed in, and about where we saw ourselves in this new world where the only money problem we had to worry about was how we were going to hold on to what we had already earned. Everyone had their own ideas about where we should go or what line of work we should get into next. But absent was the distrust that had plagued us when we first met at Katie's barbeque. The change was subtle, but it was obvious. The mothers didn't guard themselves like they used to. The children didn't sit off by themselves with the siblings they'd been raised with originally. Instead Mom and Dawn traded jokes back and forth that got the whole kitchen shaking from our collective laughter. Beth held little Karina still on her lap while Sebastian prac-ticed his boxing jabs on Logan's open hands. Eventually it was decided that Fresno would be a good place to start at until we arrived at a more definite plan. But after the final vote was taken, no one seemed afraid of what was in store for us, at least compared to how we felt a year earlier when our world lay in pieces and we were all skeptical that we could put it back together, or find any better alternative.

On the morning we were scheduled to head out, I was loading boxes into the trunk when Ellie came out to the driveway. Her new clothes suited her well, not that she would go in for anything too flashy even with extra money to throw around. She sat down on the hood and put her foot up on the bumper. She was closer to fifteen now than four-teen, and a lifetime removed from where she was when we first talked in the orchards outside Katie's.

Mom wants to know if you need more snacks for the drive up, she said. Way she's been fussing over this trip, you'd think it was a ten-hour drive instead of one.

I closed the trunk and came around to the front and stood next to her. Glad she's excited about the move, I said. She's looked a lot happier in general lately.

Ellie smiled. She is happy, she said. That's a new one for her.

Well. Things are starting to look up.

Yeah, they are. You nervous?

No. You?

A little bit. I've been wondering what your plans are for after we get settled. Whether you're going to look for your own place or not.

Been thinking about it. I still got a few months before the Army'll take me. Might see if Will and Logan need any help getting their business up and running.

That'd be a good way to spend your time. Better than getting shot at.

Yeah, I guess.

I asked her to get off the hood so I could wipe it down with a shammy. She watched me run the damp rag over the metal. I knew she was waiting for the chance to say something else.

A lot of things are going to change now, I said. But you know I'll always be around to protect you.

She laughed. If that's how you want to think of it, she said, then go ahead. But know this. I love you. You're my brother and I love you. And I figured I might as well say so if you're never going to.

All right, then, I said. I guess I love you too.

She smiled and stood on tiptoes to hug me around the shoulders.

You're still kind of a bitch, though, I said.

I know, she said. It runs in the family.

With the cars packed up, all that was left to do was round up the kids and say goodbye to the farm. But I was already itching to go. I knew enough secrets about the land not to get sentimental about putting it behind me. And besides, any chance I had to sit behind the wheel of the Lexus was one I was going to take. I pulled the small key out of my pocket and unhooked the club from the steering wheel. The first time I saw it lying in the backseat, I had no idea what it was. I had to ask Mom, and felt foolish after she explained it to me. Of course Dad would've taken extra precautions to keep his new car safe. He was always worried about his things falling into the hands of the wrong people. He wouldn't have approved of me driving his convertible. He wouldn't have approved of any of this. But his approval didn't matter anymore, if it ever did. I was driving his baby the whole way there, and not giving it up.

My brothers piled into the backseat while Mom sat up front with Karina balanced on her leg. She made the sign of the cross over her chest. She smiled at me.

You ready, mijo?

I pressed the button to let the top down. Yeah. I'm ready.

Mother. My mother. Thank you. Thank you for doing the best you could by me. It wasn't an easy life you led. It wasn't the life you expected. But thank you for helping me to become free.

Somewhere in this valley, or somewhere beyond, is the land we were promised when we made our promises to one another. A promise made not in blood, but in something stronger. Blood is weak. Blood is deceitful. They got that lesson wrong in Sunday school. Slash the vein, watch it pour. Nothing constant, nothing real. Watch it change colors in ordinary air. Watch the yellow plasma separate after a few hours on the ground. Wine becomes it in the hand of a priest. Wine betrays it in the mouth of a father. My father. Your husband. My children will know his name, but will never hear me honor it. In the vineyard, where our story began, there is too much poison to grow anything new. In the orchard, too, where our stories converged, nothing new will grow there either. But we will grow, and we will prosper, in California as well as anywhere. My sisters and brothers and mothers and me. We will finally have a home.

Our city is out there. We will find it before the end.

Our city is rising. Lay the stone.

ACKNOWLEDGMENTS

The author would like to acknowledge and thank the following people for their support during the writing process: Robert Lasner, Ryan McIlvain, Kathy Valencia, Brian Desmarais, Elise Blackwell, David Bajo, Brandon Haffner, and Matthew Fogarty.